P
Furbid...

"If you like cats, dogs, and entertaining mysteries, you're going to love *Furbidden Fatality*."
—Donna Andrews, *New York Times* bestselling author of *The Falcon Always Wings Twice* and *The Gift of the Magpie*

"*Furbidden Fatality* has everything a cozy mystery reader is looking for—a clever heroine, a puzzling mystery, and a collection of adorable animals. Deborah Blake writes with passion and charm. She's a new mystery writer to watch."
—Dorothy St. James, author of *The Broken Spine*

"*Furbidden Fatality* has all the cute cat and dog cameos you'd want in a fun pet cozy. Animal sanctuary owner Kari Stuart teams up with a knowing kitty and several pet-loving friends to collar the culprit in this fast read."
—Jennifer J. Chow, author of *Mimi Lee Reads Between the Lines*

"Blake does a great job of building up the who-done-it suspense. . . . If you're in the market for a delightful mystery with endearing characters and adorable animals, *Furbidden Fatality* is a must-read." —Fresh Fiction

Catskills Pet Rescue Mysteries

FURBIDDEN FATALITY
DOGGONE DEADLY

Doggone Deadly

 A Catskills Pet Rescue Mystery

DEBORAH BLAKE

BERKLEY PRIME CRIME
New York

BERKLEY PRIME CRIME
Published by Berkley
An imprint of Penguin Random House LLC
penguinrandomhouse.com

ISBN: 9780593201527

First Edition: November 2021

Printed in the United States of America
1   3   5   7   9   10   8   6   4   2

Book design by Gaelyn Galbreath

To everyone who ever rescued an animal—cat, dog, or other. Y'all rock. And to my own beloved kitties, who rescued me at least as much as I rescued them.

❡ One

"Quick, hide me!" Suz said as she ran into the large white tent.

Kari Stuart looked up from where she was positioning a freestanding wall featuring pictures of animals currently up for adoption at the Serenity Sanctuary, almost dropping the display on her foot. Kari wasn't sure what amazed her more—that her best friend, who was six feet tall with spiky lavender hair, thought she could actually hide behind five-foot-six brown-haired Kari, or that there was something Suz would feel the need to hide from at all. They'd been friends since grade school, and as far as Kari knew, Suz wasn't afraid of anything.

"Is there a demon chasing you?" Kari asked, shifting one side of the hinged board so the whole thing was more stable. They were on the parklike grounds of the two-year state college in Perryville, not far from their hometown of Lakeview, for the annual Tri-County Kennel Club Show. Suz was a member of the local kennel club, one of three clubs putting on the event, and she'd been roped into taking on the coordinator role when someone else backed out at the last minute. In turn, she'd persuaded (okay, bribed) Kari into helping by giving her the chance to have a fundraising and awareness-raising booth for the shelter.

"Worse," Suz said as she ducked behind one of the two long folding tables covered with white cloths. "You haven't seen me. You don't know where I am." A pile of adoption application forms on top of the table quivered, threatening to topple over into the volunteer sign-up sheet next to them.

The setup was fairly simple, in part because it had been thrown together quickly, and in part because AKC rules said that no unregistered dogs could be allowed onto the show grounds. That meant Kari had only been able to bring photos of the dogs they currently had up for adoption, along with two metal cages—now perched atop the table not lined with application and information sheets—holding four adorable kittens each.

A third cage held a half-grown black kitten named Queenie, who was definitely *not* up for adoption, since she belonged to Kari. Or vice versa. It was often hard to tell. Queenie had insisted on coming along, so she was currently lounging on a cat bed, supervising Kari as she arranged the rest of the displays.

"Miss Stuart," a piercing voice said as a statuesque and well-preserved woman in her mid-sixties strode into the tent as if she owned it. "I am looking for Suzanne. Have you seen her?"

"Apparently not," Kari said, suddenly understanding why her friend was hiding behind a table. "Is there anything I can help you with, Mrs. Weiner?"

Olivia Weiner was well-known in Lakeview, and probably admired and dreaded in about equal measure. Not only was she the president of the garden club, the literary book club, and the kennel club, but her husband, Jack Weiner, had a used-car "empire" that stretched over a half a dozen counties.

Olivia, with her professionally cut and dyed blond hair, piercing hazel eyes, and perfect figure, maintained with rigorous dieting and the religious use of a personal trainer, appeared in all of his ads along with her purebred dogs. She was wearing a floral skirt and jacket suit that had *designer* written all over it, a sharp contrast to Kari's jeans and tee shirt. No doubt Olivia achieved many good things with all the committees she worked on, but Kari had always found her a little intimidating.

"For goodness' sake," Olivia said, looking around the tent with disapproval radiating from her rigid posture. "I can't imagine why the show committee agreed to allow this. As you may know, I voted against it." She frowned at the donation jar on the end of one table and at the pictures of three grinning pit bulls, an elderly beagle with lopsided ears, and some sort of poodle-schnauzer-wandering-hound mix. "Why, most of those dogs aren't even purebred. Plus that jar is just undignified."

"And what on earth are those things?" She pointed at the cages as if offended by the existence of their non-canine occupants. An orange ball of fur opened its tiny mouth and let out a yawn, clearly unimpressed with this loud human.

Kari choked back a laugh and said with a straight face, "Those are kittens. They're kind of like dogs, only smaller. Most people find them quite adorable."

Olivia snorted. "At an AKC dog show? It hardly seems suitable." She turned around and, behind her back, Queenie hissed. Kari made a shushing motion. The kitten ignored her, as usual.

The older woman shook her head and sighed. "Well, it's

done now. What isn't done, unfortunately, are half the tasks your friend Suzanne was supposed to have taken care of before we open the gates in thirty minutes." Olivia waved a clipboard through the air, as if to prove her point. "The show judges will be arriving any minute now, and there are no water bottles in their tent. What kind of an impression is that going to make, I ask you? We have been hosting this show for over thirty years, and we are renowned for our hospitality."

"I'm sure Suz is doing her best, Mrs. Weiner," Kari said. "After all, she just got handed all this extra responsibility two days ago."

"Well, I don't have time to look for her," Olivia said, straightening her jacket. "I am being interviewed by the local paper, then recording a video for one of my husband's commercials, and I need to walk around and make sure everything looks just right. If you see her, tell her that all the remaining items on this checklist need to be completed immediately." She shoved the clipboard in Kari's direction. "And remind her that I will be at her tent to get Snowball's final grooming in exactly one hour." She took one last look at her expensive watch and stalked out.

As soon as she was gone, Suz straightened up from behind the tablecloth, rubbing grass stains off the knees of her jeans and tugging down the bottom of her red Lakeview Kennel Club tee shirt. "Sorry," she said with a wry smile. "But I was afraid that if I had to talk to Olivia one more time this morning, I was going to end up killing the woman. She has been driving me around the bend."

A chuckle from the entrance to the tent made them both jump guiltily. A tiny silver-haired woman with faded blue eyes and wearing a fuchsia track suit poked her head inside. "I don't blame you," she said. "I'm from the Saratoga Kennel Club group, and we had a few problems with her last year."

"Miriam Rosebaum, right?" Suz said, coming around the table to shake hands with the spry octogenarian. She towered over the elderly woman. "I'm Suz Holden, and this is my friend Kari Stuart."

Miriam came farther into the tent and gazed around. "Oh! Kari Stuart. You're the woman who won the lottery and bought that run-down shelter."

"I am," Kari said. "Guilty as charged."

Earlier that year, she'd stopped at the convenience store on her way home from her job as a waitress at the local diner to pick up cat litter and bought a lottery ticket on a whim. That ticket had turned out to be worth about three million dollars after taxes. Because she'd made so many bad decisions earlier in her life, Kari had been cautiously pondering the best way to spend her unexpected windfall.

Then she'd found a small black stray kitten and discovered that none of the shelters in the area had any room for the little waif. In fact, they were all completely full, except a bankrupt animal sanctuary that was on the verge of shutting down. Kari had bought it from its beleaguered and overwhelmed former owner, only to get caught up in the murder of the then–dog warden, who had his own plans for the property. By the time it was all resolved, Kari had a rebuilt and reopened sanctuary . . . and a black kitten named Queenie, who seemed to have an uncanny nose for clues and a habit of sticking that nose where it didn't belong. Thankfully, that was all behind them now.

"You should visit the Serenity Sanctuary while you're in town," Suz said. "You won't believe what Kari has done with it."

Kari rolled her eyes. "She's just saying that to butter me

up because I agreed to help her with the show at the last minute. Apparently the woman who is usually in charge got sick."

Miriam let out a cackle. "Sick of Olivia Weiner's micromanaging and constant criticism, more likely," she said. She gave Suz a pitying look. "Let me guess—you're new to the kennel club circuit."

"Just joined the year before last," Suz admitted with a wry smile. "I really love it, even though my dogs mostly aren't show quality. I've got a pug who thinks he's a Rottweiler, but other than that I have two mixed breeds of indeterminate origin, one of whom I've gotten registered under the AKC Canine Partners program so he can take part in the agility competition."

"What about you?" Miriam asked Kari. "Are you a member of the kennel club?"

Kari shook her head. "I'm just here to help out Suz and try to raise some awareness about the pets that need good homes." She gestured at the tables. "As you can see, I'm still setting up, but then I have some volunteers coming to man the booth so I can run around with Suz. I can't believe how much work goes into putting on a three-day show like this."

"We get people attending from all over the country," Suz said proudly. "There are over six hundred dogs competing each day. It's kind of amazing."

"Well, the show itself has been held for over fifty years," Miriam said. "Although it hasn't always been the same three kennel clubs taking part. I've been coming with the Saratoga group for longer than I care to count." She patted her silver hair. "I used to show bichon frises, but I switched to dachshunds a few years ago. I had a bad experience and decided to go with a simpler breed."

"Olivia has a bichon frise this year," Suz said. "She's

convinced he is championship quality, and I have to admit, he's won every show they've taken part in so far. She had a bulldog before that, but apparently her husband, the Used-Car King, complained that the dog was too ugly to use in his commercials and made her get something cuter."

A shadow flashed over Miriam's eyes, so fast that Kari almost missed it. "Bichons are adorable," the older woman admitted. "All that soft white fur and those black button eyes. Hypoallergenic, too, so they're a good choice for people who can't tolerate most other dogs. But they have their issues, like most purebreds." She sighed, and Queenie suddenly appeared and rubbed up against Miriam's ankles. The kitten had a bad habit of opening the cage when no one was looking—Kari still hadn't figured out how she did it.

"What a sweetie," Miriam said. "Is she yours?" She leaned down and picked up the kitten, who immediately settled into her arms and started purring.

"She is," Kari said. "She insisted on coming with me today, and I've found it is easier to go along than to argue, most of the time."

"Just like Olivia Weiner," Suz said through only slightly gritted teeth. She glanced at her watch and picked up the clipboard. "I'd better go take care of the rest of this stuff before she comes back looking for me again." She explained to Miriam, "Her husband's auto business is one of the major sponsors of the event, and I guess that makes her think the show belongs to her."

Miriam tittered, handing the black kitten back to Kari and then patting Suz on the arm. "Oh, no, dear, that's just the way she is. Has been for as long as I've known her. She has to be the best and have the best. It must have been difficult for her all these years to only end up with dogs that consistently came in second and third."

"Did that have something to do with the problems you had with her last year?" Kari asked. She found the dynamics around the dog show fascinating, and surprisingly intense. Some people who took part probably did it for fun, but a lot of them seemed to take the competitions very seriously indeed. "Was she a sore loser?"

"You could say that," Miriam said, cocking her head to the side so that she resembled a tiny fuchsia bird.

Suz raised a lavender-tinted eyebrow. "Really? What happened?"

"Olivia actually accused the woman whose dog beat out her bulldog for Best in Show of sleeping with one of the judges to get his vote," Miriam said.

Kari gasped, putting a hand over her mouth. "You're kidding! And was it true?"

Miriam shrugged, but her blue eyes twinkled. "I'm pretty sure Teri slept with the judge," she said with a merry laugh. "He was quite the looker. But I doubt it had anything to do with getting his vote. There was a panel of three judges, and Teri certainly didn't sleep with them all. She just had a better dog. Still, Olivia raised quite the stink, in her own snooty, dignified way. I hope it doesn't happen again this year."

"I doubt it will," Suz said. "Like I said, that new dog of hers is pretty impressive. That's one of the reasons she's dumped all this extra work on me. She's completely focused on winning with Snowball."

"What's his official name?" Miriam asked. "Maybe I'm familiar with his sire and the kennel he comes from."

"Honestly, I don't remember. Something French, I think," Suz said. "She just calls him Snowball. The name is in the program somewhere, but if I don't get that water to the judges' tent, *my* name is going to be mud. I really should get going."

Just then Sara, one of the volunteers from the shelter, came into the tent. An older woman with a bold turquoise stripe in her gray hair, she was a former ninth-grade English teacher who had stuck with the sanctuary even when it was on its last legs. She was one of Kari's staunchest supporters and had become a friend over the last few months.

"Hi, Kari," Sara said. "I'm here to mind the shop, so to speak." She looked around at the table on the right with its neatly piled paperwork and large jar for donations, the table on the left with its cages full of kittens, currently wrestling with each other in typical kitten fashion, and the display wall set up in between. "This looks great! People are going to love it."

"I hope so," Kari said. "I'd really like to see a few animals get new homes out of this. And some contributions toward the food and litter fund wouldn't hurt my feelings either."

Getting the shelter back up and running from its previous dilapidated state had made a serious dent in her lottery winnings, and while she could keep the place running for quite a while on that money, it would definitely help if they could bring in extra toward the daily expenses. Daisy, the previous owner, had warned her how much she'd be spending just on food and medical bills, and the woman hadn't been kidding. Cat litter alone could run to hundreds of dollars a month.

"Since you're here, Suz and I need to scoot," Kari said. She turned her head to look at Queenie, who had abandoned Miriam for Kari's shoulder, a favorite perch. "I don't suppose you want to get back into your cage and look adorable for the folks who come in?" People sometimes looked at her funny when she spoke to the kitten as if the little black cat understood every word she said, but in Kari's experience, it certainly seemed that way.

Queenie gave a *mewp* that sounded like *no* and hopped down into the large tote bag Kari had slung over her shoulder. Since buying the shelter, Kari had given up on smaller purses, and the tote bag had taken their place. At any given moment, it might contain anything from a wrench and a bag of dog treats to a packet of flea meds and a collapsible water bowl. Queenie seemed to think it was the perfect mode of travel and simply arranged herself on top of whatever was in there. Two pointed black ears and a pair of green eyes peered out at the world with eager curiosity.

"Is it safe to carry that kitten around a dog show?" Miriam asked, watching with amazement. "Won't she be scared of all the big dogs and the barking?"

Kari laughed. "Queenie isn't afraid of anything," she said. "She spends most of her days at the shelter, and until he left for a new home, her best friend was a pit bull named Buster. I'm more worried about her getting the dogs excited, although usually the ones who come to shows are pretty well trained and accustomed to other animals."

She tapped the top of the kitten's head. "If you're going to insist on tagging along, try to keep a low profile." The ears disappeared into the bag.

"Let's get going," Suz said, tugging Kari along as new wrinkles appeared between those lavender-tinted brows. "I've got an hour's worth of things to do and about twenty minutes to do them. And if I don't get a cup of coffee, either I'm going to die or somebody else will."

Suz, Kari, and Queenie made their way across the grounds. The college was situated next to the same river that ran from Blue Heron Lake, which the town of

Lakeview got its name from, and followed the highway from one town to the next before meandering back into the hills. The college itself was made up of standard boxy brick buildings, practical and a little boring, but the beauty of the grounds more than made up for it.

Tall trees grouped together to make up shady areas, and rolling green lawns stretched between the buildings and ran down a gentle slope to the river. Even during the summer, when most of the students were gone, the grounds were well maintained, since they were often used for events like this one. Flower beds bloomed with bright red, pink, and yellow blossoms, and wooden benches were placed by neatly raked gravel walks so visitors could sit and enjoy the view. The air smelled fresh and clean, with a faint whiff of fried food coming from the direction of the vendors' area.

For the three days of the dog show, most of the available space had been filled with oversized white tents, interspersed with the rings where the actual competitions would take place. Porta Potties were discreetly placed in twos and threes out of the way of most of the action, and a quartet of food trucks was positioned at the end of the parking lot closest to the grassy areas. Beyond them, Kari could see rows of RVs, since many of the participants traveled from show to show, and that was apparently the preferred mode of transportation for the dogs and all their equipment.

She and Suz dealt with the judges' tent and a few other small issues and stopped by various vendors' tents to make sure that everyone had whatever they needed. There were people selling handmade dog coats and collars, grooming tools, specialty treats, and anything else you could imagine buying for your pet. Kari had already succumbed to a new brush for her dog, Fred (named after Fred Rogers because as a puppy, he'd had an unfortunate tendency to destroy sweaters), and was seriously considering putting in a bulk order of cute, whimsical chew toys for the sanctuary.

They finally swung by a booth where volunteers were selling coffee, tea, soda, and water and got some much-needed caffeine. Kari thought her coffee smelled like heaven in a cup, and she wasn't sure if she wanted to drink it or just stand there and inhale the aroma. Sadly, they had to keep moving, so they headed back toward Suz's tent, which she had set up so she could do grooming between bouts of running around.

On the way, they passed Olivia, who was standing in front of a signboard that said *Jack Weiner, the Used-Car King. Proud supporter of the Tri-County Kennel Club Show. If you buy a Weiner, you'll be a winner!* She was holding an adorable white bichon while speaking directly to a cameraman. Or trying to, rather, since there was some kind of ruckus coming from the direction of the parking lot that made it impossible for her to be heard clearly.

A ruddy-faced man with a bristling white mustache and a slight paunch stood nearby, a scowl on his homely face and beefy arms folded over his chest. Going by the picture on the signboard, Kari assumed this was the Used-Car King himself, although he wasn't currently wearing the oversized crown along with his trademark plaid suit.

"This will never work," he said in a loud voice. "We can't possibly film with all this racket. What the heck is going on, Olivia? I thought you were in charge of this shindig. Can't you shut those people up?"

Suz and Kari exchanged worried glances and changed their trajectory to head in the direction of the unhappy couple. Jack Weiner was a major contributor to the show, providing many of the prizes that were given out to winners in the name of the local kennel club. Keeping him happy may not have been on Suz's official checklist of duties, but it might as well have been.

"Is there a problem, Mr. Weiner?" Suz asked as they came up. But the growing noise from the direction of the campus entrance made the question fairly superfluous.

"There you are," Olivia snapped, as though Suz were somehow late for an appointment. "You have to do something about this. A bunch of hooligans have set up across the street from the parking lot and they're accosting people as they come in. It's making a terrible first impression. Not to mention that we're trying to film one of my husband's commercials and I can't even hear myself think. I want you to call the police and have them arrested."

"I'm not sure the police are the answer." Suz ran a hand through her hair so that it stood up on end even more than usual, and Queenie poked her head up to see what was upsetting her friend. Kari gently pushed her back down again.

"Why don't you go film over by the river?" Kari suggested. "It's much quieter and you can see people walking their dogs in the background without having them upstage your own beautiful baby." She smiled at the bichon, which panted happily at her.

Jack grimaced but nodded his head and tugged Olivia by the arm, jerking his head at the man holding the camera to indicate that he should follow them. "We'll move," he said. "But you'd better deal with that rabble out front."

"And don't forget to meet me at your tent, Suzanne, so you can give Snowball his final grooming," Olivia said over her shoulder as she was hustled away.

"Argh," Suz said. She turned to Kari. "Do you mind coming with me to check out what's going on?"

"Not at all," Kari said. To be honest, she was kind of

curious. Maybe there had been an accident, or two contestants were coming to blows before the show had formally gotten underway?

The noise grew louder as they approached the entrance to the campus, where today a couple of volunteers were checking in participants, directing visitors to parking spots, and selling the thick program books that listed all the contests and entries for each of the three days of the show. Suz and Kari walked over to one of the volunteers, a woman named Chloe who Kari recognized from when she'd arrived earlier.

"What on earth is going on?" Suz asked. They all turned to stare across the street, Queenie included. Her pointed black ears swiveled in the direction of the mob from which most of the noise was emanating.

Despite the air of chaos, on closer examination the crowd turned out to be about a dozen people, most of them waving placards and shouting at the cars as they turned to go into the campus. The signs said things like *Breeding pedigree dogs is mad science* and *Animal shows are animal abuse*. There was even one that read *For every purebred dog you buy, a shelter animal dies*, with a heartbreaking picture of a sad puppy on it.

"SHAFFT," Chloe said, rolling her eyes.

"Excuse me?" Kari said.

"SHAFFT," Chloe repeated. "Save Helpless Animal Friends From Tyranny. It's an animal rights organization, but they're known for being kind of rabid. I'm sure their hearts are in the right place."

"They're against dog shows?" Kari said. She didn't think anyone could object to watching adorable and mostly pampered pets show off their beauty and skills. Apparently she was wrong.

"The SHAFFT motto, the same as the one PETA uses, is 'Animals are not ours to eat, wear, experiment on, use for entertainment, or abuse in any other way,'" Suz explained. "I'm guessing they think what we're doing falls under entertainment."

"It's abuse, that's what it is!" a man shouted through a megaphone. Kari started, then realized that he couldn't have overheard them. Queenie growled quietly, as if in response.

The man, who appeared to be the leader of the group, was tall and skinny, with thinning light brown hair. Kari thought he might be in his late fifties. The voice coming through the megaphone was surprisingly sonorous and resonant for such an unprepossessing body, and it quivered with righteous anger.

"Who's that?" Suz asked, pointing in his direction. Next to him, a thin woman with frizzy red hair waved her sign with such abandon, she almost smacked him over the head with it.

"Shawn Mahoney," Chloe said in a disgusted tone. "That's his wife, Minnie. He's a custodian at the high school, and my kids say he is always trying to convince the administration to make school lunches vegan. He and his group have harassed local pig farmers, protested at horse auctions, and petitioned to have the yearly children's fishing derby canceled. But this is the first time they've ever shown up here."

"Oh, great," Suz said. "I don't suppose we can call the police and have them arrested for, I don't know, disturbing the peace or trespassing or something?" She clutched her head with the hand not holding the clipboard. "They're sure disturbing mine."

Chloe shook her head. She was wearing a Lakeview Kennel Club tee shirt in lime green and had braided a matching ribbon into her long blond hair, which fluttered with the movement. "They know what they're doing. As long as they stay across the road, they're not on private property. So while they're annoying, they're not actually doing anything illegal. There's nothing we can do."

Suz watched them for another few minutes. "Well, most people seem to be ignoring them. Maybe they'll get bored and go away."

"Maybe," Chloe said, but she didn't sound hopeful.

Just then, a large white SUV with magnetic signs that said *Blue Skies Kennel* stuck to each side drove up. The sight of it seemed to send Shawn Mahoney into a renewed frenzy.

"Animal abuser!" he yelled into the megaphone. "Shame on you!"

"Crap," Suz said. She approached the car as it came to a halt at the entrance to the campus, followed by Chloe with her clipboard.

"Hi," Chloe said, looking down at her paperwork. "You must be Francine Carver, right? I have you down here with the kennel name and address."

A slightly plump redhead with green eyes hidden behind large black-framed glasses stuck her head out the window. "Yes, that's me. I'm here to handle Olivia Weiner's dog for her. Do you know who she is?"

Suz and Chloe exchanged sideways looks. "Everyone knows who she is," Chloe said in a dry tone. "I can direct you to her tent." She handed over a copy of the program and a sheet of paper with a map of the grounds on it and pointed out where Olivia's tent was located.

"What the heck is going on here?" Francine asked, swiveling her head around to look at the protesters. "I'd heard this was a classy show."

Suz gave her an apologetic smile. "It is, I promise. But apparently as long as they stay on public property, there's nothing we can do about these yahoos. Don't worry, though. They can't come onto the campus, so once you're actually inside, you won't even know they're there."

Mahoney picked this moment to cross the road. Ignoring Suz and Chloe, he shouted at Francine, "We know all about your kind! You run a puppy mill! Produce elitist dogs for rich people, when you should be helping dogs who can't find homes. Because of people like you!" Spittle formed at the corners of his mouth.

Francine sputtered, her face turning an alarming shade of red that almost matched her short, wavy hair.

"Breeding kennels should be outlawed!" he went on. "If it weren't for you, shelter dogs would be adopted. Instead, they're euthanized because the shelters are full. Meanwhile your type is getting wealthy enslaving overbred dogs." His face was turning red too, and he waved the megaphone around in an alarming manner. "Animal lives are as important as human lives! People like you should be killed for the good of all dogs!"

"That's enough," Suz said, stepping in between him and the car and glaring down at him from her considerable height. "Get back across the street or I'm calling the cops. Now."

For a moment, Kari thought he was going to argue with the lavender-haired Amazon, but he took another look and wisely thought the better of the idea and retreated to the safer company of his companions.

"Sorry about that," Suz said to Francine. "Look, if you can't find Olivia at her tent, she should be at mine for Snowball's grooming in about ten minutes. You'll be able to meet up with her there if you haven't found her before then." She pointed to the spot on the map while still keeping a wary eye on the protesters. "I'm really sorry you had such an unpleasant start to your day. I find it's best to just ignore those kinds of crazy people."

"Thanks," Francine said. "It's not a big deal." But her face still showed a tinge of heightened color, and Kari could see her hands shaking slightly where they rested on the steering wheel. She muttered under her breath, so quietly Kari could barely hear her, "Damn it. I knew I should have said no to that woman. I *hate* dog shows."

Kari blinked, startled, and was about to say something when Francine put the car in gear and drove through the entrance, almost running Suz's foot over in the process.

"Well, that was fun," Suz said, turning narrowed eyes on the SHAFFT folks and making Mahoney flinch. "Let's hope the rest of the day goes a little more smoothly."

"I'm sure it will," Chloe said.

She was wrong.

¶ Two

Ten minutes later, a frazzled Suz checked the last item off her list and rushed into her own tent, Kari hot on her heels. The kitten peeked her black head over the edge of the tote bag, but hurriedly stuck it back down again at the sound of distressed barking and an angry human voice.

"Will you sit down!" This shrill command was followed by a high-pitched yelp.

Kari and Suz screeched to a halt inside the white fabric walls, stunned by the sight of Francine standing next to a trembling white bichon, her hand held high. The dog was perched on Suz's grooming table, the leash pulled tight, and the duo had clearly been waiting for Suz to arrive.

Suz cleared her throat. "What do you think you are doing?" she asked. "Were you about to strike that dog? Because I will report you to the stewards."

"I have been training and raising dogs professionally for years," Francine said, lowering her hand to pat the bichon on the head. "I would never do that."

Kari shook her head. "It certainly looked like it to me. And we heard the dog cry out in pain."

Francine curled her lip. "Don't be ridiculous. Snowball is just a little high-strung. These kinds of animals make all kinds of noises to get attention." She patted the dog again, although Kari couldn't detect anything that looked like affection in the gesture.

"Sure," Suz said. "Whatever. But I won't hesitate to inform Olivia if I see anything I think is inappropriate. We take these kinds of things very seriously around here."

Francine smiled, but there was a glint of menace in her green eyes that didn't quite match the meek personality she had projected earlier. "I take things seriously too," she said in a quiet voice. "If I were you, I'd keep my nose out of other people's business."

Then she shrugged, as if dismissing the entire incident. "Now, are we going to get this handsome boy looking his best for his big weekend?" She leaned over the dog. "You'd like that, wouldn't you, sweetie?"

Suz and Kari exchanged glances. The woman changed moods faster than an agility dog jumped through hoops. Even Queenie muttered a feline comment from the depths of Kari's bag before hopping out to sit on top of a supply cabinet so she could supervise.

"If you're all set here, I'd better go check on the sanctuary tent," Kari said. "Queenie, come on."

The kitten didn't budge. Instead, she settled down with her head on her front paws, watching the grooming table with interest.

Suz laughed. "Apparently she doesn't trust me to work without her. Why don't you leave her here and come get her when you're done?"

"If you're sure," Kari said. "I won't be long." She turned

to the kitten. "Be good." She'd had a lot of cats in her life, but never one who was quite this determined to get her own way. It was amusing and challenging in about equal measures. But she wouldn't have traded Queenie for any other kitten in the world.

The Serenity Sanctuary tent was bustling when she got there. The members of the public who had come to watch the events had started to arrive, and show attendees mixed and mingled with old friends and new. The rescue tent seemed to be drawing a lot of attention, and the donation jar was starting to fill up.

"How are things going?" Kari asked Sara.

Sara gave her a big grin, flipping the turquoise streak in her cropped gray hair. She wore a shelter tee shirt in a matching turquoise and a pair of tan Capri pants. Cute white-and-blue sandals completed her ensemble. "I think we're a success," she said.

"We've already got two applications for kitten adoptions and one man who is interested in coming to the shelter to meet one of the dogs." She pointed at a picture on the board of a black-and-white pit bull with a lolling tongue. "On top of that, we have a couple of folks who filled out applications to come to the shelter and volunteer, including one woman who leads a Girl Scout troop who wants to bring her girls to walk the dogs."

"That's great!" Kari said. They were always short-handed, and having someone to take the dogs out into the fenced runs and walking trails would free up people who were trained to do the other jobs that needed to be done. "Is there a badge for that?"

"I think it falls under community service," Sara said.

"But if it doesn't, I'll happily create a badge to give them myself."

Kari chuckled. "I would too, although my sewing skills are less than impressive. It looks like you have everything under control here. If you don't need me, I'd better get back to Suz. She has her hands full, and like any badge I might sew, I think she is starting to fray around the edges."

"Oh dear," Sara said. "And the show has only just started."

"I have a feeling it is going to be a long three days," Kari said.

She headed back toward Suz's tent to pick up Queenie, most of her mind on whether to get a snack from one of the healthier vendors or give in to the heady aromas coming from the truck selling fried dough. She finally decided on the latter, justifying it by telling herself that it was only once a year, and besides, she was doing so much running around, she would burn off the extra calories by the end of the morning.

Between the visit to the shelter tent, the stop for her snack, and all the people she ran into who wanted to chat with her about the sanctuary, ask about her lottery win, or show off how gorgeous their dogs were (and admittedly, they were all pretty adorable), it was almost an hour before Kari made her way back to Suz's tent.

She was nearly there when she was sidetracked by the sound of raised voices. Francine, a newly clipped Snowball in her arms, was standing face-to-face with Miriam. The diminutive but feisty elderly woman was up on her tiptoes, one finger pointing at the little white dog, her voice high and verging on hysteria.

Francine, on the other hand, was clutching the dog to her chest and trying to move past the octogenarian, clearly trying to disengage herself from the confrontation.

"Is there a problem here?" Kari asked, walking up to them. People were starting to pay attention, and the last thing they needed was some kind of unpleasant incident to mar the opening day of the show.

"Not at all," Francine said, her eyes a little too wide behind her black-rimmed glasses. "This woman has just confused me with someone else."

"I have *not*," Miriam said, her small, square chin thrust out assertively, like some kind of miniature bulldog-poodle cross. "I know that bark. And I know you too, Lois Keller. You can change your hair and eye color and wear those ridiculous glasses and put on thirty pounds, but after what you put me through, I would know you anywhere."

Kari blinked. *What the heck was going on here?*

"I'm sorry, Miriam," she said in a gentle voice. "I'm afraid you're mistaken. This woman is named Francine Carver. She's the owner of Blue Skies Kennel."

Miriam's thin lips twisted. "That might be what she is calling herself now, but when I first met her, her name was Lois Keller. She was a breeder, all right. She sold me a dog with serious issues. Nearly broke my heart, not to mention my bank account. My dog was a bichon, and he had the same abnormally deep bark this dog has. It caught my attention from way over there." She pointed at a show ring across the way. "I've never heard another dog this size who sounded quite like it."

"She's crazy," Francine said. "I've never met this woman before in my life."

"Ladies? What seems to be the issue?" Suz asked, appearing out of the crowd that was starting to gather, drawn in by the raised voices.

"This is Lois Keller," Miriam said, her voice quavering with emotion. The finger she was using to point shook with agitation, or possibly fatigue. "She was barred from all AKC events. I'm going to have her kicked out of this show. She should be run out of town! She should be arrested!"

Suz gave Kari an alarmed look, glancing around at the increasing mass of bystanders, many of them hanging on every word.

"Miriam, I think you've confused Francine with someone else. This isn't even her dog. It belongs to Olivia Weiner. Francine is just handling the dog for Olivia," Suz said.

"I know what I know," Miriam insisted, crossing her arms over her scrawny chest. "I recognized the sound of that bark, and then when I got closer, I recognized Lois."

Francine let out a sigh. "I'm sorry, but I can't believe you think you can distinguish one dog's bark from a hundred others in the middle of a dog show. It's a warm day. Maybe you need to get a cold drink and sit in the shade for a while."

"I am not some crazy old woman!" Miriam said. She gave Suz a beseeching look. "I'm telling you, this is Lois Keller, and somehow this dog is related to the dog she sold me years ago. She shouldn't be allowed here."

Kari put her arm around the older woman. "I'm sure we'll get this sorted out," she said. "In the meanwhile, you need to get back to your own dog, and Francine needs to get Snowball back to Olivia. Let's go someplace where there aren't quite so many people, shall we?"

Miriam shook off Kari's arm. "I'll go," she said, giving Francine a hard stare. "But this isn't over." She stalked off, pushing her way through the crowd of mesmerized onlookers.

"No, it is not," Francine said, thinning her lips and glaring at Suz. "I don't know what kind of circus you are running

here, but I don't expect to be accosted by hysterical old ladies. I promise you, I'm going to have a few choice words
with Olivia about your complete lack of control over this
show." Shaking her head in disgust, she clutched Snowball
even closer and took off in the opposite direction.

Without anything left to watch, the remaining people
quickly went back to whatever they had been doing before
they'd been distracted by the altercation.

"Wow," Kari said. "That was . . . unexpected. Miriam
seemed so together when I met her earlier."

"Some folks get very overwrought at these shows," Suz
admitted. "They're just fun for me, but for people like Miriam and Olivia, they are as important as the Oscars or the
Olympics. Emotions can ride pretty high."

"Yeesh," Kari said. "It kind of makes me glad that Fred
is a completely untalented mutt with no aspirations higher
than stealing the cats' toys and burying them in the back-
yard."

Suz patted her on the shoulder. "And bless you for that.
I need one sane person around me for the duration."

"Well, 'sane' might be an overstatement," an amused
voice said from behind them. "But she's probably less nutty
than some of the rest of these folks."

Kari spun around, a big smile on her face. "Angus!" she
said. "I didn't know you were going to be here today."

Dr. Angus McCoy (and yes, he had heard all the "Dr.
McCoy" jokes) was one of the vets who took care of Kari's
pets, and he volunteered his time tending to the animals at
the shelter as well. He made it possible for them to provide
free spaying and neutering for any dog or cat they adopted
out, as well as offering low-cost spaying on a sliding scale
to members of the public who couldn't afford to pay full
price for their own animals. He and Kari shared the goal of

reducing the numbers of unwanted kittens and puppies, as well as finding homes for the ones who already existed.

They had also shared a couple of dates over the last two months, but they were both so busy, things hadn't gotten any further than that. Kari wasn't sure yet if there was potential for something more serious, but she did know that she found his shaggy red hair, twinkling eyes, and infectious smile attractive enough to try and find out.

He grinned at her, nodding at Suz, whose animals he also treated. "I'm the vet on duty for the show. The AKC mandates that there be a veterinarian on call for all dog shows, and the local kennel club prefers to have one on-site." He was wearing his everyday attire of jeans and a blue polo shirt that brought out the color in his eyes, but he also had a lanyard around his neck with a badge that said *Official Show Veterinarian*.

"I thought Dr. Grody was going to be here," Suz said. "I just talked to him last week and he said he was all set."

Angus brushed a lock of hair out of his face, a gesture Kari always found endearingly boyish and adorable for some reason. "He was, but then his daughter went into labor a month earlier than expected, and he and his wife had to leave for Boston right away to be with her. So he called and asked me to sub. I would have thought Olivia would have let you know."

Suz rolled her eyes. "Yeah, you would think that. But she has been pretty preoccupied. Thanks for stepping in though, Doc. I really appreciate it."

"No problem," he said. "I love these shows. So many beautiful dogs." Someone walked by with a naked-looking Chinese hairless crested on a bright lime-green leash and he gave a small shudder. "Okay, and some not so beautiful ones. Although I know some people love them. And to be fair, all the ones I've met are very sweet. I just prefer my dogs to actually have fur on places other than their ears and tails."

Kari laughed. "Me too. I'm not a big fan of the hairless cats either, although sometimes when I'm sweeping up enough cat fur to make an entire new animal, I think they might have some good points."

"What was that big fuss about?" Angus asked, a more serious expression on his face. "I could hear it from two tents away. I was worried someone's dog had gotten hurt."

"I think it was just a misunderstanding," Kari said. "Do you know a local breeder named Francine Carver?"

He nodded, that one hank of hair sliding back into his eyes again. "Sure. Bichons, right? She comes into the offices occasionally if there is something serious going on, but like many breeders, she handles most of the smaller things herself. She seems quite competent. I will say that even for bichon frises, her dogs all look remarkably alike. I always have to check the charts to find out which one I'm dealing with." He grinned at them. "For all I can tell, she could be bringing in the same dog over and over again and telling me it is one of the others."

"We'd better get back to my tent," Suz said, looking at her watch again with a tiny wrinkle between her brows. "I have another owner bringing her dog in for a trim in ten minutes, and then I really should make the rounds and check that everything is running smoothly. Or at least as smoothly as possible, when you have hundreds of dogs, thousands of people, and Olivia Weiner going around stepping on everyone's toes." She glanced at Angus. "Oops. You didn't hear me say that last part."

He bit back a smile, but one dimple made a quick appearance to betray his amusement. "No worries," he said.

"I think I'm going deaf in that ear from all the barking. I heard nothing."

Suz sighed in relief, but started edging in the direction of her tent.

"Can I walk you ladies there?" Angus asked. "I don't have anywhere to be right now, and this might be the only chance I have to see Kari if things get busy." He winked at Suz. "And now you know the real reason I agreed to fill in for Doctor Grody."

Kari could feel herself blushing and ducked her head to pretend she was looking for something in her bag. It had been a long time since a man had given her butterflies in her stomach. At least in a good way. After a disastrous early marriage had ended in an acrimonious divorce, she'd pretty much avoided any serious romantic involvements, preferring to go it on her own rather than risk giving up her hard-won autonomy.

But Angus McCoy didn't seem the abusive, controlling type—although that kind rarely did when you first met them, in her experience—and so far hadn't set off any of her alarm bells. Plus, her animals liked him. That was a major recommendation as far as she was concerned. Even Suz approved, and she'd hated Kari's ex from the moment she'd met him.

The three of them walked back to Suz's tent, which was close enough that she had heard the shouting from there. Inside, Queenie was curled up on a nest of towels, looking sweet in the way that only kittens can. Kari's heart contracted at the sight of her. Kari hadn't intended to get another cat, but she thanked her lucky stars every day for whoever had abandoned the tiny black kitten in back of Kari's former apartment.

Queenie woke up as they came in and sat up to give

them a great big yawn that revealed a pink tongue and rows of sharp white teeth. Then she meowed at Kari, as if to say, *Where have you been?*

"Sorry it took me so long," Kari said. Usually she tried not to speak to her animals as if they were human beings around other folks, since that tended to get her odd looks. But both Suz and Angus did the same thing, so Kari didn't worry around them. Besides, she was pretty sure that Queenie understood every word she said. Even if the kitten only paid attention to the ones she felt like listening to. "I got sidetracked by a few things."

The kitten gave another yawn, unimpressed by Kari's excuses.

"I did happen to find someone selling organic cat treats," Kari said, pulling a colorful box decorated with pictures of salmon and chickens out of the depths of her bag. "I mean, if you think that would help you forgive me for taking so long."

Queenie promptly jumped from the pile of towels to the grooming table and sat down with her tail twitching slightly.

"Wow," Angus said. "You've got her really well trained."

Kari snorted, taking a couple of treats out of the box and giving them to Queenie one by one. Queenie plucked each one out of her hand and crunched away on it with apparent enjoyment.

"I'd say it is more like she has me well trained," Kari said with a laugh. "After all, she's not fetching me treats, is she?"

Angus grabbed one of the snacks and gave it to the kitten with a bow. "You get more beautiful every time I see you, Queen Nefertiti," he said. The kitten's purr was so loud, it practically shook the table.

"Stop sucking up to my cat," Kari said. But she could feel her smile getting wider. Her animals were definitely the way to her heart. That and chocolate.

A low buzzing noise made everyone except Queenie jump.

"Drat," Angus said, peering at the pager attached to his belt. "It looks like there is a crisis at Ring Four. Something about an argument between a Bernese mountain dog and a schnauzer." He rolled his eyes. "How much do you want to bet that the schnauzer started it?"

He gave Queenie one more treat, then hurried out of the tent.

Kari tried not to sigh like a lovesick teenager, but her friend grinned at her anyway. Before Suz could start to tease her, they were interrupted by an angry whirlwind as Olivia stormed into the tent, Francine hot on her heels.

"What on earth do you call *this*?" Olivia asked indignantly, holding a bemused-looking Snowball out at arm's length.

Suz and Kari exchanged glances, and Kari just barely managed to keep herself from rolling her eyes. Queenie licked one velvety paw, seemingly uninterested in the loudly squawking human.

"Um, your dog Snowball?" Suz said, clearly at a loss to understand what the other woman was so upset about. "Is there a problem?"

"I'll say there is a problem," Olivia said indignantly. "You have always been very reliable up until now, but I can't believe you chose today of all days to botch my dog's haircut. You know as well as I do that imperfections of any kind could cost me the title of Best in Show. How could you?"

Suz opened and closed her mouth a couple of times before she could even make any words come out. "I don't know what you're talking about. I gave that dog exactly the trim we agreed upon."

Francine plucked Snowball out of Olivia's hands and plopped him on the table, Queenie adroitly hopping onto Kari's shoulder to get out of the way.

"Really?" the breeder said in a triumphant tone. "This is your idea of a correct cut for a bichon?" She pointed at a ragged area under the dog's belly where the fur was clearly uneven. The glint in her eye made Kari wonder if Francine could have done something as nefarious as messing up the cut herself to get back at Suz for yelling at her for mistreating the dog.

"I didn't do that!" Suz sputtered. "I would never make that big a mistake on a clip." She yanked on her hair, making the lavender strands stand up even more than usual. "I don't know how that happened, but I swear, the dog didn't look like that when he left my tent."

Olivia puffed out her chest and waved her arms. "Well, he clearly looks like that now!" she said, her voice going up at the end to a pitch that made Queenie duck her head into Kari's neck. Olivia flailed around so wildly, one arm caught the edge of a portable cart that was holding a number of grooming tools. Scissors and combs and clippers went flying through the air to land on the grassy ground.

"Crap!" Suz said. She and Kari scrambled to pick them all up. Olivia bent down to help, but got in the way more than she actually assisted.

"You really need to keep your things better organized," the older woman said, plopping what Kari knew to be an expensive set of clippers down with a thud. "Someone could get hurt if you are so careless with them."

Suz ground her teeth together so hard, Kari was afraid

she'd crack a molar. But when the groomer spoke, her tone was even and polite.

"Absolutely," Suz said through tense lips. "I'll get right on that. And I don't know what happened with Snowball, but if you leave him here, I'll fix that cut so it is fit for the show ring." Kari knew there was no way her friend was going to let the dog be seen with a clumsy chop job and let Olivia blame her for it to the whole world.

"See that you do it correctly this time," Olivia said with a sniff, hefting her colorful designer purse higher up on her shoulder. "I've got some important things to deal with, but I'll be back in an hour."

She swept out of the tent with Francine following her. As soon as they were out of hearing range, Suz let out a huge groan.

"I can't believe that woman," she said. "I swear, when Snowball left here earlier, he was perfect."

"I believe you," Kari said, giving her friend a hug. They walked out of the tent to watch Olivia stalk off across the green to yell at a vendor. Francine veered off in another direction, but she didn't make it far before she was stopped by a large, muscular man who seemed to loom over the breeder in an almost threatening manner. He was tall and imposing, with a shiny bald head, and even from this distance Kari could tell his nose had probably been broken multiple times.

"Do you know who that is?" Kari asked Suz. "He doesn't look like the dog show type, somehow."

Suz put her hand over her eyes to cut the glare as she gazed into the sun. "Huh. I don't recognize him from here, but we do get all sorts." She peered a little closer. "It's hard to say from this distance, but it looks like they're arguing about something. Do you think we should go check and make sure Francine is okay?"

But before they could make a decision, Francine wheeled around and took off, walking away from the strange man as fast as she could. If Kari didn't know any better, she would have said the woman looked scared.

Three

A few hours later, Suz and Kari met up at Ring Three, where the non-sporting breeds were being shown. They were both munching on aromatic sausage, onion, and pepper rolls, since neither of them had gotten lunch, and Kari was trying to convince Queenie, who was perched inside her tote bag, that none of those things were good for cats. Judging by the kitten's disgruntled expression, she wasn't buying it.

Kari couldn't blame her. The rolls were delicious, made by a vendor who used her own homegrown pork and vegetables and baked her own crusty wheat rolls. The sausages were slightly spicy, and the onions and peppers were sweet and flavorful. Suz and Kari had agreed they were far better than the usual county fair versions—which was really saying something.

Despite everything that had happened earlier in the day, the two friends had showed up to be supportive of Olivia, along with a number of the other kennel club members. She was standing next to them, practically holding her breath as Francine led Snowball through his paces in the ring.

The rings were fairly simple, nothing more than circular areas on the grass demarcated by ropes strung on posts, with a few openings for people and their dogs to come in and out through. Various equipment was tucked along the side of each one for whichever trials the dogs might be performing, and there was a chair for the judge, although they usually spent most of their time on their feet.

"He looks good, doesn't he," Olivia said in a loud whisper. "I mean, really, really good."

Kari had to admit that he did. No matter her faults, Francine was a consummate professional when she was handling a dog in front of a judge. Her short hair was tucked back behind a brown velvet headband, and her drab khaki clothing and low, practical shoes made it easy for her to blend into the background so all you focused on was the dog.

Snowball was in his element, and he flew around the ring with his tail held high, following each command to the letter and looking every inch the top of his class. His fur, Kari was happy to see, looked perfect too, after Suz's careful repair job.

"He does," Suz said. "You've really done a fabulous job with him, Olivia. It's hard to say for sure, but I think the judge agrees."

Snowball finished his final circuit of the ring and stood patiently while the judge, a stern-looking woman dressed all in black despite the heat of the summer's day, gave him a thorough going-over, checking for conformation to breed standards and general health.

Then they had to watch three more dogs in the non-sporting group do the same thing, and then all fifteen dogs who were competing ran around the ring together before the judge announced the winner for that group—Snowball.

Olivia was practically incandescent with joy. "I knew it!" she said gleefully, clasping her hands together. "I tell you, this is finally my year. Snowball is going to win Best in Show today, and together, we're going to go all the way to the top!"

"The top?" Kari asked. She couldn't help being glad for Olivia, no matter how big a pain the woman might be. This was clearly incredibly important to her.

"Westminster," Olivia said in reverent tones, like another woman might say, "Paris," or maybe, "George Clooney."

Suz looked at the dog with a critical eye and gave a tentative nod. "The Westminster Dog Show. That's the top, all right. But you're not wrong. He is awfully good. He might just have what it takes. Congratulations, Olivia."

Francine headed in their direction, proudly holding up the blue ribbon that designated Snowball's first-place win. Snowball trotted beside her, head high and pink tongue lolling. He clearly knew he had done well.

But before Francine got to them, she was intercepted by the same large man they had seen her arguing with earlier. He pointed at the dog, then back at her, his face drawn into an angry grimace.

"Who is that?" Olivia asked. "That man with Francine. He looks quite disreputable."

Suz shook her head. "I don't know. But we saw him earlier. I don't think he's good news, whoever he is." The sound of increasingly loud voices reinforced that suggestion.

Since Francine seemed to be stuck in place, the other three moved in her direction. As they drew closer, it became clear from the man's loud voice and use of profanity that the conversation was as adversarial as it seemed. The judge, who was getting ready to examine the next group of dogs, cast a disapproving glance toward the shouting pair, and Suz and Kari moved even faster.

"Good job with Snowball," Suz said to Francine as they got closer, then turned to the bald man. "Is there a problem here?"

"No problem," he growled. "The *lady*"—this was said with a clearly sarcastic tone—"the lady and I have some unfinished business, that's all."

"I've never met this man before in my life," Francine said. But Kari noticed that the hand holding on to Snowball's leash was clenched so tightly, the knuckles had turned white.

"Do you want me to call the police?" Suz asked. She pulled out her cell phone and poised one finger over the 9.

To Kari's surprise, the guy just let out a deep laugh. "You go right ahead, sweetheart. I guarantee you, that's the last thing she wants." He turned back to tower over Francine. "You haven't heard the last of me. I want my money back—or else. And I'm not going away until I get it." He swiveled on one huge, boot-clad heel and stomped off in the direction of the parking lot.

"What on earth was that about?" Olivia asked, reaching out to snatch Snowball's leash from Francine's grasp. "I have never seen such goings-on at a dog show in my life." She didn't wait for Francine to answer before turning to Suz and saying through gritted teeth, "You are doing a simply dreadful job of running this show. You've allowed that man to completely ruin my moment."

"But I—" Suz sputtered. Her mouth opened and closed again like a fish out of water. "Olivia, I didn't do anything!"

"No, you didn't, did you?" Olivia said. Glaring at Francine and Kari just for good measure, she stalked off, practically dragging Snowball as his little legs trotted as fast as they could to keep up with her indignation-fueled pace.

"Good grief," Francine muttered under her breath. "That woman is a piece of work. 'Thank you for the good job, Francine. Great work winning the blue ribbon, Francine.' Pfft." She looked up at the other two and said, "I need a cup of coffee," and took off too.

Suz and Kari were left standing by themselves, gazing at each other in stunned silence. After a minute, Kari said, "Well, that was fun. Want to go pet some cute kittens? It might be therapeutic."

"Yes, please," Suz said, shaking her head. "And remind me never to volunteer for anything ever again."

At around five, an exhausted and frazzled Suz was back at the Serenity Sanctuary tent, sitting on a stool drinking a bottle of cold water Kari had forced on her and watching as Bryn Jenkins, one of the shelter workers, got the kittens ready to go back home for the night. Ever helpful, Queenie was napping on top of one of the piles of tee shirts they were selling, which bore the sanctuary logo of a cat and dog in silhouette in front of a hand-drawn heart. Bryn was wearing one in vivid red to help promote them, along with her usual ripped jeans.

Bryn had been one of the most loyal volunteers during the shelter's previous existence, sticking with former owner Daisy even when there wasn't a penny in the coffers and they were slowly going under. Young, competent, and dedicated, she was studying to be a vet tech at Perryville State College, whose grounds they were on today. She hadn't been thrilled about Kari buying the sanctuary, and it had taken them a while to arrive at a level of trust. These days Bryn worked part-time at the shelter when she wasn't taking classes, and she was doing an informal apprenticeship with Angus when he came to take care of the animals.

Unlike her occasionally strained relationship with Kari, Bryn got along with Suz just fine. In fact, Kari suspected Suz's influence had a lot to do with Bryn's improved attitude toward Kari, the person who had replaced the boss Bryn had adored after Daisy had moved away to live with her sister.

Right now, Suz was teasing Bryn, flicking drops of water from her sweating bottle onto the younger woman's neck and making her giggle. They were quite the contrast—the tall, pale, spiky- and lavender-haired Suz and the more petite Bryn, with her dark hair in its many tiny braids, light brown skin, and delicate jeweled nose stud. But their matching grins made Kari smile too. Even Queenie picked up her head and let out an amused-sounding meow.

"Hey." One of the other members of the local dog club came through the entrance to the tent. "Did you hear? Olivia's dog won Best in Show for the day! And a couple of other ribbons earlier on. She's over the moon." She picked up some of the show booklets they had stacked on the table. "I promised I'd pick her up a couple extra of these as mementos. Apparently she wants to send them to her family and friends who weren't here."

"That's great," Suz said, holding the cold bottle up to her own neck for a second. The weather had gotten pretty warm as the day progressed, and they were all a little overheated. "Tell her we send our congratulations."

"Maybe the win will finally put Olivia in a better mood and she'll be less critical of you," Bryn said hopefully after the bearer of good news had left the tent.

Suz snorted down her long nose. "Maybe. Probably not.

Either way, I have a whole list of things to do to get the show shut down for the night, and no matter how good a mood she's in, Olivia won't be happy if I don't get them done." She took another long swig of water, and straightened up. "Kari, any chance you can come help?"

"I don't see why not," Kari said, taking a drink from her own water bottle and thinking wistful thoughts about a cold beer. She was definitely going to have one of those as soon as she got home. "Bryn, have you got everything under control here?"

Bryn nodded, braids bouncing with the motion. "Sure thing. All I have to do is put the sides of the tent down and tie them shut for the night, then put the kittens in my car to go back to the shelter. It won't take me long."

"Great," Kari said. "I don't suppose you want to stay here until I get back? I could come pick you up before I leave," she said, looking down at Queenie. In answer, the little black fuzzball simply yawned and jumped into Kari's tote bag.

"That's what I thought," Kari said. "Thanks for everything, Bryn. I'll see you tomorrow."

The two friends walked over to the judges' tent and made sure they all had rides back to their various bed-and-breakfasts or hotels. A couple of the judges had traveled to Perryville in RVs and were already "home" for the evening.

Kari had been surprised to discover that many of the people who acted as judges for the AKC circuit traveled across the country to attend various shows. According to the booklet for this weekend's events, there were eight judges total, and they came from six different states, including New Jersey, Ohio, and one who drove all the way from Seattle, Washington. Suz said they were paid a small amount, plus expenses, by the clubs putting on the shows, but that most of them did it for love of the dogs.

Hence the special care taken to make sure that they all had everything they needed. Suz and Kari tidied up the tent, took one errant golf cart back to its corral at the front gate so it would be ready for the judges to use the next morning, and packed up the remaining ribbons and paperwork. These had to be returned to the supply tent and put in their proper places so they'd be easy to grab when they set everything up for Day Two first thing tomorrow.

As they strolled across the short green grass to the supply tent, which had purposely been set off to one side, away from the more active show rings and participants' tents, they could see volunteers from the local club picking up garbage and gently escorting the last few stragglers back to the parking lot. There was also rather a lot of poop scooping going on, even though the dog owners were supposed to clean up after their own animals. Kari decided she was grateful to be helping Suz instead.

Despite the long day and the many dogs, the air still smelled fresh and clean, in part because of the breeze coming off the river. Kari caught a faint whiff of greasy fried goodness coming from the direction of the food trucks, but thankfully they'd shut down for the night too, so she didn't have to worry about being tempted. After all the fattening things she'd already eaten today, she was ready for a nice healthy salad for dinner. And that beer, of course. Everyone knows that beer has no calories if you drink it at the end of a really long day.

"That's odd," Suz said as they approached their goal. She shifted the box of ribbons she was carrying. If it was anything like the one Kari had, it had magically grown heavier as they'd crossed the expanse of lawn.

"What's odd?" Kari asked. As if they'd summoned her, Queenie poked her head up over the edge of Kari's bag and added her own questioning "Mew?" Then she hopped out of the bag and headed toward the tent. "Queenie, come back here, you monkey!" As usual, the kitten completely ignored her.

"The tent is tied closed," Suz said, putting her box down on the ground and pointing at where the front section had been fastened to the left-hand side. "No one was assigned to do that, since I knew I'd be the last one coming here." She shrugged and reached for the bottommost ties. "I suppose one of the volunteers just got carried away." She laughed as Queenie wiggled underneath as soon as there was a tiny bit of space.

"Oh, for goodness' sake," Kari said, sighing at her kitten's antics. She usually found them pretty amusing, but it was late and she was tired, and she really didn't feel like chasing a cat. She helped Suz open the next few ties and ducked in after the kitten.

The inside of the tent was dim, with only the ambient light coming in through the white canvas sides and a slice of brighter sunlight slipping though the small section they'd opened up. She couldn't see a small black furry miscreant anywhere among the shadowy forms of boxes and bags of supplies and whatever that was lying in the middle of the floor.

"Did you knock something over already?" Kari called out to the kitten. "You were only in here for a minute and a half." As her eyes adjusted, she walked over to the pile of cloths that were clearly out of place in the otherwise neatly organized tent and let out a muffled scream.

"What is it?" Suz asked, appearing at her side and looking down. "Oh, crap. Crap, crap, crap." The box of ribbons slipped out of her hands and landed on the grass on its side, colorful rosettes in red and purple and green slithering out to lie on the ground in ironic tribute.

"You can say that again," Kari said. At her feet, Queenie let out a hiss and a loud meow, and Kari bent down to pick her up so she wouldn't touch anything.

Not that the kitten could do anything to hurt Francine. The woman was clearly past any worries about help or harm, her body lying crumpled on its back, eyes open and staring at nothing, a pair of grooming shears with lavender handles protruding from her chest.

Somehow, Kari had a feeling her own worries were only beginning.

Four

There was no way they were staying inside the tent with Francine's dead body. It wasn't as though anyone was likely to disturb it if they left it, so Kari and Suz walked out of the tent and called 911 from the other side of the canvas walls.

Suz calmly described who they were and where they were calling from and promised they would wait where they were. Once she hung up, she consulted a complicated spreadsheet on her phone and then called the volunteer who was stationed at the entrance to warn him to expect official visitors and ask him to send them to the supply tent. She didn't tell him why.

"This is like the worst case of déjà vu ever," Kari said, hugging Queenie to her chest. She wasn't sure if she was trying to comfort the kitten or the other way around. This was the second time she and Queenie had found a body together. The last time it had been a nasty dog warden who had been trying to sabotage the shelter, and Kari had been one of the primary suspects until she had accidentally stumbled across the real murderer while looking for clues.

At least this time there was no connection between her and the victim. Although she wasn't sure the same could be said for her best friend.

"Um, I hate to bring this up," Kari said. "But were those—?"

Her question was cut off by the arrival of three men striding purposefully in their direction. Two of them were relatively young, wearing matching crew cuts and Perryville police uniforms. Kari had never seen them before, but that wasn't surprising, since she didn't spend much time in the neighboring town, and always tried to stay on the right side of the law.

Unfortunately, she knew the third man all too well, although she had never seen him dressed in civilian clothes—in this case, a short-sleeved button-down shirt and blue jeans so neat they might have been pressed. In his late fifties, he had the look of an ex–high school jock gone only slightly soft around the edges.

"Oh, no," she said.

"Isn't that Sheriff Richardson?" Suz asked. "What is he doing here?"

"Attending a dog show, believe it or not, Ms. Holden," the sheriff said, his sharp ears missing nothing, as usual. "I overheard the call on my radio as I was heading home, so I turned around and came to see if I could be of any assistance. The Perryville chief of police is a pal of mine, and I told him that some of the folks taking part in the show came from my jurisdiction and I might know them." He cocked an eyebrow in Kari's direction. "The two of you in particular. These gentlemen were already in the neighborhood, so they caught the call."

The taller of the two Perryville cops stepped forward, obviously trying to regain control of the situation. "Are you the ones who reported finding a dead body?" he asked. "I'm Officer Kent, and this is Officer Clark."

Suz bit her lip.

"Don't," the officer sighed. He had blond hair so light it looked almost white, and pale lashes that gave him a permanently startled look. His partner, on the other hand, had straight black hair and Asian features. They both looked like they were young enough to be attending college, not policing one. "We know. We've heard all the Superman jokes. Just answer the question."

Kari coughed into her hand to cover up the laugh she couldn't quite keep down. But then she remembered what was in the tent, and any urge for humor fled faster than a speeding bullet.

"Yes, we're the ones who called," Suz said. "She's in there, toward the middle of the tent." She pointed with a finger that only shook a little.

Kent rolled his eyes, clearly not believing them. "You're sure it isn't just a pile of rags or something else that looks vaguely like a person? You wouldn't believe how many calls we get about dead bodies that turn out to be an old black garbage bag containing nothing more interesting that someone's discarded winter clothing."

Sheriff Richardson nodded at Kari. "Actually, Ms. Stuart found a murder victim a couple of months ago. And Ms. Holden is hardly the hysterical type who jumps at shadows. I suspect that if these two say there is a body, there really is one."

"Really?" Clark said, looking suspiciously at Kari. "So you make a habit of finding dead people?"

"Two isn't exactly a habit," Kari muttered. "And it isn't as though I do it on purpose."

He scowled at her, as if he couldn't decide if she was being facetious or not.

"Let's just go inside and check, shall we, gentlemen?" Richardson said in a firm tone that no young officer in his right mind would ever argue with. "Once we know what we're dealing with, we can figure out if we need to question these ladies any further."

Kari was pretty sure she knew the answer to that one.

A couple of minutes later, all three cops came back out of the tent looking grim, and in Kent's case, even paler than before, if that was possible. Clark walked back in the direction of the parking lot, talking rapidly on his phone. Kent and the sheriff walked over to where Kari and Suz were standing, the kitten back on her perch on Kari's shoulder. Kari knew that set of the sheriff's jaw all too well.

"There's a dead body in there," Kent said, sounding almost as if he had expected them to be lying and was indignant that he'd been proven wrong.

"We did say so," Suz said in a mild tone.

Richardson rolled his eyes. "The woman didn't have any identification on her, and we didn't find a purse, although obviously we haven't searched the entire tent yet. Do you happen to know who she was?"

"Her name was Francine Carver," Kari said. "She is—I mean was—a dog breeder. She was showing a dog today for Olivia Weiner."

Richardson made a note in his ever-present notebook, and Kent rapidly pulled his cell phone out and started tapping on the keyboard.

"How did you happen to find the body?" the sheriff asked. "Were you looking for Ms. Carver?"

"Not at all," Kari said. "As far as we knew, she'd gone home with everyone else. Suz is part of the kennel club putting on the show, and she got stuck doing a bunch of organizational jobs at the last minute, so I was helping her out. This tent"—she pointed to the one they were standing next to—"is where various supplies are kept. We were returning a couple of boxes of ribbons and paperwork to keep them safe until tomorrow."

"Would those be the ribbons that are all over the ground next to the victim's body?" Richardson asked. Kari couldn't tell if his tone was disapproving or just curious. Kari was still clutching her carton, not knowing if it was okay to put it down or not.

"Sorry," Suz said, flushing. "I got startled when I saw the body and dropped the box. I hope I didn't mess anything up." She shuddered. "The only dead person I've ever seen was my grandmother, and she died peacefully in her sleep."

"Unfortunately for Ms. Carver, that clearly wasn't the case here," Richardson said. "But I don't think the ribbons will be a problem, now that we know they weren't in place at the time of the murder." He stared from Kari to Suz and, after a moment's hesitation, back at the kitten sitting on Kari's shoulder. "Did any of you touch anything when you were in there?"

Suz shook her head. "We undid the tent ties when we got here, but I didn't touch anything else. Kari went in first, though."

"The kitten ducked under the edge of the tent as soon as we had it open," Kari explained. "I followed her in to keep her out of trouble. When I found her, she was sitting next to the body. But I don't think either of us touched anything. I picked her up right away so she wouldn't contaminate the scene any more than she already had. Sorry."

"The tent was closed up when you got here?" Kent said.

"It was," Suz said thoughtfully. "And it shouldn't have been, since I was planning to come back here. We just assumed someone had been trying to be helpful, but maybe not . . ."

Richardson raised an eyebrow. "You're suggesting the killer closed up the tent after murdering Ms. Carver?" He rubbed his chin thoughtfully.

"What difference would that make?" Kent asked. "Would the killer's fingerprints be on the tie strings?"

"That's always a possibility," the sheriff said. "But I'm also more interested in what it would say about the killer, if in fact it is true."

He gazed at the tent. "It would indicate either that the crime was premeditated or else that our killer is very calm under pressure. Most people who commit murder on the spur of the moment tend to panic and either run away or try to cover up the crime. Stabbing someone in the chest with a pair of scissors would normally indicate an impulsive act, where someone picked up whatever was handy and struck out with it. Maybe a robbery gone wrong, since her purse is missing. But that doesn't jibe with neatly closing up the tent afterward.

"Are scissors normally kept in the storage tent?" he asked Suz.

"No, they're not," she said. Kari winced, knowing what was coming.

"In fact," Suz said, "I'm pretty sure they're mine." She twisted her hands together in front of her, and it was all Kari could do not to reach out and hug her friend. But she had a feeling the cops might frown on that.

"Wait," Kent said, his homely face lighting up with excitement. "You're admitting to murdering her?"

Suz sighed. "No, of course I'm not. I had nothing to do with it. But I'm sure you noticed the color of the scissors, right?"

"They were some kind of light purple," Kent said, scrunching up his forehead. "I've never seen scissors like that before. Aren't they usually silver or black?"

"Mostly, yes," Suz said. "The ones in the tent"—Kari noticed she didn't say *in Francine's chest*—"those looked like the ones I use for my grooming business. I order them in my signature lavender shade from a specialty online shop, and you have to buy them in sets of eight pieces. These ones are longer and thinner than your average pair of scissors, and sharper than usual for making precise cuts. They also have cushioned plastic handles because I use them all day. They aren't the kind of thing someone would be able to just walk into a store and pick up."

"Interesting," Richardson said. He made another note on his pad. Kari had painful memories associated with that thing from when she was a suspect, and she had to make an effort not to twitch. Queenie nuzzled her ear as if sensing her person was in need of comfort.

"So, Ms. Holden," he went on, "who could have had access to those scissors, assuming it wasn't you who used them on the victim?"

"Yes, let's assume that," Suz said in a wry tone. As Richardson had pointed out to the younger officer, Suz was pretty hard to rattle. She'd grown up as a gay woman when that wasn't always readily accepted in a small town, not to mention being a foot taller than most of her classmates by the time she hit high school. Plus she dealt with Dobermans and mastiffs for a living. It would take more than being accused of a murder she knew she hadn't committed to keep her from being snarky.

"Unfortunately," she said, "we had more than a thousand people through here during the day. Any one of them could have, theoretically at least, gone into my tent and picked up a pair of scissors."

"That seems very irresponsible," Officer Kent said, trying to sound stern. "Leaving a pair of sharp scissors out where anyone could get at them."

"Normally I would have had them locked up in my portable case when I wasn't there," Suz admitted. "But today was crazy, and I spent a lot of time running in and out of the tent to handle issues. Then I'd go back to work on a dog, then run out again for a few minutes. It just didn't make sense to keep putting them away every single time."

Richardson shook his head, his graying brown hair cut short and neat, although not as dramatically as the Perryville cops'. Kari had the irreverent thought that it looked as precise as one of Suz's efforts, but decided it would be best to keep that to herself.

"So in theory, someone could have waited until you left on one of your errands, strolled into your tent, and taken them," he said. "But if the scissors are as distinctive as you say, wouldn't whoever took them know that the blame would land squarely on you?"

Kari's jaw dropped. "Are you saying someone is trying to frame Suz?"

"It's possible," Richardson said. "But it is also possible that it was just a matter of convenience and accessibility."

"Or that you did it, figuring we'd believe you wouldn't be stupid enough to use a weapon that could be traced back to you," Kent added.

"Or that," the sheriff agreed. Kari couldn't tell from his

expression whether he thought that was likely or not. She knew from experience that he was nearly impossible to read.

"Do we know when the victim was last seen alive?" Kent asked.

"Good question," Richardson said in an approving tone. "When was the last time either of you saw her?"

"I think it was around three o'clock," Kari said. "She showed Olivia's dog at two, and they finished up the judging a little before three."

"Olivia Weiner, you said." Richardson made another note. "Would that be the wife of the Used-Car King, Jack Weiner?"

"I love his commercials!" Kent said, showing more animation than he had during most of the questioning. "That one where the bulldog was driving the truck was a hoot."

Richardson rolled his eyes. "You're still new at this," he said to the younger cop. "But you'll find that having someone wealthy or influential involved in one of your cases only complicates things." He grimaced. "And I've met Olivia Weiner. She is *definitely* going to complicate things."

"You can say that again," Suz muttered.

"So the victim was working for Mrs. Weiner?" the sheriff asked, ignoring Suz's last comment.

"Yes," Suz said. "Francine was handling Snowball, Olivia's bichon frise. From what I understand, Francine breeds that type of dog, although this particular one wasn't one of hers, so when Olivia's regular handler had an accident and couldn't come, Olivia asked Francine to step in."

"Were they friends?" Richardson asked.

"Oh, I don't think so," Kari said. "I'm not even sure they liked each other very much. I think it was strictly a professional relationship."

"I see." Richardson jotted down a couple more things.

Kari wished she could look at the paper. For all she knew, he was writing limericks and just scribbling on the pad to make them nervous. In her case, it was kind of working.

"And can you tell me where you were between three and the time you found the victim?" he asked Suz, not glancing up from the notebook. "Which was?"

"Five forty-seven, according to the dispatcher," Kent put in helpfully.

"Thank you," Richardson said dryly. Kari was pretty sure he'd wanted Suz to answer that herself. "Now, about that alibi?"

Suz ran one hand through her hair. "Like I said, I was running around all over the place. I was mostly done with my grooming appointments for the day, but I had to check in on the judges, deal with a number of small crises, and settle an argument between two vendors who both thought they were the only ones who were allowed to sell organic dog treats. There are plenty of people who saw me, but I have no idea exactly when or, honestly, even in what order. By that point in the day, it was all starting to blur together."

"I see," he said. More notes. He gazed at Kari. "And were you with her that whole time?"

Kari grimaced. "No, I wasn't. I went back to the sanctuary tent for a while. Suz came in around five fifteen as we were shutting down for the day, and I made her drink a bottle of water. Then we went out to deal with the last few things. I was with her from then on."

"So no one can vouch for your whereabouts between a little after three and five fifteen?" Kent said. He tapped that into his phone, obviously taking Richardson's example to heart.

"Not every single minute," Suz said. "But there were plenty of people who saw me."

"And we'll be talking to as many of them as we can find," Richardson said. "We'll put together a timeline. It would help if you could write down what you do remember about where you went and who you saw. But let's face it—it wouldn't have taken long to duck into this tent, stab the woman, close it back up, and get back about your business."

"Did you have any beef with the victim?" Kent asked, narrowing his eyes at her.

"No, I didn't," Suz said. "I only met her for the first time today, and we didn't have many interactions. But there were definitely a few people who did."

Five

"Would you care to explain that statement, Ms. Holden?" Richardson said, pen poised over his notebook.

"Well, there was the bald guy she had a fight with," Suz said. "I don't know who he was. We saw him talking to her earlier in the day, and it didn't seem like a friendly conversation. But we weren't close enough to hear anything. Then, after she finished up with Snowball in the ring, he came up and accosted her when we were standing right there.

"You can ask Olivia," Suz added. "She was there too, and she got mad at me because I somehow hadn't prevented them from making a scene in public and disturbing the show. She accused me of allowing them to ruin her 'moment.'"

"Her moment?" repeated Kent, looking confused.

"Olivia's dog won the event," Kari explained. "She was really excited and happy, and then Francine and this mystery man caused a fuss. It kind of took the wind out of Olivia's sails. I don't know why she blamed Suz, though. Except that she seems to be holding her responsible for every little thing that goes wrong with the show."

"Huh," Richardson said. From what he'd said, he'd obviously met Olivia before. Maybe that's why he didn't ask any more questions. About that, anyway. "So you have no idea who this guy was?"

"Never saw him before," Suz said, and Kari nodded her head in agreement.

"He said something about wanting his money back," Kari added. "Francine looked a little scared, I thought. I didn't blame her either. He was pretty intimidating. Looked like a boxer or a bouncer or something. He was a little under average height, but his muscles had muscles, and it looked like his nose had been broken a couple of times. Like Suz said, he was completely bald. He took off after the confrontation, but he said she hadn't heard the last from him."

Kent gave Kari a dubious look. "Are you sure you aren't making up this conveniently threatening thug to take the suspicion off your friend?"

Kari stifled a sigh. "Like Suz said, Olivia was right there. And lots of other people saw them. This guy wasn't exactly subtle. Just ask around."

"I assure you, we will," Kent said stiffly. "We take murder very seriously here in Perryville."

Like she thought it was a laugh riot? "That's good to know," Kari said. "Have you had many?"

"Excuse me?"

"Murders. To take seriously. I was just wondering if you've had a lot of them," she asked.

Richardson bit his lip, but Kari could see the corners of his mouth curve up despite his best efforts.

"Uh, well, no. I mean, not since I've been on the force. Perryville is a pretty peaceful town," the young cop said, a flush moving up from the base of his neck. "But I assure you, we're going to take *this one* very seriously."

"I'm sure you are," Kari said. She thought for a moment. "In that case, you might also want to check into the SHAFFT guy at the front gate."

"Shaft guy?" Kent repeated. "Like the one in the movie? Or some guy holding a large pole?" He had one finger poised over his phone.

Richardson let out a sigh. "SHAFFT, Officer Kent. Save Helpless Animal Friends From Tyranny. It's an animal rights group known for being somewhat extreme in their approach to protecting anything from chickens to endangered species." He turned to Kari. "Are there SHAFFT folks here?"

She nodded, making Queenie hold on a little tighter to her perch on Kari's shoulder. "Ow, watch it." Kari put one hand up to steady the kitten. "Sorry, claws. Uh, yeah, they were making a big fuss at the front gates when we got here this morning. Waving signs and yelling at the people coming in. There was one guy, I think he was in charge, who really got into Francine's face. Accused her of running a puppy mill."

"Interesting," Richardson said. "I saw them when I got here for the show, but they weren't there when we answered your call. Must have left for the day. I don't suppose you got this gentleman's name?"

"I think maybe Chloe, who was at the front gate, knew who he was. If she mentioned his name, I don't remember it," Kari said. "But I can tell you that he told Francine animal lives are just as important as human ones and people like her should be killed for the good of all dogs."

One bushy graying eyebrow went up. "Did he, now? I would definitely like to have a chat with him. I'm sure we'll be able to find out who he is."

"If not, I'm willing to bet they'll be back tomorrow

morning," Kari said. "They didn't strike me as the kind of group to only come for the first day of a three-day show."

Just then Kent's radio squawked, and he talked into it for a minute. "Clark's got the medical examiner and the ambulance," he said. "He wants to know if you want them to drive up here or walk."

"Tell them to drive as close as they can get," the sheriff said. "There aren't many people still around, but we should probably keep as low a profile as possible. No point in walking through the place with a body bag on a stretcher."

Paved roads ran throughout the campus, and many of the tents had been set up in the wide expanse of lawn between them. The supply tent was farther back than most, since they'd had volunteers to help them haul everything in when they set up the night before and lined up to help them lug it all out at the end of the show. It wasn't a place that the attendees or general public would need to access, so it didn't matter that it was out of the way and a bit inconvenient to get to. Until now.

A few minutes later, a squad car drove slowly up the nearest road, followed by a gray sedan and an ambulance with no lights or sirens. Sadly, Kari thought, Francine was well beyond needing either.

"So Ms. Carver had run-ins with an unidentified bald man and someone from the local SHAFFT group," Richardson said as they waited for the newest arrivals to join them. "Is that it for any problems that you know of?"

Suz and Kari exchanged looks.

"What?" the sheriff asked. "What aren't you telling us?"

Kari started to shrug and then stopped when Queenie dug her nails in again. "It's nothing, I mean . . ."

"She's old," Suz added, probably equally unhelpfully. "And tiny. There's no way she had anything to do with it."

Richardson heaved a sigh and crossed his beefy arms over his chest. "Ladies, I think you know by now that I prefer to have all the facts and be allowed to make my own decisions about how pertinent something might or might not be to a case." He stared from Kari to Suz and back again. "Now, who are we talking about, exactly?"

Suz ran a hand through her hair and scrunched up her face. Kari nodded at her. If they didn't tell him, someone else would. And really, there was no way tiny, sweet Miriam could have killed Francine. Was there?

"Earlier in the day, a woman from the Saratoga Kennel Club got into a disagreement with Francine," Suz said, reluctance visible in every line of her long body. "Well, it wasn't even really a disagreement, because it was completely one-sided."

"This woman's name?" Richardson asked, pen ready over his notebook.

"Miriam Rosebaum," Kari said. "But she's over eighty and about as big as my thumb." She held up her thumb as if to demonstrate how small Miriam really was. "I can't see how she would be able to kill someone young and healthy like Francine."

"You would be amazed how tough some of the seemingly harmless little old ladies turn out to be," Richardson said. "I had a case years ago when a seventy-five-year-old great-grandmother bludgeoned her son-in-law to death with a cast-iron frying pan. Mind you, it turned out he deserved it, but even so, she weighed all of about one hundred pounds dripping wet and she smashed his head like a melon." He shook his head ruefully. "I no longer make any assumptions about murderous ability based on age or size."

Suz pointed a finger up and down her own tall and muscular frame. "As long as you don't assume anything about someone just because they happen to be large and strong," she said. "As for Miriam, I've known her for a few years, although not very well. She's a regular at the show. I've never seen her get so upset before. But Francine swore it was a case of mistaken identity, and I'm sure Miriam ended up feeling embarrassed about making a fuss over nothing."

Officer Clark walked over to them, accompanied by a short, pudgy, middle-aged man with slightly overexuberant eyebrows. Kari recognized him as Doc Phelps, who acted as the county coroner. They were trailed by two men from the local fire department carrying a stretcher. They were dressed in jeans and tee shirts instead of their gear, so they had undoubtedly come with the ambulance. In a town as small as Perryville, the firemen often doubled as EMTs, and most of them were volunteers. These guys had either been on duty or had been pulled away from their day jobs to come deal with this thankless task

The sheriff held up one hand to signal them to wait. "What kind of mistaken identity are we talking about here, Ms. Holden?"

Suz cast an unhappy glance at Kari, clearly not comfortable with the thought of getting Miriam into trouble. But it wasn't as if they had a choice.

"Miriam accused Francine of being someone else. A breeder who had sold Miriam a dog with serious issues, apparently, and who had later been banned by the AKC. Miriam insisted that Francine had changed her hair and eye color somehow and put on a lot of weight, but Miriam swore she would recognize the woman anywhere. Francine said she was wrong and walked away, and that was it." Suz fiddled with the line of studs that ran down the side of her ear. Today they were all shades of red, to match her tee shirt. "I can't imagine it was anything worth killing over."

"Very little is, Ms. Holden," Richardson said. "And yet people murder each other every day. Go figure."

He turned to the other men. "Doc, if you could certify the death and give me an estimate on the time of death, that would be great. We already took our pictures when we first got here, but Clark can take a few more after you okay the boys to move the body. I think you'll find the cause of death is pretty obvious, but let me know if you find anything unexpected.

"You can pick up all those ribbons and rosettes on the ground near the body and put them back in the box they came out of," he said to Clark. "They weren't there at the time of the murder. Ms. Holden dropped them when she and Ms. Stuart found the body."

Suz bit her lip. "There should be a clipboard in there too. I propped it on top of the box while I was carrying it. It has some information I really need for the next couple of days. Is there any chance I can get it back?"

Richardson pondered her request. "Come by in the morning. I'll see what I can do. In the meanwhile, though, if you have a copy in your computer, you might want to print it out just in case." He made another note, this time in larger letters, so Kari assumed it was a reminder to himself rather than a fact about the case.

"Speaking of information, do you happen to know if Francine Carver had a next of kin? I'll also need an address for her."

Suz and Kari looked at each other.

"I don't know about next of kin, sheriff," Suz said. "Maybe Olivia would have the answer to that, since she worked with the woman. But I have a list of all the attendees back at my tent, and Francine's address and phone number should be on it. I could go get it for you."

"Why don't we both go," Richardson said. Kari suddenly realized he probably wanted to get a look at Suz's tent. Or else he didn't want to let her out of his sight, for fear she would hide some kind of evidence. Either one would mean that he was seriously considering Suz as a suspect. Suddenly the remains of the sausage roll Kari had eaten felt like a ball of lead in her stomach.

"I'll come too," she said. "If that's okay."

The sheriff rolled his eyes, but didn't say anything to stop her. So they all walked across the green to Suz's tent, which was most of the way across the quad. Fortunately the campus was largely deserted except for a last few kennel club members standing around and chatting in small groups, so there weren't many people to question the presence of the police and an ambulance.

In Lakeview, with its diner grapevine, the news would be all around town by nine in the morning. Kari didn't know if the same thing was true of Perryville, but she knew Suz would be grateful for any delay in the upheaval that was sure to occur as soon as word spread of a murder at the dog show.

Back at Suz's tent, she found the stack of paperwork she was looking for right away and handed Francine's information over to the sheriff. He took it, but then spent a minute gazing around, his glance moving from the grooming table in the middle of the space to the display of neatly hung lavender leashes and collars, the portable sink, and the three-drawer rolling cabinet full of tools. The tools themselves had all been put away and the cabinet locked with a padlock.

"You've put everything away," he said.

Suz nodded, clearly puzzled by the comment. "Of course. It was the end of the day."

"And you didn't notice you were missing a pair of scissors?" The doubt in Richardson's voice was impossible to ignore.

"What?" Light dawned in Suz's eyes. "Sheriff, you have to understand—I have a number of scissors in different sizes and shapes. I brought duplicates of a few of the ones I use the most, in case one went dull or got broken. I did actually notice that I was short one of my larger pairs, but I thought I'd just forgotten it back at my shop."

Kari thought that sounded like a perfectly reasonable explanation, but Richardson didn't seem as impressed.

"I assume I don't need to tell you not to leave town, Ms. Holden," he said. "You are still very much a person of interest in this case."

"But, Sheriff—" Kari said.

Suz just shook her head. "I hope by 'don't leave town,' you mean the area, since I actually live in Lakeview, not Perryville."

"Don't get smart with me," he said without any particular severity in his tone. "But yes, I will allow you to sleep in your own bed tonight." He held up the piece of paper she'd given him. "Thank you for this. Now let's get back to the crime scene. I want to check a few things with the coroner, and then you are both free to leave for the day."

Six

Back at the supply tent, Doc Phelps was talking into a small recording device. Making some kind of official notes for the case, Kari guessed. The two EMTs were gone, taking the body with them, thank goodness, and Officers Clark and Kent were at the entrance to the tent, its front flaps now reopened to let in more light, taking pictures of the area where Francine had been found. Yellow crime scene tape had been put up around the tent, and orange cones labeled *PPD* (Perryville Police Department, she assumed) marked the area off.

The sheriff walked Suz and Kari over to stand a couple of feet away.

"Try not to touch anything, but see if you can tell me if anything is missing or out of place," he said to Suz.

"Can I get a little closer?" she asked.

He gave a tired-looking shrug. "I don't see why not. There were so many people in and out of there today—volunteers setting up, you coming in and out to fetch things, and obviously the victim—it isn't as though you are likely to mess up any viable footprints."

They all moved a couple of steps closer, and Suz peered around the interior of the tent. "Honestly, Sheriff, I don't see anything that looks any different than the last time I was in here. And really, there was nothing worth taking. It's all basic supplies like extra copies of the show booklet, paper plates and cups and napkins for the booth selling coffee, additional ribbons, things like that."

"That's what I figured," Richardson said. "But in my job it pays to be thorough, so it was worth checking."

"Of course," Suz said. But Kari thought her usually energetic friend looked drained, with drooping shoulders and fine lines appearing around her eyes where there were usually none.

The coroner finished up and strolled over to join them. He nodded at Kari, who he'd met the last time she'd found a body. "Miss Stuart. We've got to stop meeting like this."

She gave him a wry smile. "I couldn't agree more. Nice to see you, Doc."

He held out one hand and scratched the kitten under her chin. Loud purring ensued. "I seem to remember this young lady from our previous encounter." He had a slightly formal, old-fashioned way of speaking that Kari found oddly calming. "One or both of you really needs to get a better hobby. Myself, I enjoy putting together model planes."

Kari laughed, envisioning Queenie with the multitude of tiny pieces. "I'll keep that in mind."

Richardson heaved a sigh, no doubt wanting to get on with things so he could get home to his dinner. Kari couldn't blame him.

"Do you have a time of death for me, Doc?" He glanced at his watch.

"Hot date, Sheriff?" the coroner asked. He himself was wearing a loose tan jacket and plaid pants, and Kari guessed he'd been called away from the golf course. A pair of bifocals perched on the end of his diminutive nose.

"Hardly," Richardson said. "My dog, Duke, has been inside for hours, and I'm hoping I can make it home before he makes a mess. I don't mind so much, but he always feels bad about it and slinks around with his head down for the rest of the day."

The sheriff had a big golden retriever, Kari knew, named Duke after John Wayne. She had always considered his obvious affection for his dog to be one of his more redeeming features, along with his absolute dedication to fairness and the law. Even when that dedication made her life miserable.

"Well, then, I'll make this quick," Doc Phelps said. "Not that it is very complicated anyway." He peered nearsightedly at an official-looking piece of paper on a clipboard. "As you know, establishing time of death is often much more difficult than it looks on television, and in this case the body being in a hot tent complicates things a bit. But based on body temp and the lack of rigor mortis, I'd say she died less than two hours before she was found. The wound looks very fresh, so possibly less than that."

"That fits with the timeline so far," Richardson said. "Ms. Stuart and Ms. Holden said they saw the victim a little after three, and they found the body at about five forty-five, assuming they called it in immediately, as they claimed."

Suz and Kari exchanged glances, but didn't bother to proclaim their innocence yet again.

"The cause of death was pretty much what it looked like," Doc said, apparently oblivious to the tension in the atmosphere. "Stab wound to the chest. Punctured the heart and would likely have been nearly instantly fatal. There was some postmortem bleeding, but not much. The murder weapon itself would have contained most of the flow." This fact seemed to make him quite cheerful.

"So the murderer might not have gotten any blood on him- or herself?" Richardson said, gazing thoughtfully at Suz's red tee shirt, which was a little the worse for wear after her long day of dealing with dogs, people, and messy food truck fare. The shirt had at least three brownish-red stains on it. One of them Kari knew to be chili sauce from a chili dog (Suz could put away as much food as any three men and never seemed to gain an ounce, a fact that Kari had always found unfair in the extreme). "Or perhaps just a small drop or spatter?"

"Distinctly possible," Doc said. "It did soak into the victim's shirt in the area around the wound, but most of that probably happened as the woman was dying, with just a little seepage afterward."

Kari suddenly didn't care quite so much about getting home for dinner anytime soon.

Richardson narrowed his eyes at Suz. "I don't suppose you'd be willing to allow us to take the shirt you're wearing and test it for blood. If, as you said, you never touched the body, there shouldn't be any of the victim's on it."

Suz grimaced. "If it will get me out of here and home with a glass of wine, you can have my pants too. It has been a really long day." She grasped the bottom hem with both hands and got ready to lift the shirt over her head.

"Whoa!" Richardson said, his eyes wide.

The coroner actually took an involuntary step back, although the two young cops' heads swiveled around so fast Kari was worried they might give themselves whiplash. She tried not to laugh.

"Uh, Sheriff, there should be some extra Lakeview Kennel Club tees in one of the boxes in the supply tent. If you'll allow me to, I'd be happy to fetch one," she said.

"Thank God," he muttered under his breath. "Clark, escort Ms. Stuart into the tent and let her take a shirt. Make sure she doesn't touch anything else."

Clark looked disappointed, but he complied, and a couple of minutes later, Suz ducked behind the tent and came out with the old shirt in her hand and the new one safely covering all her slim Amazonian splendor. She handed the piece of clothing to the sheriff, who handed her back a receipt and popped the shirt into a plastic evidence bag.

"You can go," he said. "But I expect to see you back here in the morning."

Suz snorted. "If I'm not here, Olivia will have my head. I think you can plan on it."

"Oh, no," Kari said. "Speak of the devil."

"Crap," Suz hissed. "I thought she'd left for the day."

Even the normally stoic sheriff blanched noticeably as Olivia Weiner stalked up to the group in front of the tent. Unlike Suz and Kari, her attire was as pristine as when she started the day, and her back just as rigidly straight. Two spots of color were visible on her perfectly smooth face.

"Sheriff, I demand to know the meaning of this," she said, planting herself a foot away from him and ignoring everyone else. She placed her hands on her narrow hips, causing the large bag over her shoulder to sway dangerously. "People are talking about police and ambulances, and all sorts of ridiculous rumors are springing up. Would you believe that one of the vendors told me someone has been murdered? Here? At *my* dog show? It's outrageous."

Kari thought she saw the sheriff take a deep breath and brace himself before answering, although he was pretty subtle about it. Queenie growled softly, and Kari shushed her. That kitten really didn't like Olivia. Kari didn't blame her.

"Ms. Weiner—" Richardson started to say.

"Mrs. Weiner, if you don't mind," Olivia said, raising her chin. "I don't hold with any of this modern nonsense. I am very proud to be married."

"Lucky guy," Kent muttered. Kari didn't shush him, but it was a near thing.

"Of course," Richardson said smoothly. "Mrs. Weiner, I'm afraid that the person you spoke to was not mistaken, although how he or she heard about it so fast is a mystery."

He glared at Clark, who was holding a cup of takeout coffee in one hand, the aroma gently scenting the air around them. Kari guessed that the cop had picked it up from one of the vendors still packing up at the edge of the parking lot while he was waiting for the coroner and the ambulance to arrive. She suspected he was wishing now that he'd left it in his car.

"There has been a murder?" Olivia said, her tone marginally less aggressive. "Not anyone associated with the show, I hope."

"The victim was a woman named Francine Carver. I'm told she was actually working for you." The sheriff's keen eyes were focused on Olivia, waiting to see her reaction. She didn't disappoint.

"What? Francine! No, you must be mistaken. I just spoke to her a couple of hours ago." Olivia looked around as if Francine would magically appear. "Are you sure?"

"Suz and I found the body, Olivia," Kari said as gently as possible. "I assure you, there is no mistake."

"You!" Olivia shrieked, pointing one perfectly manicured finger tipped in pale pink at Suz. "I might have

known you had something to do with this. You were angry
with her because she showed me the mess you'd made out
of my dog's haircut. You must have killed her to keep her
from telling everyone how incompetent you were."

The sheriff raised one eyebrow but didn't interrupt.

"Olivia, if I were going to kill someone over a cut a
customer was unhappy with, I would have done it a long
time ago," Suz said dryly. "Besides, as you know, I fixed the
problem, which I did *not* cause in the first place, and you
went on to win Best in Show with the dog. I assure you, I
wasn't in the least bit worried about Francine saying anything to anyone."

"Then why did you two fight earlier in the day?" Olivia
asked triumphantly. "People heard you yelling at her in
your tent."

"I wasn't yelling," Suz said. "But yes, I did raise my
voice, because she was handling Snowball too roughly. She
was a professional and knew better. You should be grateful
that I was looking out for your dog instead of accusing me
of things based on ridiculous assumptions."

"You had an argument with the victim?" the sheriff said,
a dangerous undertone in his voice. "And you didn't think
it was a good idea to mention this to me?"

Kent bent over his phone again, typing madly. Kari
wanted to grab the thing out of his hands and toss it to the
ground. She also wanted to give Olivia a swift kick in the
shins, but she restrained herself.

"I'd forgotten all about it," Suz said, a little sheepishly.
"It has been a really long day, and finding Francine's body
kind of knocked it out of my head. It really wasn't that big
a deal. She was being too rough with the dog, I told her off,
she got mad at me, but then I groomed Snowball and we all
just got on with our lives." She swallowed hard as she real-

ized how wrong that had turned out to be. "Well, I thought we had, anyway."

"I see," Richardson said, making another note. "I'm going to need you to stop by the police station so we can take your prints, Ms. Holden."

"Well, of course they're going to be on the scissors," Suz said, looking worried for the first time since the sheriff had started questioning her. "They're mine, and I used them all day."

"I realize that," he said. "It is just for elimination, in case we find multiple prints on the scissors or anywhere else."

Kari didn't feel reassured, and from the look on her face, neither did Suz.

"This is going to be terrible publicity for the show," Olivia said. "One of our own kennel club members suspected of murder." She pursed her lips and shook her head, aiming an acid-bearing glance at Suz. "I knew I should never have allowed the committee to put you in charge when that ninny Caroline got sick."

"Does that mean you don't want Suz to keep doing all the work of running the show for the next two days?" Kari asked sweetly. "I'm sure you can find someone else to take her place and she'd be happy to just enjoy the show."

Suz gave her a smile, only slightly crooked around the edges.

"Oh, ah, no," Olivia said, clearly thinking rapidly about the odds she'd be stuck doing everything herself after all. "I'm sure Suzanne is innocent of all the charges against her. There's no reason she can't keep on with all her little duties, as long as she keeps a low profile."

Richardson snorted, possibly at the idea of Suz ever having anything that resembled a low profile, but then said to Olivia, "I assure you, Mrs. Weiner, no one has been charged with anything as of yet. We are still in the early stages of our investigation."

"Very well," Olivia said. "I'd appreciate it if you could keep this as quiet as possible, Sheriff. You know my husband, the Used-Car King, is the main sponsor of this dog show, and he will be very unhappy if his name is associated with anything untoward."

She yanked her purse back up on her shoulder and said to Suz, "I suppose I'll have to find someone else to handle Snowball tomorrow, now that Francine has let me down. I definitely can't run the show too, so I'll expect to see you in the morning." As she turned away, Kari heard her mutter, "If you haven't been arrested." As Olivia started walking away, she pulled out her phone and started barking orders at someone on the other end.

Clark gazed after her, his mouth gaping open until he shut it with an audible snap. "I'm surprised she wasn't the murder victim," he said, looking somewhat stunned by the force of nature that was Olivia Weiner. "Now, *that* would have made sense."

Richardson shook his head, grimacing at the statement, but also not disagreeing.

"Did Mrs. Weiner have any problems with the victim?" he asked Kari and Suz.

"Not that I know of," Suz said.

"Me either," Kari agreed.

"Ah, well," Richardson said. "That's all I need from either of you tonight. You're free to go."

"Thanks," Suz said. "But what about Francine's dogs?"

Seven

"Excuse me?" Clark said, rocking back on his heels. "What dogs? I thought the dog she had at the show belonged to Mrs. Weiner."

Kari refrained from rolling her eyes. Barely. "Francine Carver was a dog breeder. That means, presumably, that she has a kennel full of dogs at home that will need to be taken care of, unless there is someone else who lives there who can do it."

"Oh," Clark said. "Uh, do we know if anyone else lives there?"

"That's a good question," Richardson said. He glanced down at his notebook. "We're still looking for a next of kin or emergency contact. Without the victim's purse or her phone—which presumably was in the missing purse—we don't have any of that information yet. There was nothing personal listed on her website. I checked."

He turned to Suz. "Do you happen to know if she lived alone?"

"No idea," Suz said, fiddling with one of the studs in her

ear. "As I said, I just met her today, and our interactions were minimal. Maybe Olivia would know." She sighed. "I suppose you want me to call her."

"If you would," the sheriff said, not unsympathetically.

Suz pulled out her cell and made a face, but placed the call anyway. She asked the question, then listened to a brief answer, shaking her head as she hung up. "Sorry, Sheriff. Olivia said she's only been to the kennel once, briefly. She didn't see anyone else there, but they didn't discuss personal matters, so she really couldn't say." It sounded like a direct quote.

Richardson shrugged. "I guess you and Kent will have to go check out the house," he said to Clark. "Maybe you can find some information that will tell us who to notify about her death while you're there."

The two Perryville officers exchanged glances. Kent shuffled his feet and Clark ran one hand through his short, dark brush of hair. "Uh, couldn't you go, Sheriff?" Clark asked. "I mean, it is in your jurisdiction, and we should probably keep searching for evidence here."

Kari suspected the issue was more likely to be that neither of the younger officers wanted to be stuck telling a grieving husband that his wife had been murdered, if there happened to be one. She couldn't really blame them, although it seemed as though they would have to learn to deal with such things sooner or later.

It was impossible to tell if Richardson shared her thoughts on the matter, since his poker face gave away nothing, as usual.

"Fine," he said. "I'll go out there and see what I can find out, and tend to the animals until they can be transferred to someplace more suitable, assuming that there isn't anyone living at the kennel. Even if no one else lives there, perhaps she has an assistant or something."

He gazed at Kari speculatively. "Ms. Stuart, would your shelter be able to take the dogs in, if it turns out to be necessary? The county would pay for their upkeep, of course, until a legal owner is found or the court releases them for adoption."

"As long as there aren't too many of them," Kari said. "Most small breeders don't usually have more than five or six adults and whatever puppies haven't been sold yet, but you never know. Still, if there turn out to be more than we can fit into our space, I could probably find other places that will take them."

"There might also be other breeders who would be able to take them in on a short-term basis," Suz said. She waved one long-fingered hand at the tents set up around them. "Many of whom are probably here this weekend, if we need to ask."

"Good point," the sheriff said. He rubbed one hand over the five o'clock shadow just beginning to appear on his square chin. Kari wondered if he'd been up late the night before with a case or just needed another cup of coffee. "I don't suppose you and Ms. Stuart would be willing to come along to the kennel and lend me a hand. I know something about dogs, of course, since I have one of my own, but I confess, I find the thought of numerous dogs and puppies a bit daunting. It would go a lot faster with three of us."

Kari was tired after a long day running around the show. Her feet hurt, and her own animals would be waiting for her to come home and feed them. She suspected Suz was even more worn-out than she was. But she wasn't about to pass up a chance to check out the dead woman's place and maybe find something that would clear her friend, or at least point a finger in someone else's direction.

"Sure," she said. "I'm happy to help. At least then I'll get some idea of how many dogs there are."

"I'm in," Suz said, rubbing the small of her back. "What's an extra hour?"

Kent looked disapproving. "Sir, isn't that a little unorthodox? Taking a murder suspect to the victim's house?"

Richardson heaved a sigh that sounded like it came from the soles of his shoes. "First of all, Ms. Holden is a person of interest, but not as of yet an official suspect. Second, do you want to come with me and feed, water, walk, and clean up the poop from however many dogs there are at this kennel, if it turns out there is no one else there to do it?"

Kent turned pale. "No, sir," he said, taking an involuntary step backward. Clark just shook his head.

In a slightly gentler tone, Richardson explained, "Ms. Holden is a dog groomer, and Ms. Stuart runs an animal shelter. They're as close to experts as I'm going to get at this time of day. Hopefully once we get there, I'll be able to find the name of a relative or neighbor who can take over the responsibility for the dogs, assuming there isn't someone already there. In the meanwhile, these two are what I've got. Unless you have any more objections, we'll get to it."

"No, sir," the officers said in unison.

Richardson gave them a benign smile. "Look on the bright side," he said. "The last time I investigated them for murder, it turned out they weren't guilty. So there's that."

Kent and Clark gazed at him, speechless. Kari had to bite back a laugh.

"Come along, ladies," Richardson said, and they all walked off toward the parking lot, leaving the Perryville cops standing there with their mouths open.

* * *

Kari and Suz decided to follow the sheriff out to Francine's house in Suz's car. They figured it would be easier than forming a small parade of vehicles, and it would be simple enough for Kari to leave her car in the parking lot at the college and have Suz pick her up in the morning, since they were both going back to the show.

It was after seven by the time they all set out, but the early-August sky was still light, so there was no problem keeping Richardson's aging blue sedan in view. In the meanwhile, they got to enjoy the drive, which wound past fields full of huge, round hay bales; clusters of black-and-white cows making their leisurely way back from milking; and stalks of corn reaching green fingers up toward the clouds.

Either Francine's place was well off the beaten path or the sheriff was taking a roundabout route, because once they left the campus, it seemed as though they were traveling on a series of back roads and rarely used county highways. Here and there a farm or a small, isolated house made it clear that there were some people living out here, but for the most part, the twenty-minute drive was rarely interrupted by any other vehicles.

Kari was grateful that at least they were heading more or less in the direction of home, so with any luck it wouldn't take them long to get back to Lakeview once they finished up at the kennel. She'd long ago given up on the idea of anything resembling a healthy dinner and was now fervently looking forward to a bowl of organic popcorn drenched in butter and a glass of wine in front of a mindless movie.

"There," Suz said, after it seemed as though they would

be driving forever. She pointed at a small, barely noticeable sign that said Blue Skies Kennel in an Old English font. The sign had a picture of a white dog under an improbably blue sky, which Kari supposed made sense, given the name.

They turned right and bumped down an uneven gravel driveway surrounded on either side by green lawns that were overdue to be mowed and a few gnarled apple trees laden with half-ripe fruit.

"Huh," Kari said. She wasn't sure what she'd been expecting, but this wasn't it. You would think that a place that was both home and business would be kept up a little better, but maybe Francine didn't have many prospective customers making the trip to the back end of nowhere.

"A lot of breeders do most of their sales long distance, with people in other states," Suz said, as if reading Kari's mind. They'd been friends for so long, that sort of thing happened all the time. "The prospective buyer looks at the bloodline and pictures and gets the dog shipped to them without ever meeting it."

"Then how do they know if they'll be a good fit?" Kari asked, somewhat indignantly. At the shelter, they had a room set aside for people to spend time with the animals they were considering adopting, and they encouraged taking walks with the dogs or sitting with the cats.

Kari had been told by Daisy, the former owner of the shelter, that the more time someone spent with a potential pet, the better the likelihood was that the adoption would stick. There was nothing more heartbreaking than when someone brought back an animal because it turned out not to be a good match, although Serenity Sanctuary had a policy that ensured people could do so, rather than dumping the dog or cat somewhere unsuitable.

Suz shrugged, causing the car to veer alarmingly to the

right as it hit a dip in the driveway. "People who buy pure-breds aren't always looking for a companion, although of course some of them are." She nodded through the windshield. "At least the house looks like it is in better shape than the grounds."

It was actually quite charming, Kari decided, although not exactly bursting with personality. A low white ranch-style house, it had black shutters and a small outbuilding attached by a breezeway, which was presumably the actual kennel. A lone chimney, inactive in the end-of-summer heat, was silhouetted against the evening sky, and a single pot of red geraniums hung from a cast-iron hook next to the front door.

The place looked deserted. There were no cars in the driveway other than the sheriff's dusty sedan, and no lights were visible in the house. When Suz and Kari got out of the car, they could hear the faint sounds of barking from the direction of the kennel, but otherwise the house was completely silent.

"Doesn't look like anyone else lives here after all," Richardson said, gazing around. "I hope she has a key hidden somewhere out here so I don't have to call a locksmith."

"You aren't going to just break down the door?" Suz asked.

Richardson sighed. "I really wish people wouldn't watch those idiotic cop shows. I can only break into a house if I am convinced that there is a criminal inside and I have a warrant or if there is some indication that someone inside is in imminent danger."

"What about if the door is unlocked?" Kari asked. She had tried it out of curiosity, and the knob had turned easily in her hand.

Richardson raised an eyebrow, but tried the door himself. "Interesting," he said. "Mind you, lots of people in the country don't lock their doors, no matter how often we tell them that's a bad idea."

Kari tried not to look guilty, since she rarely locked the door to her own small farmhouse.

"Try knocking," Suz suggested.

That did seem like a reasonable place to start. Kari banged on the door a couple of times, but nothing happened. She looked over her shoulder at the sheriff, who shrugged.

"I can't do anything official," he said. "But if you're feeling neighborly and worrying about the dogs . . ."

Kari took the hint and opened the door, sticking her head inside and yelling, "Hello! Anyone home?" She waited to hear dogs barking, but the house was completely silent.

"Well, I'm not going to let a bunch of animals starve," Suz said, and pushed her way inside. After a moment's hesitation, Kari and Richardson followed her in.

"Is this illegal?" Kari whispered to the sheriff.

"It's a gray area," he said. "But I suspect that under the circumstances, Judge Simmons would approve of me entering the building to check on the welfare of the victim's animals."

Kari nodded, having met the judge once. She'd actually liked the woman, despite having had to stand up in her court to answer charges related to one of the dogs then at the shelter. Kari remembered the judge mentioning that she sat on the board of a shelter in a nearby town outside her jurisdiction, so Richardson was probably right.

The entryway was narrow and only contained a wooden coatrack, currently holding a woman's tan raincoat, a short denim jacket, and a slightly battered umbrella, and a woven rubber mat with a pair of muddy boots sitting on it. Kari thought the back door was probably the one that really got used, since that was the way things usually work in the country.

They walked through to a medium-sized living room. Large windows on either end let in plenty of light, which reflected off of clean white walls and a row of small mirrors set over a broad fireplace. A tan leather couch and matching recliner faced a large-screen television, and a wooden table next to the sofa held a cup half filled with what looked like cold coffee and an old copy of *Dog Fancy* magazine. There were a few pictures of adorable white bichons on the walls in various poses, all clearly professional shots, but nothing else that gave the visitor any sense of the person who lived there.

"Huh," Kari said. "How long ago did you say she moved here?"

Suz glanced around the room. "I think Olivia said two years, maybe? Something like that. Maybe she is just one of those people who likes things clean and neat."

Kari snorted, thinking about the slightly chaotic and admittedly messy work in progress that was the house she'd moved into a couple of months ago when she bought the sanctuary. "Maybe she has a maid?" Kari had thought about hiring someone to clean, but decided against it when she realized she'd have to clean up before she could let anyone in.

"Maybe she's just getting around to unpacking?" Richardson said, pointing at a couple of boxes Kari hadn't noticed, tucked into a corner. A set of decorative candlesticks that looked as though they might have come off of the mantel could be seen sticking up out of the open flaps.

"Or planning to move?" Suz suggested. She pointed to a door at the side of the room, and they all walked over to discover another short hallway. One direction led toward what looked like it might be a couple of bedrooms and a bathroom, while the other opened into the kitchen. They tried that first, figuring there might be a contact list next to the phone or attached to the refrigerator door. That's where Kari kept hers.

The kitchen was almost as tidy as the living room, although there were a dirty pan and a plate in the sink, along with another coffee cup. Just one, Kari noticed. Plain wood cabinets were painted a light olive green, and a small darker green table with four chairs sat in the middle of the room.

"That's odd," Suz said in a puzzled voice.

"What is?" Richardson asked, his eyes darting around the room.

"No dogs," Suz said. "There are no dog bowls in the kitchen or dog beds in the living room. In my house, there are half-chewed toys in every room too."

Kari nodded. "*That's* what feels so off about the place." She'd been sensing something, but hadn't been able to put her finger on what it was. "She's a dog breeder, but she doesn't have any dogs of her own? How weird is that?"

Richardson raised an eyebrow. "Surely not everyone who breeds dogs is required to have one."

Suz snorted, tossing her lavender hair. "I wouldn't call it a requirement, but most people who like dogs enough to raise them professionally also like them enough to have two or three. Or six. They certainly have their breeding dogs in the house from time to time. But there isn't even a water bowl on the floor."

Richardson sighed. "Okay, I admit it is a bit unusual, but it also isn't any help, so why don't we head out to the kennel and deal with the dogs out there, and then we can come

back in here and see if we can find any indication of someone to call."

There were definitely dogs in the kennel, since they
could hear the barking from where they stood at the entrance to the kitchen, even though the door to the breezeway that connected the kennels to the house was across the
room.

They had started in that direction when suddenly the outside door opened and a man walked in. He wore a cap with
a brim pulled down over his face and a large pair of sunglasses, but Kari could still see what looked like old scars,
puckered and red and angry looking. She also saw the gun in
his hand, although he quickly tucked it into a pocket of the
loose beige jacket he wore as soon as he spotted the sheriff's
badge, which he'd hung on a lanyard around his neck.

The man wasn't particularly threatening looking other
than the scars—about average height with shaggy brown
hair and the slightly curved posture and pale complexion of
someone who spent most of his days at a desk bent over a
computer. He was dressed in khaki's and a lightweight tan
shirt that looked like it was missing a pocket protector. If it
hadn't been for the gun and the scarring, she might not have
given him a second look.

"Who are you?" the man asked, a belligerent edge to his
voice. "And what are you doing in Francine's house?"

Richardson stepped forward. Kari noticed that although
he didn't mention the weapon, he carefully put himself between her and Suz and the strange man.

"I'm Sheriff Dan Richardson," he said. "This is Kari
Stuart and Suz Holden. They're here at my request. I'm
sorry if we startled you. We did knock, but there was no
answer."

"Francine is at a dog show all day," the man said shortly.

"She should be back soon. I actually expected her about an hour ago."

"May I ask who you are?" Richardson said. "And if you live here?"

"My name is Herman Blue, and I'm Francine's friend and a silent partner in the kennel. I don't actually live in the house, although Francine and I go in and out of each other's places all the time. I have my own house farther back on the property." He pulled the cap down a little lower over his face. "I like my privacy, and Francine likes hers."

He looked from the sheriff to the women and back again. "I don't understand. What are you doing here? Are you looking for Francine? Is something wrong?"

Richardson glanced at Kari out of the corner of his eye and gave a small nod. Maybe he thought the news would be better coming from someone less official? Kari swallowed hard.

"I'm sorry, Mr. Blue," she said softly. "But I'm afraid that Francine is dead. We came here to check on the dogs and see if we could find out who we should notify about her death."

All the color drained out of Herman's face, making the scars stand out even more. "Dead?" he whispered. "She can't be dead." He walked over and sank into one of the kitchen chairs, as though his legs couldn't support him anymore.

Kari took a couple of steps in his direction, only stopping at a warning look from the sheriff. "I'm so sorry," she said. "Are you all right?"

To her surprise, the man burst into tears. "Oh, Francine," he said. "This is all my fault."

Eight

Every line in the sheriff's body stiffened as he shifted into high alert. "Your fault?" he said in a quiet voice. Kari had gotten to know that stance all too well when she had been part of a murder investigation. "How so, exactly?"

Herman Blue shook his head. "I can't tell you."

"Can't or won't?" Richardson asked, taking a couple of steps closer until he was standing in front of the table where Blue was sitting, slumped with his head in his hands.

"Can't," Blue said. "I'm not allowed. You could get me killed."

Kari and Suz exchanged puzzled glances and Suz made a *Do you have any idea what the heck he is talking about?* face.

"If you're in some kind of trouble, I might be able to help," Richardson said. "Unless, of course, that trouble is the murder of Francine Carver, in which case the best thing you can do is confess and turn yourself in."

"I would never hurt Francine," Blue said, a stricken look

in his eyes. To Kari, he seemed sincere, but she'd grown up with an emotionally abusive alcoholic father and spent her younger years with a controlling husband, and she was more aware than many that even the most hurtful of people could feel genuine remorse when the shouting was all over.

"I loved her."

"If that's so, then I'm sure you want to do everything you can to help us find the person or persons who killed her," the sheriff said in a reasonable tone.

"So she really was murdered?" Blue whispered. "There is no chance it was an accident?"

"None whatsoever, unfortunately" Richardson said. Kari noticed he didn't mention the exact cause of death. At the moment, the only ones who knew about that were the police, the coroner, her, and Suz. "Now, about this secret— the reason you believe you were responsible for her death?"

Herman picked up his head and stared at Kari and Suz. "Not in front of them," he said. "The fewer people who know, the better."

"We can wait for you outside, sheriff," Kari said. But just then Queenie poked her head out of Kari's bag. The kitten gazed around the room, her green eyes zeroing in on the scarred man, and before Kari could stop her, the black kitten had jumped out of the bag and onto the table. She proceeded to stroll across it as if she owned it and sat down in front of Herman, rubbing her head up against his hand where it rested on the table.

"Hey," he said. "Who is this?" He scratched under her chin and she started to purr.

"I'm sorry," Kari said, reaching out to pick up the kitten. But she aborted the gesture at a subtle jerk of the head from Richardson. "That's Queenie. I'm afraid she has a mind of her own sometimes."

"All of the time, more like," Suz muttered.

"She's so soft," Blue said, sounding calmer. "What a sweet kitten."

"I would have thought you'd be more of a dog man," Kari said, although she and Suz had both dogs and cats. Still, the man was a silent partner in a kennel.

"Oh, no," Blue said. "Francine was the one who was into dogs. I've always liked cats. They're so independent and fierce." His tiny, fierce new friend snuggled even closer, and he sighed. His shoulders slumped even farther. "I guess I can tell you, Sheriff, but you have to promise never to share this information. I wasn't kidding when I said it could get me killed. I'm afraid that's what happened to poor Francine."

The sheriff sent Kari and Suz outside to wait with the kitten while he sat down at the table with Herman Blue. As soon as the women were out the door, Queenie jumped down from Kari's arms and scampered around the corner of the house.

"Queenie, come back here!" Kari hissed as she and Suz hurried after her. "Where are you going?" Kari had visions of chasing a tiny black ball of fur into the next county. Who knew what whim motivated a cat.

But Queenie hadn't gone far. When they caught up with her, the kitten was sitting underneath a window that was partially open, allowing them to hear the conversation taking place in the room on the other side. In fact, if Kari stood right at the edge of the far side of the window frame, she could even catch a glimpse of the occupants.

"You sneaky little devil," she breathed. Suz held a finger to her lips, either because she was trying to listen in too or as a warning that they didn't want the sheriff to catch them eavesdropping. Or both. But Kari wasn't about to pass up a chance to find out what was going on. Not with Suz's freedom and good name at risk.

"My name isn't really Herman Blue," Herman was saying. Kari could feel her mouth drop open. "Although all my identification says it is, and if you put my fingerprints into the system, that's the name that will come up."

She could just see Richardson give him a keen look. "Ah," he said. "Witness protection program?"

Blue nodded slowly. "I used to be an accountant for some particularly unethical businessmen. I won't tell you any specific names."

"Mob?" Richardson asked shortly.

Blue shrugged, but didn't answer. Instead, he just continued to tell his story. "I turned state's evidence, and when I was coming out of the courthouse after the last day of the trial, someone threw acid on me."

He reached up and touched the scars on his face with a rueful smile. "I was never all that outgoing to begin with, but after that, I just wanted to hide. So the feds found Lakeview and set me up in this place. I still do some forensic accounting work for the government, but it is all via email. I never leave the house if I can avoid it."

Richardson looked thoughtful. "Then how did you meet Francine Carver?"

Blue's eyes darted to the floor and back again. "We actually went to college together. She was a close friend and we stayed in touch."

"Even after you were put into the witness protection program?" The sheriff raised one bushy eyebrow.

"I know, I know. It's against the rules." Blue waved a hand through the air. "To be honest, I was never all that concerned with following rules and regulations. I suppose that's how I ended up working for the mob in the first place. To me, it was just another job, and it paid really well, which is how I could afford this place."

He shook his head. "Anyway, Francine and I were really careful, and I didn't figure anyone was likely to listen to her phone calls or read her emails, because we hadn't seen each other in years. When she called me one day and told me that her life had kind of blown up in her face and she needed a place to start over, I offered to let her come here. Even fronted her the money to start up a new kennel."

"You let her have this house *and* you helped her set up a kennel?" Richardson voiced the doubt Kari had been feeling. "That must have been some friendship."

Color spread over Blue's face, patchy where it met up with ridged and mottled tissue. "Well, it was nice to have some company, and she didn't care about my scars. And this place was way too big for me anyway. So I moved into the smaller house out back. It was no big deal." He pulled out a large white handkerchief and blew his nose. "Unless they tracked her here and killed her to punish me. If that's true, I'll never forgive myself."

"There are reasons for all those rules you like to ignore, Mr. Blue," Richardson said grimly. "Although I'd have to say, it seems unlikely that the mob was behind this. It doesn't seem like their style. But I'll look into it." He stared at Herman without blinking. "Can you tell me where you were today between three and five in the afternoon?"

"I was here," Blue said, a slightly bitter tone to his voice. "I am always here. But of course, there is no one to back up my story."

"I'm going to need the name and contact information for the U.S. Marshal assigned to your case," the sheriff said. Blue opened his mouth as if to protest, then just sighed and nodded. He rattled off a name and number by heart, and the sheriff wrote it down.

"Now, can you tell me if Ms. Carver has any family or a next of kin who I should notify of her passing?" Richardson asked, his pen still poised over his ever-present notebook.

Blue stared at the ground again for a minute before looking up to meet the sheriff's eyes. "No," he said. "There's no one. She was all alone in the world except for me. And the dogs, of course."

"No boyfriend?" the sheriff asked.

"Boyfriend!" Herman started so hard, he almost knocked over the table. "Why would you say that?"

"Ms. Stuart saw her arguing with a large, muscular bald man at the dog show," Richardson explained. "It was apparently pretty heated, according to the people who witnessed it, so I wondered if he was a boyfriend and they'd had some kind of spat."

"A large bald man?" Blue turned as pale as he had been red a few minutes before. "Uh, no. I have no idea who that could be. Francine didn't know anyone like that."

The sheriff gave a look that told Kari he wasn't buying Herman's denial any more than she was. "I see," Richardson said. "Thank you. If you think of anyone else we should talk to, please let me know."

Blue nodded, his head bobbing up and down. "Oh, you bet, Sheriff. Definitely. Anything I can do to help catch whoever did this."

"Just out of curiosity, Mr. Blue," Richardson said, tucking the notebook back into the top pocket of his shirt, "did Ms. Carver normally carry a purse?"

The scarred man blinked. "A purse? Of course she carried a purse. Gigantic red leather thing. You never knew what she was going to pull out of it. Why do you ask?"

Kari looked down at her own handy tote bag, still slung over her shoulder. Maybe all animal people carried bags full of treats and toys and other handy things.

"We didn't find one at the scene," the sheriff explained. "Her phone is missing too, so it might be inside."

"Maybe it was just a robbery gone wrong, then," Herman said, perking up, possibly at the thought that his misspent past hadn't led to his friend's murder.

"That's one of the options we're looking into," Richardson said. "I'll be in touch." He rose from the table and cleared his throat. "Maybe Ms. Stuart and Ms. Holden would like to come back inside now." He directed his comment toward the front of the house in a voice loud enough to reach them if they had actually been standing there. But Kari had a feeling he knew exactly where they were.

Oops. She and Suz exchanged guilty glances and hurried back around the house, through the front door, and into the kitchen.

"All done?" Kari asked in as perky a tone as she could manage. The kitten had regained her favorite spot on Kari's shoulder, and Kari put one hand up to steady her.

"Do you want us to help you with the dogs?" Suz asked. "We'd be happy to lend a hand."

"No, no," Blue said, suddenly herding them back in the direction of the front door. "I've got it all under control. I occasionally help out with them when she's busy. Thank you for coming."

And then they were standing outside, with the door slamming shut behind them.

"That was interesting," the sheriff said as he escorted them to Suz's car.

"Which part?" Suz asked, pulling her keys out of her pocket. "The part where he said he was responsible for her death, or the part where he hustled us out of the house so fast I almost lost a shoe?"

"Or the part where he lied about not knowing who the guy was that we saw Francine arguing with?" Kari added, opening the passenger side door.

"We don't know that he lied," Richardson said, crossing his arms across his chest and glowering at them. "And I want you to forget everything you overheard. Some of that was classified information. I assure you, I will be looking into it. You, on the other hand, will be going to your respective homes and keeping out of this investigation. Ms. Holden is in enough trouble already. I appreciate you both coming out here with me, even though it turned out that I didn't need your canine expertise. But don't take this little excursion as carte blanche to poke your noses in where they don't belong. Remember what happened the last time you did that."

He stared at Kari, who had almost been killed while trying to find out who murdered the town dog warden. As if that was something she could ever forget.

"Well, I did solve the case for you," she said brightly, then slammed the door shut before he could respond.

"You should probably drive before he arrests me for being a wiseass," she said to Suz. Suz drove.

They were most of the way back to Kari's house before it occurred to her that Suz was being way too quiet. Definitely not her normal state. Queenie, who had been sitting calmly on Kari's lap (she didn't mind riding in the car, unlike Kari's other two cats, who considered it to be a form of torture worthy of a call to Amnesty International), picked up her head, looked at Suz, and said, "Murp?"

"You're awfully quiet," Kari said, scratching the kitten behind the ear. "Queenie wants to know if you're okay." She normally made the kitten ride in a carrier in the car, since that was safer if there was an unexpected accident, but the carrier was back in her own car, parked at the college.

"I'm tired," Suz said. "It was a long day." She took her eyes off the road briefly to smile at her passengers, but the ebbing light didn't make her expression any more convincing.

"It was a long day," Kari agreed. "But I don't think that's what's bothering you. Talk to me."

Suz was one of those people who hardly ever talked about their emotions. She tended to keep everything inside, even with her best friend. But Kari had a feeling this was one of those rare times when it would be better to keep pushing. As if to confirm her thinking, Queenie let out another meow, this one even louder.

"See," Kari said. "Even the kitten thinks you should let us know what's really on your mind."

Suz sighed as she turned onto Goose Hollow Road, slowing down for the curves, which were famous for having deer lurking behind every bend.

"It's just, well, it's kind of disconcerting to realize one of my shears was used as a weapon," she said, eyes firmly aimed ahead of her. "I love my work, and getting that first set of lavender-handled tools was my way of celebrating when I was finally able to open my own shop. It makes me happy every time I pick one up, and I'm afraid I'll never look at them the same now that one of them has been used to murder someone."

Kari hadn't thought of it that way. She felt awful that someone would not only take a life with those scissors, but also steal away her friend's joy in using the tools of her trade. Especially since Kari had a sneaking suspicion that the killer's choice of weapon hadn't been an accident.

"That sucks," she said, as Suz pulled into the parking lot at the shelter. The shelter itself was silent, shut up for the evening with the new security lights gleaming on the freshly repainted building. Kari's little farmhouse, which had come with the sanctuary, was off to the left down a narrow walkway edged with flowers and tall grass. A few chickens rambled along, waiting to be shut up in their coop for the night. The sound of their sleepy clucking and a chorus of crickets greeted them as Suz brought the car to a halt.

"It does," Suz said. "But I'm sure I'll get past it."

"I've been wondering," Kari said slowly. "Why those scissors?"

Suz stared at her. "What do you mean?"

"Well, think about it," Kari said. "We know that someone brought the shears to the supply tent—probably the murderer, although I suppose there is a small chance that for some reason Francine had them and whoever killed her just picked them up. But why those particular scissors? Were they just handy, or did someone choose them in particular because they knew how distinctive they were and that they would quickly be traced back to you?"

Her friend's mouth dropped open. "You think someone purposely set me up to look like the murderer? Why would anyone do that?"

Kari narrowed her eyes, staring out at the chickens without really seeing them. "I don't know. But we are going to find out. I like the sheriff, but I don't have much faith in those two Perryville cops, and I know from experience that once the cops decide you're a suspect, it can make your life pretty miserable."

She picked up the kitten and grabbed her bag as she

prepared to get out of the car. "You are suspect number one right now, and there is no way we are leaving your future in their hands. Starting tomorrow when you pick me up in the morning, we're going to put our heads together and figure out exactly what they're missing. Deal?"

Suz blinked rapidly, a few unshed tears dangling on the edges of her lashes. "Deal," she said. "I'll bring the coffee."

"Better make it a double," Kari said with a grin. "It is going to be another long day."

Nine

Kari was up by six the next morning, since she wanted to go by the shelter for a while before Suz came to pick her up for another day at the dog show. She fed the cats—the orange brothers, Westley and Robert (both named after characters from her favorite movie, *The Princess Bride*), and little Queenie, whose kitten chow had to be given to her in the living room so the other two wouldn't eat it out from underneath her.

Her dog, Fred, who was surprisingly laid-back, got his food in a corner of the kitchen away from the cats, and they all studiously ignored each other.

After a quick shower, Kari pulled her slightly too-curly dark hair back into a braid to keep it out of the way and threw on a pair of denim Capri pants and a blue scoop-neck tee shirt with a picture of a cat that read *Do you think my human knows I'm letting her live in my house?* Considering the amount of walking she had done the day before (and the possibility of dog poop), she opted for sneakers instead of sandals, despite the warmth of the day.

Then she grabbed a travel mug of coffee and walked down the path toward the shelter, followed by a prancing Queenie, who as usual somehow managed to get out the door despite Kari's best attempts to leave her behind.

"You can come down to the shelter with me," Kari said sternly, gazing down at the stubborn little ball of black fur. "But you are not coming to the show today. There is just too much going on." Queenie ignored her, dancing off in temporary pursuit of a butterfly before coming back to walk slightly more sedately at the heels of Kari's sneakers.

As always, the sight of the newly renovated Serenity Sanctuary lifted Kari's heart and made all the hard work and stress worth it. Run-down and on the verge of closing when she bought it, the sanctuary had been started by Daisy with more enthusiasm than money. She hadn't had much of either left when Kari found her way there, but Daisy's vision of a place that rescued the animals that couldn't be accommodated by the other local shelters—the overflow of kittens, the desperate cases, the ones no one had room for—was still strong.

Kari had vowed to continue that mission. By using her unexpected lottery winnings to fix up the place, and with the help of the stalwart volunteers who had stuck with the rescue even when things got bad, the Serenity Sanctuary had been given a second chance at life.

Now the outside gleamed with fresh yellow paint, and the dog yard had a strong new fence that went all the way around the back of the building. Both the dog runs and the pathways used for walking the animals could be accessed from the back door. Off to the left side of the rambling one-story building was an entrance that led to the big feline room, where all the adult cats lived in (relative) harmony.

But Kari's favorite part of the shelter was the front entrance. The door had been repainted a shiny black and adorned with the Serenity Sanctuary logo, with safety glass at the top that gave you a glimpse into the wonders that waited inside. She had helped design the main room and was justifiably proud of the way it had turned out.

As she walked in, the first thing she saw was the set of new cages that lined the side wall. This was where the kittens, and sometimes mama cats with babies, were kept. A few adult cats were there as well, either those who couldn't get along with the others in the big room or those who needed special care but weren't infectious in any way. (Sick cats stayed in the upgraded medical room, unless they were ill enough that they had to be at the vet's.)

Kari loved the big, fancy cages that had one level for sleeping and another for playing and litter boxes. The cages stacked on top of each other and had wood fronts that softened the look of all that wire. Each one had a card with the name of the cat or kittens in residence, along with a picture and their age, sex, and personality traits. This really helped prospective adopters to get to know them, and medical notes or instructions for feeding were a boon to the volunteers.

The entire room felt fresh and clean, with the walls painted a soothing light blue and a new linoleum floor in a restful blue-and-white pattern. An L-shaped oak desk greeted visitors, with one side facing the front and the other used for dealing with paperwork by Kari and the other shelter workers. There was an amazing amount of paperwork involved in running a shelter, Kari had found. She had her own smaller desk in the far corner, but she was much more likely to be found hanging out up at the front with whoever else was working at the time, if she wasn't there on her own.

This morning when she walked in, Bryn and Sara were

in the middle of feeding the kittens and mama cats. At the moment, they had over twenty kittens, most of them still with their mothers, although there were two that a Good Samaritan had found abandoned and had brought in to be cared for until they were old enough to be spayed or neutered and put up for adoption.

All the mothers would be spayed as soon as their kittens had been weaned, and anyone adopting a kitten was required to have it spayed or neutered before the adoption was final. There were already too many unwanted cats and dogs in the world, and part of the sanctuary's mission was ensuring people could afford to have their animals fixed so they didn't add to that problem.

Tripod, the three-legged yellow cat who had come with the shelter when Kari bought it, supervised the workers from the top of the couch they kept for visitors, and he occasionally let out a brisk meow if he thought Bryn and Sara needed guidance. Because he was missing a number of teeth, he had an unfortunate tendency to drool, so they tried to keep him away from the paperwork.

The couch had a rotating series of washable covers, so it was a reasonably safe spot for him to sit. Between the drooling and only having three legs, he was considered to be unadoptable and was one of a small number of cats who would likely spend their lives at the shelter. Luckily, they were so spoiled by the volunteers and workers, they didn't seem to mind.

"Good morning," Sara said in a cheerful voice. The turquoise streak in her short gray hair had been joined by a thin purple one, and she was wearing a matching short-sleeved blue-and-purple flowered top over a pair of jeans. She adroitly kept a trio of kittens from escaping while she put bowls of fresh wet food and clean water into their cage.

After breakfast, all the occupied cages would be sanitized and given fresh bedding, toys, and bowls of water and dry food for the day.

"Hey, Kari," Bryn added. Her many tiny braids were tucked under a bandana while she worked, and the stud in her nose winked as it caught the light. "We weren't sure you would be in this morning. Don't you have to be at the dog show all day?"

"I do," Kari said. "I had to leave my car there last night, so Suz is picking me up in a little while. It's a long story." She really didn't want to get into the fact that she'd stumbled across another body. Finding the dog warden murdered out back by their fence had been bad enough. She didn't want them to think she was starting a macabre new hobby.

"Anyway, I figured I'd check in before I go and make sure you don't need anything here."

"We're good," Sara said. "Jim and Stacy are out back taking care of the dogs."

Jim was one of the few volunteers left from earlier days, a disabled veteran who said that being around the animals was more like therapy than work. Stacy, on the other hand, had joined them soon after they'd reopened. She was in her sixties, loved dogs, and said that spending a few hours a week away from her newly retired husband would probably keep her from smacking him over the head with one of his own golf clubs. Kari was *mostly* sure Stacy was kidding.

"Did you eat any breakfast?" Sara asked, closing the cage she was dealing with and then squirting sanitizer on her hands. They had to meticulously clean their hands between doing each cage to avoid inadvertently spreading an illness through the shelter. Kittens, especially strays, often dealt with upper respiratory and gastrointestinal issues when they were still young and vulnerable. "Stacy brought blueberry muffins from the bakery."

Apparently it was a rhetorical question, since Sara walked over to the front desk and plopped one onto a napkin before handing it to Kari, who took it gratefully. Not only had she not eaten breakfast but the bakery's muffins were famously delicious.

"Thank you," she said with her mouth full. Swallowing, she added, "I was going to grab something from one of the food trucks when I got there, but this will hold me over until then."

"You're welcome," Sara said. She gave Kari a keen-eyed look. "How are you doing? I stopped at the diner this morning to pick up a roast beef sandwich for lunch, and the place was all abuzz with news of the murder at the dog show yesterday afternoon. I can't believe you found another body."

Kari sighed, blowing muffin crumbs all over the floor. Oh, well. It would get mopped soon anyway. She sank onto one of the new ergonomic stools behind the desk, and Queenie jumped up to sit on the counter in front of her. No doubt waiting for more crumbs, since the tiny black kitten had an unusual fondness for blueberries.

"I'm okay," Kari said. She should know by now that nothing of importance ever happened in or around Lakeview without the news somehow magically making the rounds of the diner crowd by early the next morning. "And technically, Queenie found the body, although Suz and I were the ones who called the cops."

The kitten sat up straighter, as if she knew they were talking about her. Which she probably did. She meowed at Sara, who nodded.

"You're right, Queenie. That deserves a treat, and I'll bet no one thought to give you one at the time." Sara grinned and reached into her pocket, pulling out a baggie filled with the homemade liver treats she made for the shelter cats. Kari thought they smelled vile, but the cats seemed to love them. Queenie took hers daintily, ate it with gusto, and then settled down to wash her face as if she'd just eaten a five-course meal.

"So this woman who died, did you know her?" Bryn asked as she filled another set of stainless steel bowls with dry food out of one of the central bins. "Sara said she was some kind of trainer?"

"A breeder, actually. Her name was Francine Carver," Kari said, taking a long drink of coffee. This was clearly going to be the kind of day that required copious amounts of caffeine. "Although she wasn't at the show with her own dogs. Olivia Weiner hired her to handle her bichon frise, Snowball."

Sara wrinkled her nose and made a noise in the back of her throat that reminded Kari of one of her cats getting ready to cough up a hairball. "Olivia Weiner. She's still president of the kennel club, isn't she? It figures that she wouldn't want to do the work of handling her own dog. But I thought she had bulldogs. She always had one in those annoying ads her husband runs."

Bryn and Kari exchanged glances and Bryn raised one eyebrow. Sara was a pretty easygoing woman, and there was hardly anyone she didn't like. Clearly they'd found the exception to the rule.

"She used to have bulldogs," Kari explained. "But she never managed to get one that was quite good enough to be a champion. And I guess her husband thought bulldogs were too ugly for commercials, or something idiotic like that. So Olivia got a bichon instead. It seems to have paid off, since Snowball won a bunch of first-place ribbons yesterday and then got Best in Show at the end of the day."

"Olivia must have been thrilled," Sara said in a dry tone. "Being the best and having the best was always very important to her. When her son was in my class, I gave him a D minus on a paper and she tried to have me fired for incompetence. Insisted to the school board that if I was any good as a teacher, her brilliant, perfect son would never have gotten a failing mark."

Ouch. Well, that explained it.

"Yikes," Kari said. "She's definitely not an easy woman to deal with, although she really was thrilled about the dog's win. You know, until Francine turned up dead and ruined Olivia's day."

The door from the back hallway banged open and for a moment they could hear the cacophony of two dozen dogs all clamoring for food at the same time. Then, mercifully, it swung shut again as Jim walked into the room.

"Hey, are you talking about the woman who got killed at the dog show yesterday?" Jim asked.

He was long and lanky, with sandy brown hair and hazel eyes. Tattoos of trees and vines covered both arms and ran down onto his hands, and he walked with a slight limp courtesy of his second tour in Afghanistan. He didn't talk much, as a rule, and tended to disappear when there were visitors, but he was great with the dogs and was always happy to pitch in and do whatever was needed.

"We were," Kari said.

He pushed his hair out of his face and grimaced. "Is it true what they're saying down at the diner? That Suz was found standing over the body with her hands on the murder weapon?" Suz was one of the few people Jim seemed at ease with, probably because she never asked him questions or treated him any differently than anyone else.

Kari scowled at Sara, who had clearly left out an important piece of the gossip. "Really? The diner grapevine is saying Suz was the killer, and you didn't think to mention that little tidbit?" She turned to Jim. "Of course it isn't true. Suz was with me when we found the woman, and she was already very thoroughly dead."

Kari wasn't sure if she was allowed to say anything about Suz's scissors being the murder weapon, although it was clear that someone somewhere along the line had let something slip, or the rumor mill wouldn't already be associating her friend with the murder. Still, Kari was pretty sure that Sheriff Richardson would consider discussing details of the crime to be a major no-no.

"Suz had nothing to do with Francine Carver's death," she said instead. "I'm surprised at you for even considering the idea."

Jim held up his hands. "Whoa, don't kill the messenger. I was just asking because I heard a couple of the regulars talking about it. I know Suz wouldn't kill anyone." He stopped and thought for a minute. "Well, not anyone who didn't deserve it, and if she did, she'd definitely confess to it right away."

Kari had to admit, that sounded about right.

"And I didn't say anything about it because I thought it was just plain stupid," Sara said. "Those people at the diner need to get their heads out of their—"

Luckily, Kari's cell rang before Sara could finish her sentence. Queenie sprang up onto Kari's shoulder.

The caller ID said it was Suz. "Hey, are you on your way to pick me up?" Kari asked. "We were just talking about you."

The voice on the other end was barely coherent. "What?" Kari said. "Suz, calm down."

The kitten reached out and batted at the phone, putting the call onto speaker, almost as if she wanted to listen to the conversation. Sara, Bryn, and Jim all crowded in closer.

"You are *not* going to believe what those cops have done now!" Suz said. The murmuring of multiple voices could be heard somewhere behind her.

"They haven't arrested you, have they?" Kari asked, already grabbing for her bag and her keys before she remembered that her car was still stuck at the college in Perryville.

"What?" Suz sounded even more indignant. "No, of course not. I came over to the campus early to check on things and the police have put crime scene tape all around the supply tent and they won't let us use it for the rest of the show." She was so incensed, she was practically sputtering.

"I have two volunteers frantically searching for a replacement tent to use instead, and I finally convinced the sheriff to allow me to take out all the ribbons and other supplies we can't replace. But they're insisting on bringing them out the back of the tent and looking through every single box before we remove it. It is going to take me forever to get it all shifted." Suz said something indistinct, probably to someone standing next to her. "I'm sorry, Kari. I'm going to be really late picking you up."

Bryn waved a hand to get Kari's attention, and then pointed at herself and made a motion like turning a steering wheel.

"Hang on a second," Kari said into the phone. "Sara, can you do without Bryn's help for the rest of the morning?" Kari had been planning to man the Serenity Sanctuary tent until volunteers could get there later on.

"We'll manage," Sara said, and Jim nodded an assertive agreement.

"Don't worry about it," Kari said to Suz. "Bryn can drive me over and take over the booth so I can come help you. I'll meet you at the supply tent, okay?"

Sara leaned in closer to the phone. "Have you eaten anything, Suz?" Kari had to choke back a laugh. Sara was the resident mother hen and took care of everyone, Suz included.

"Uh, no?" Suz's voice sounded vaguely apologetic as it echoed up out of the phone.

Sara rolled her eyes and went over to pack up a few more muffins for Kari to take with her.

"Hang in there," Kari said. "We're on our way." She ended the call and looked around for the kitten. Queenie was already sitting inside the top of Kari's bag.

"Oh, no," Kari said. "I already told you. You have to stay home today. Things are going to be too chaotic."

The kitten opened her mouth and let out a yawn before settling further into the bag. Bryn smothered a snort behind one hand. "Why do I think you have already lost this argument?" she said. She took the bag of muffins Sara was holding out. "Come on. The sooner we get going, the sooner we can check on Suz. And you know that kitten always gets her way."

Kari would have liked to have disagreed. But really, it was true.

"Okay," she said to Queenie, picking up the bag. "But try and stay out of trouble."

She could hear Sara's laugh behind her as they walked out of the room.

🐈 Ten

The drive from Lakeview to Perryville was just as beautiful as it had been the day before, but Kari wasn't in the right frame of mind to enjoy it. Half her head was busy trying to figure out what she could do to help out Suz with the dog show, and the other half was trying to figure out how she could get her friend off the suspect list for Francine's murder.

She wondered if the cops had tracked down the large bald man they'd seen Francine arguing with—or if they'd even taken Kari seriously enough to check into him at all. As she and Bryn drove past the small group of SHAFFT protesters, already in place with their placards and a few signs with grisly pictures of tortured animals, she also wondered if Richardson had talked to the guy who had yelled threats at Francine.

She wasn't sure she'd have the nerve to ask, even if she ended up seeing the sheriff today. But maybe she could do a little poking around while she was running errands for Suz.

It was still early, so only the parking spaces nearest the entrance were filled, probably by vendors and a few of the people who would be showing their dogs in the earliest competitions of the day, eager to get a head start on prepping for the show.

As Bryn started driving toward that area, Kari noticed a white SUV with a distinctive sign on the side parked at the far end of the lot.

"That's weird," she said. "It looks like Francine Carver's car is still here. Maybe the cops didn't think to search for it last night. Or they know it is there but haven't bothered to have it towed away yet. I guess that if her purse still hasn't turned up, they probably don't have the keys."

She thought for a second. "Can you park down there so I can take a look?" Kari asked Bryn. Not that there was likely to be a note from the killer tucked conveniently under the windshield, but hey, if Francine hadn't locked her doors, it wouldn't hurt to take a peek inside, right?

But when Bryn pulled her tiny VW Beetle up next to the larger SUV, it was clear someone had beaten them to it.

"Uh-oh," Bryn said. "I'm guessing the cops didn't do that." She turned the car off and they both got out to examine the damage.

The passenger side window had been smashed, and glass adorned the black pavement, glittering in the early-morning sun like diamonds. It crunched under Kari's feet as she went closer, and she was glad she'd worn her sneakers and not sandals with their open toes. Peering inside, she could see that the glove compartment was hanging open and empty, only a few scattered items on the seat in front of it remaining of whatever had been inside.

"Wow," Bryn said.

Kari nodded, revising her estimate of the amount of caf-

feine needed to get through this day sharply upward. She
pulled her phone out and called Suz, since Richardson
wasn't on her speed dial list.

"We just found Francine's car in the lot," she explained
to Suz. "It has been broken into. Are the cops still there, or
should I call 911?"

"I'm standing right next to them," Suz said, not sounding particularly happy about it. "We're still sorting through
the stuff I'm trying to get out of the tent. Hang on, and I'll
tell the sheriff."

She went silent for a moment and then came back. "He
says he'll be right there," Suz said. There was a muttered
rumble in the background. "Don't go anywhere. Don't
touch anything." That was undoubtedly a direct quote from
the sheriff. Great.

Kari hung up and glanced at the SUV. She couldn't see
anything that looked like an obvious clue, unfortunately.
Apparently they were just going to have to wait.

A Perryville squad car drove up a few minutes later, and
Kent, Clark, and Richardson got out of it and headed
toward where Kari and Bryn were sitting in Bryn's car,
conspicuously not touching anything.

"Good morning," the sheriff said, in a tone that made it
clear it was anything but. "Would you ladies like to tell me,
for the record, what happened here?"

Kari got out of her side of the car, slinging her bag (with
Queenie still inside) over her shoulder, and Bryn walked
around to join her.

"I have no idea what happened here, besides the obvious," Kari said, a trifle sharply. She didn't enjoy the implied
accusation. "When we arrived a few minutes ago, I noticed

Francine's car over here at the end of the lot. I recognized
it from when she drove in yesterday. I thought it was a little
odd that it was still here, so I asked Bryn to park next to it
so I could take a look."

She gestured at the damaged window. "It was clear that
someone had broken into the car, so I called Suz and asked
her to let you know."

Clark and Kent had given the SUV a cursory glance and
then strode over to join the sheriff. Kent gave Kari what he
probably thought was a piercing look, although it reminded
her more of Fred when he had indigestion.

"So, first you find the body," the Perryville cop said.
"Then you conveniently 'find' the victim's car broken into."
He made finger quote marks in the air when he said the
second *find*. "And by a remarkable coincidence, your best
friend's scissors are used as the murder weapon." He stared
at her. "Maybe the two of you were in on it together."

There was a long pause. If this was a television show,
now would probably be the time when Kari confessed to
the entire crime. But since it wasn't television, and she
hadn't actually done anything wrong, she just stared back
at him calmly.

The sheriff sighed. Loudly. "I should probably explain
to you that it has been my experience that Ms. Stuart has an
unfortunate habit of being in the wrong place at the wrong
time. Put another way, she sometimes sticks her nose where
it doesn't belong. But I think it is unlikely that she broke
into Ms. Carver's car and then called us to tell us about it."

He gazed pointedly at Kent. "Wouldn't you agree?"

The young officer stuck out his jaw, but didn't argue,
although he still looked dubious. "Right. Let's say we buy
her story for the moment. Who is this?" He pointed at Bryn.

Kari bit her tongue so she didn't say something rude,

like *My getaway driver.* Instead, she settled for the truth. "This is Bryn, Bryanna Jenkins. She works for me at the shelter. Since Suz couldn't get away to pick me up, Bryn drove me over."

Switching gears, she pointed at the open glove box. "Do you think that maybe someone killed Francine because they wanted something she had, and when they didn't find it on her or in her purse, they searched her car?"

"Was Ms. Carver a wealthy woman, that you know of?" Clark asked. "Was she likely to be carrying around valuables?"

Kari shrugged, eliciting a squeak of protest from her bag that made Clark look at her funny. "I don't know, but I doubt it. Most people don't get rich being dog breeders. Her dogs would probably have been the most valuable thing she owned, and it isn't as though there would have been one in the glove compartment. Although, as I said, I just met her yesterday. For all I know she is a runaway heiress."

"The only thing running away here is your imagination," the sheriff said with a grimace. "It's much more likely that someone random happened to notice the car sitting out here overnight and decided to break in to see if there was anything worth stealing. I doubt it has anything to do with the murder."

He scowled at Kent and Clark. "Mind you, it should have been towed to the impound lot last night. Let's make sure that gets done now, shall we?"

"Maybe it was one of the SHAFFT people," Kari suggested. "I noticed they were back at the front gate. Since their leader yelled at Francine yesterday about being a breeder, maybe they saw the sign on her car and came back later to trash it."

Richardson nodded reluctantly. "That is certainly one of

the possibilities we'll be looking into. They are on the list of people we plan to talk to, so you can bet I will be bringing up this new incident when I do."

"Are you going to take the people you want to talk to in to the police station?" Kari asked. She sincerely hoped she wasn't going to end up spending half the day there, going over her statement again.

"We are not," Richardson said. "We've set up a picnic table"—he winced when he said the words—"over next to the crime scene. That way we can keep an eye on the supply tent, which is still evidence, plus talk to everyone involved in the case. Most of the people we need to question are already at the dog show. It just seemed simpler."

"Ah," Kari said. "That makes sense."

Richardson gave her a wintry smile. "I'm so glad you think so, Ms. Stuart."

She made an effort not to grimace. "Do you need us for anything else, Sheriff? It's just that we promised to help Suz get things set up, and I'd like to get going."

He shrugged. "I assume you'll be here at the show all day long?" Kari nodded. "Fine. Then I'll let you know if I need to talk to you later. In the meanwhile, you and Ms. Jenkins can go. Thank you for alerting us to this issue." He nodded in the direction of the damaged vehicle.

Then he turned to Clark. "Anytime now on calling that tow truck, Clark. Unless you want to stand out here in the parking lot all day and guard it."

This time it was the young officer's turn to wince, after which he swiveled on his heel and headed for his car, no doubt to use the radio.

Kari and Bryn headed across the grass toward the supply tent, where as expected they found Suz yanking on her lavender hair until it stood straight up from her head. Today's row of earrings was red, which she'd told Kari she wore when she thought she'd need extra energy. That was a pretty safe predication under the circumstances, Kari thought.

Suz was wearing jeans, running shoes with rainbows painted on them, and a tee shirt with a picture of Wonder Woman wielding a sword on it. It was her version of wearing battle armor.

"Thank goodness you're here," she said when she spotted Kari and Bryn. "Did someone really break into Francine's car? And can you carry these boxes over to the new replacement supply tent? It's really just an E-Z UP, but it will have to do. I had them put it right next to my grooming tent, since I'm in and out of there anyway, and that way I won't have to worry about anyone else complaining about it being put too close to their spot."

She plopped a box into each of their arms and went on without stopping for breath or waiting for Kari to answer either question. Kari assumed the second one was rhetorical anyway. Suz grabbed another box and they all trotted over to where the new tent stood—more of a canopy than a tent, really, although you could put sides on if you needed to. Thankfully, the weather was supposed to be in the mid-seventies and clear, so Suz hadn't had to take the extra time to do that.

"Put that one down over there," Suz said to Bryn, pointing at a stack of boxes labeled *First-Place Ribbons*. She put down her own burden and gave the younger woman a smile, only slightly strained around the edges, followed by an affectionate tug on one of her braids. "And thanks for coming to help out. I really appreciate it."

Bryn smiled back shyly. "You know I'm always happy to pitch in. Besides, I was going to be manning the shelter's tent later anyway. Coming early got me out of cleaning litter boxes, so maybe I should be thanking you."

Suz laughed, and Kari was glad to see some of the tension ease out of her face.

Kari glanced around at the E-Z UP. Despite the chaos surrounding the move, the impromptu storage area was neatly organized into a section on the left for ribbons and rosettes, one on the right for the prizes that would be given out to select winners (all donated by local businesses, including the Used-Car King), and a table toward the back that held stacks of extra paperwork and programs.

"Aren't you worried about those blowing away if the wind picks up?" Kari asked Suz.

Suz nodded, her forehead wrinkling. "I am, actually. The original supply tent was enclosed, so it wasn't an issue."

"Why don't I run to the shelter's booth and get a few of the rawhide chew toys we are selling?" Bryn suggested. "They're heavy enough to hold the papers down, and if we don't sell them, we can always use them at the sanctuary."

"Good idea." Kari nodded. "Why don't you go grab a few and stick them in one of the tote bags we've got for sale? That way we can pack them up easily at the end of the day tomorrow. You can meet us back at the original supply tent for another load when you're done here."

Bryn took off down the path that led to the sanctuary's tent, and Suz and Kari headed back where they'd come from.

"In answer to your question about Francine's car," Kari said to her friend as they walked past people leading every kind of dog imaginable. In the three minutes it took to get from one tent to another, she spotted a stately black standard poodle with a perky topknot, an adorable Yorkie sporting a tartan collar, a cheerful pug, and two yellow Labs pulling their owner along on matching leashes. "Yes, someone definitely broke into it. The passenger side window is smashed and the glove compartment was hanging open. There was no way to tell if anything was taken."

"Do the cops think it had anything to do with her murder?" Suz asked, waving at a woman wearing a volunteer badge on a lanyard around her neck. Suz wore one like it on a rainbow-colored lanyard that matched her sneakers. Kari had hers tucked into her back pocket in case she had to prove it was okay for her to be someplace, but otherwise she didn't want anyone coming up and asking her for information she didn't have.

Kari rolled her eyes. "Kent and Clark apparently think I did it, since stumbling across both the body and the car must be too big a coincidence. As for the sheriff, he seems to think it was just a random crime of opportunity. But he did say he would question the SHAFFT protesters about it, since I pointed out that they had specifically targeted Francine when she arrived yesterday."

"Yeah, he told me he was going to be talking to various folks he had questions for," Suz said as they approached the murder site with its crime scene tape flapping colorfully in the breeze. Next to it, Kari could see Kent and Richardson sitting at the picnic table the sheriff had mentioned. Across from them one of the other show participants was just getting up from the bench. Kari guessed that Richardson was questioning everyone who had seen Francine (or Suz) later in the day, trying to establish a timeline.

Kari and Suz approached the table so Suz could get Richardson to authorize the release of the last few boxes of supplies. As they got there, Clark hustled up with a disgruntled-looking Miriam in tow. Today the tiny woman from Saratoga was wearing a purple track suit with sequins around the collar, white sneakers, and pearl earrings. Her fine white hair was windblown, and she kept pushing it out of her face.

"I keep telling you, I don't know anything useful," she was saying to Clark, who looked as though he would rather be dealing with a three-hundred-pound biker than an irritated grandmother. "I'm showing my dog in an hour. I have better things to do than talk to the po-leese."

Richardson rose from his side of the table and took a step forward to meet them. "I'm so sorry to inconvenience you, Mrs. Rosebaum. I just have a few quick questions and then you can be on your way."

Miriam made a face, but sat down, nodding at Kari and Suz, but focusing her laser gaze on the sheriff, who waited until she was seated before taking his place again. Kent, sitting next to him, was busy typing things into a tablet, apparently having been relegated to note-taking duty.

Richardson asked a few basic questions, starting by confirming Miriam's background and participation in the show and when she last saw Francine. Then he said, "So, Mrs. Rosebaum, I have been told by numerous witnesses that you had a rather heated confrontation with the victim. What can you tell me about that?"

Miriam's thin lips turned down in a scowl, accentuating the way her bright pink lipstick had feathered into the creases around her mouth. "'Victim.' That woman was no victim. She was a darn crook, that's what she was. And her name wasn't Francine Carver when I knew her. It was Lois Keller."

The sheriff raised an eyebrow. "Is that so?"

"Yes, it *is* so," Miriam sputtered. "Why the heck would I say it if it wasn't? What, you think I'm some kind of senile old biddy who needs her eyes checked?" She gave him a glare that would have melted paint off a brick wall. "I'm telling you: look into that woman's background and you'll find out she wasn't who she pretended to be."

"You're saying Ms. Carver wasn't a dog breeder?" Richardson said.

For a second, Kari thought the elderly woman was going to spit on the ground, but she clearly thought the better of it. "She was a dog breeder, all right. But she was also a thief and a cheat. I knew her under her previous name, and she sold me a dog that turned out to have serious health issues." Her faded blue eyes filled with tears. "I was very fond of that dog."

Suz sat down on the bench next to Miriam, since otherwise she towered above her. "Was that the bichon frise you were telling us about yesterday? The reason you switched to a less problematic breed?"

Kari waited for Richardson to tell Suz to butt out, but apparently he was content to have her asking questions. Maybe because he could tell she knew which ones to ask.

Miriam pulled a tissue out of her sleeve and blew her nose, but when she spoke, she sounded more angry than sad. "It was. Samson was a wonderful dog, but he turned out to have PRA. It was devastating, I'll tell you. I really thought he was championship material."

"PRA?" Richardson asked. "What's that when it's at home?"

"Progressive retinal atrophy," Suz explained. "It is a genetic defect that leads to blindness. It is degenerative, there is no real treatment, and the dogs always go blind in the end. It's really heartbreaking. Plus, because it is genetic, you absolutely cannot breed a dog who has it, so if you're talking about a show dog, like Miriam's, you've also lost any potential for the animal to sire offspring."

Richardson shook his head. "That sounds terrible. I can certainly see why you would be upset, Mrs. Rosebaum. But why blame this breeder, the one you claim was actually Francine Carver? She couldn't have known about the issue when she sold you the dog, surely."

Miriam practically growled, making Queenie hunker down even further in the tote bag still slung over Kari's shoulder. She hadn't had a chance to drop the kitten off at the sanctuary's tent yet. The kitten seemed to be listening, although she was keeping an unusually low profile.

"I have no idea if she knew about that or not. But when she sold me the dog, she said it was the progeny of a specific champion dog. After the vet told me about the PRA, I had Samson DNA tested, and the tests proved that the sire could not have been who she said it was." The tiny woman swelled with anger, her otherwise pale cheeks flushed red.

"You had better believe I called her on it too. I demanded my money back, but nothing could make up for the fact that the dog could no longer compete, couldn't be bred, and was going blind. I had to return him to her kennel.

"She wouldn't give me my money back otherwise, and I couldn't afford to get another show dog without it. Some people who compete have a lot of money, but I'm not one of them. There wasn't any way I could have managed the inevitable vet bills, which would have been huge, but she promised me she would have him neutered and take care of him until he couldn't manage anymore."

Sympathy squeezed Kari's heart. She couldn't imagine how hard that had been, not just to invest all that time and hard work in training a dog you thought would be a winner, but no doubt getting attached as well, and then having it all vanish. Plus finding out you'd been lied to from the beginning. No wonder Miriam was still livid, even after a few years had passed.

"That is all very unfortunate," Richardson started to say, but Miriam cut him off with an abrupt wave of one gnarled arthritic hand.

"More than just unfortunate," she said. "It turned out that Lois had faked the paperwork for a number of other dogs as well, all of them supposedly with this same championship sire. She was kicked out of the AKC and banned for life." Satisfaction gleamed in those pale blue eyes. "Too little too late, but it was something."

She went on. "Then a bunch of the folks she'd sold dogs to sued her, so she was in and out of court, and no one would buy her dogs anymore. She couldn't make any money. Rumor has it that she emptied the joint bank account she shared with her husband and just disappeared." Miriam crossed her arms over her flat chest and thrust out her chin, looking for all the world like a stubborn bulldog. "Served her right, losing everything. I can't honestly say I'm sorry."

"I don't understand what this has to do with the murder victim," Kent said, slightly plaintively. He'd been madly tapping on the tablet, trying to keep up with Miriam's stream of vitriolic comments.

"Haven't you been paying attention, young man?" Miriam snapped at him. "Francine Carver was Lois Keller. She'd changed the color of her hair, put on a few pounds, and her eyes were a different shade, but I'd have known that crooked liar anywhere."

She glared from Kent to the sheriff and back again, as if daring them to contradict her. "So yes, I confronted her and accused her of breaking the AKC rules, since banned former members aren't allowed on show grounds ever again—not even as spectators, and certainly not as dog handlers."

"From what I've heard, Ms. Carver denied it and said she'd never met you before," the sheriff said. Suz and Kari nodded in agreement. "Swore it was a case of mistaken identity."

"Huh," Miriam said. "Of course she'd say that. But I'm telling you, it was her."

"So how far away were you when you theoretically recognized her?" Richardson asked. Miriam was wearing thick bifocals. "Some of these same witnesses told me you came barreling across the grass past three tents or more. Surely if she has changed as much as you said, you couldn't have spotted her from that far away."

To Kari, it was clear he wasn't buying Miriam's story at all, although it was equally clear that Miriam believed it. There was no way the elderly woman was faking that much anger.

"It wasn't her I originally recognized," Miriam explained patiently, as if she was talking to a not very bright four-year-old. "It was the bark of the dog with her. My Samson had a very distinctive bark, unusually deep for that breed. I'd never heard another bichon with one like it, until yesterday. So I went to investigate the dog that was barking, and that's when I saw Lois, who had the dog on a leash. It took me a minute, but then I could tell it was her, even with all the ways she'd tried to change the way she looked."

"A dog bark," Richardson said. "You identified her as this other woman because of a dog bark?"

Miriam stood up so suddenly, Suz almost fell off the bench. "I really don't know why you're bothering to question me. For one thing, if you were doing your job, you would have discovered her real identity by now. Don't you people check fingerprints anymore?"

Richardson sighed. "We don't need to check fingerprints when we have a positive identification of the victim," he said. "Not to mention that most law-abiding citizens aren't even in the system. Unless you're been arrested or worked for the government, you're not likely to have your finger-prints on file either. Now that you've brought up this issue, we'll certainly look into it, and I'll ask the coroner if Fran-cine Carver was wearing colored contacts when she died. But even if she was, that doesn't necessarily mean she was trying to disguise her appearance. Plenty of people wear them for cosmetic reasons."

"Piffle," Miriam said. "This is why I didn't come to you in the first place. I knew you wouldn't listen to me." She shook a finger at him. "Just you wait until you're my age and everyone treats you like you've lost your marbles. Now if we're done here, I have to get back to my dog."

"I just have one or two more questions," Richardson said. "Perhaps you could tell me where you were between four and six p.m.?"

Miriam heaved a sigh. "You must be joking. You think I killed her? I'd probably break a hip just trying. Not that I'm sorry she's dead. Not one little bit." Her eyes shifted to where Suz was sitting. "Mind you, I don't know why you're questioning me at all. I'm not the one who threatened to kill someone yesterday."

Eleven

Both cops instantly went on the alert, sitting up straighter, and in Kent's case, actually reaching for his gun.

"What?" he said. "Someone threatened to murder our victim? Why are you just telling us this now?"

Richardson didn't get quite as excited, but he did give Miriam his full attention. "Exactly who are we talking about, Mrs. Rosebaum?"

Miriam pointed at Suz, who simply raised an eyebrow.

"I overheard Suz telling her friend that she was on the verge of killing Olivia Weiner," the elderly woman said. Kari couldn't tell if she was being serious or just yanking the cops' chains. So to speak.

"If wanting to murder Olivia was a crime," Kari said with a laugh, "you would have to arrest nearly everyone at this show."

Richardson made a sound like a balloon losing air. "If Mrs. Weiner had been our victim, Ms. Holden's threat, if it was one, might have some bearing. But since last I saw, Mrs. Weiner was alive and well and berating the guard we left at the gate for having egg on his tie, I hardly think it is pertinent." He glared at Kent, who had continued to take notes. "Don't write that down, Kent."

The sheriff turned back to Miriam. "Just for the heck of it, can you describe this dog you saw with Ms. Carver, the one you said had the distinctive bark that made you think it was somehow related to the dog you used to have?"

Miriam snorted. "White and fluffy? Honestly, I used to raise bichons, and even I can barely tell one from the other. They're adorable, have black button noses, and have a lot of soft white fur."

Suz reached into the bag slung over her shoulder, making Kent twitch, and pulled out the show program. "Hang on, let me check something." She flipped to the day's schedule. "Ah, there you go. You can see for yourself if you want. The group the bichons are in will be starting soon. There are three of them entered in the non-sporting category. They're first up in the ring closest to the parking lot."

Richardson heaved himself off the bench and gestured at Kent to come with them. "If you don't mind, Mrs. Rosebaum. Just this one last thing and you can get back to your plans."

He, Kent, Miriam, Suz, and Kari walked toward Ring One, with Queenie poking her head out of Kari's bag to look around with avid interest. Along the way they passed dozens of people walking dogs, some of them dressed in costumes (the dogs, not the people) or carrying bags full of supplies (the people, not the dogs). They also passed Ring Three, where the entries for the Doberman class were lining up in a black-and-tan row, and Ring Two, where six dachshunds were parading around like tiny miniatures of their larger cousins.

"This place is like a three-ring circus," Richardson muttered under his breath. "How on earth does anyone know where they're supposed to be at any given time?"

Suz waved her program at him. "Didn't anyone give you one of these?" she asked. "It tells you which competitions are where, and when." She laughed. "And really, it is a five-ring circus, since we have as many as five different competitions going on in the five different rings at the same time. It can be a little overwhelming, I'll grant you."

"Each breed gets its own time in the ring?" Richardson said. "No wonder you need five of them."

"Not just each breed," Suz said. "There are also competitions for the different types of dogs, like terrier, hound, toy, the working dogs, herding dogs, non-sporting, and sporting. Each group has a judge, and they each get their own awards. Plus there are skill groups, like the dogs who compete in agility." She sighed. "I'm supposed to be entered in that competition with my own dog this afternoon, but I doubt I'll be able to make it."

"But you're running the show," Kent said, sounding slightly incredulous. "Isn't it kind of unfair to have your dog entered too?"

"She's not actually running the show," Kari put in. "Just in charge of making things go smoothly." She remembered that they were dealing with a murdered woman and missed a step, almost tripping over her own feet. "As smoothly as possible, anyway."

"Only the senior members of each kennel club are not allowed to participate," Suz added. "And that's only on the day when their particular club is putting on the events. So tomorrow, when our club is hosting, Olivia, as president, and Caroline Rogers, who is the show chairperson, won't be showing their dogs." She made a face. "Of course, Caroline is the one who called in sick and stuck me with this job, so she isn't going to be here anyway."

They got to Ring One just as the judge, a tall, thin woman wearing a crisp white blouse and dark gray slacks, was examining each dog in turn as it ran around the circle with its handler, then stopped in front of her to be checked out more closely.

"She's looking to make sure that they fit the conformation for the breed," Suz explained. "Every breed has its own specific parameters, and a dog has to fit within them in order to have any chance of winning a ribbon. The judge will also look at how well they behave, how good they look when they're moving and sitting still, things like that. Some people handle their own dogs, but others prefer to use a professional because they can show off a dog to its best advantage."

Across the ring from them, Olivia, in a cream-colored linen suit and her usual perfectly coiffed hair, was watching both the judge and her competition with a critical eye. She must have found someone to step in and handle Snowball for her at the last minute, since Kari saw the dog trotting around with a woman she didn't recognize. Olivia took her eyes off the dogs long enough to spot the cops, Kari, Miriam, and Suz across the ring. She aimed a seething glare in Suz's direction but stayed where she was.

"Jeez," Kent muttered. "I'd be more worried about her murdering Ms. Holden than the other way around."

Kari was pretty sure she heard Richardson choke back a laugh, although when she glanced over at him, his face was as placid as always.

"The dogs do look remarkably similar," he said. "I don't see how the judge can possibly pick one over another."

"Really?" Suz sounded genuinely surprised by his comment. "That one in the blue collar has legs that are out of proportion with the rest of his body." She pointed at another. "And that one is too squirmy. He needs to have more training in maintaining a sit command before he can progress much further." She pointed at the one the judge was indicating. "See, there's Snowball, Olivia's dog. He's clearly superior to the others in both behavior and conformation. It looks like she is going to have another good day."

In fact, Olivia was being handed a first-place ribbon and beaming from ear to ear.

Richardson shook his head. "It might be clear to you, but they still all look the same to me." He turned to Miriam. "Are you sure that the dog you say you heard barking is one of these three?"

Miriam pressed her thin lips together, peering at the dogs as they left the circle. "Honestly, no. I assumed at the time that it was one of the dogs entered in the show, but now that I know Lois—or Francine, if you insist—is breeding bichons near here, I suppose it could have been one of hers that she brought to the show for some reason. I can hardly walk up to those three owners and ask them to make their dogs bark for me, can I?"

"How on earth are we going to know if it was one of the murdered woman's dogs?" Kent asked Miriam plaintively. "Even if we went to her kennel and checked all the dogs there, how would we be able to tell if one of them was somehow related to your former dog? Or if your dog was actually at the kennel and being bred, even though it wasn't supposed to be?"

"Oh, if my dog is there, you could identify him by his microchip," Miriam said, as if she couldn't believe the young cop didn't know that. "I have all my animals micro-chipped when I get them."

"Huh?" If anything, poor Kent looked even more con-fused than before. His hand edged toward his phone, as if he was tempted to Google it but was afraid of being caught. "Is that some kind of computer thing?"

"A microchip is a small chip that is implanted under an animal's skin," the sheriff explained. "It is registered with information about the owner and the animal's name, so if the dog—or cat or whatever—is ever lost, the chip can be scanned if the animal turns up someplace and the owner contacted. My dog Duke has one."

"Here," Kari said, pulling Queenie out of her tote bag, to the kitten's evident delight. "Once the animals get big-ger, you usually can't even tell it's there, but since Queenie is still pretty small, you can actually feel the tiny bump under her skin." She guided his hand to the back of the kit-ten's neck, where you could detect the little implant right under the surface. "The vet put it in for me on her first visit."

"Huh," Kent said. He petted Queenie. "So can you track an animal using this microchip thingy?"

"It's not a GPS," Richardson said. "All it does is provide identification. And for that, you have to use a special scan-ner. Vets' offices have them, places like that."

"Oh, heck. We're going to have to haul a bunch of dogs to the vet?" Kent's face was almost comically alarmed. "That will take forever. And my car will smell like dog."

Kari rolled her eyes. She didn't have the heart to tell him that the dogs at Francine's kennel probably smelled better than most of the people that usually rode in his vehicle.

"We have a handheld scanner at the shelter," she said

instead. "We use it to make sure that animals brought in as strays don't actually belong to someone. We actually had a dog once who had somehow made it over three hundred miles from home. His owner was beside himself with joy when we were able to call and tell him we'd found his pet."

She glanced at Suz, figuring anything that would send them looking in a direction other than her best friend had to be a good thing. "I could check out the dogs at Francine's kennel for you, if that would be helpful. If Miriam comes along, she can identify her own dog if it's there, if the chip has been removed for some reason."

Kari wasn't sure if she believed Miriam's story about Francine being someone else, although it was clear Miriam was convinced that was true. If the chip reader didn't turn up Miriam's dog, and she saw with her own eyes that he wasn't at the kennel, maybe she'd be able to let the whole thing go.

She suspected Richardson shared her thinking on at least the Miriam part of that equation, because he nodded reluctantly. "I suppose we should follow up on the possibility, although it doesn't seem likely to me," he said. "I'll check in with you later, when I've dealt with the next bunch of interviews I've got lined up."

"What on earth is going on here?" a sharp voice asked from behind them. They all turned around, Kent so quickly he practically fell over. Olivia stood there holding her first-place ribbon in one thin hand and Snowball's leash in the other. Kari suspected that a woman who had had less Botox would have been frowning.

"Mrs. Rosebaum raised some questions about a bichon she saw Francine Carver with yesterday, so Ms. Stuart and Ms. Holden were kind enough to bring us over and explain some of the variations between the different dogs," the sheriff said in a mild tone.

Olivia stiffened and pulled Snowball in a little closer to her linen-clad leg. "Well, Ms. Holden, for one, has better things to be doing with her time," she said, raising her chin. "And having uniformed police officers lurking at the edges of the ring is very disruptive. I can't imagine anything that Miriam would have to say would warrant an armed investigation."

Richardson's shoulders tensed, but he simply said politely, "We certainly had no intention of disrupting anything. Congratulations on your win. That's a fine-looking dog you have."

Olivia's tight lips relaxed into a smile that practically made her face glow. "Why, thank you, Sheriff Richardson. He is quite special, if I do say so myself."

"Yes, he's a lovely dog," Miriam interrupted, thrusting her diminutive body forward. "But that is no excuse for working with Francine Carver. The woman was using a phony name because she'd been kicked out of the AKC for falsifying papers. She should never have been allowed on the grounds of this show."

Olivia blinked. "What on earth are you talking about, Miriam Rosebaum? Francine was a perfectly legitimate breeder and handler. You need to be careful about what you say. This is a very well-respected dog show, and we can't have people going around spreading absurd rumors."

"It is *not* an absurd rumor," Miriam said. She shook her fist at Olivia. "Just you wait. When I get home from this show, I'm going to contact the AKC and suggest that they insist on DNA testing for every animal Francine sold before she died. I am not going to let anyone else get ripped off the way I was."

Olivia tossed her head. "Really, Miriam, you are being ridiculous. But if you want to make a fool out of yourself, no one is going to stop you. Thankfully, my dog came from a different breeder, so it has nothing to do with me." She glanced over Kari's shoulder and perked up. "Now, if you don't mind, I see Charlotte Phelps. She won this event last year, and I should go show her my ribbon." She stalked off, Snowball trotting obediently at her heels.

Kari had kind of been hoping to hear him bark, just in case Miriam wasn't crazy, but the dog didn't utter a sound. Kari was beginning to think Miriam had imagined the whole thing. Maybe she had heard another, larger dog bark and mistaken it for whichever bichon Francine had been with at the time.

"I really don't understand what all the fuss is about," Kent said, his plain face bewildered. "They're just a bunch of dogs."

"There is a surprising amount of money at stake," Suz said. "Both what people have spent on these dogs and in breeding fees if an animal is a successful champion. But more than that, some people invest a huge amount of time, effort, and emotion in the dogs they show. You saw how excited Olivia was to finally have a winning streak after years of coming in second and third. It is a big deal."

"It is a big pain in my butt," Richardson muttered under his breath. He nodded at Kari and Miriam. "I'll talk to you ladies later about taking a chip scanner over to the victim's kennel. Right now, Officer Kent and I have to get back to picnic-bench central."

He turned on one heel and strode off, the younger officer hustling to keep up with his fast pace. It reminded Kari a little of Snowball scurrying after Olivia, and she had to bite back a laugh.

"Miriam—" Suz started to say after they'd left.

"They'll see," the elderly woman said. "They'll see I

was right." She pushed one hand through her white hair, and Kari thought she saw Miriam tremble. But whether that was due to anger or just age, she couldn't tell.

"I have to go get my dog ready," Miriam said. She gave Kari and Suz a grin that was more like the perky woman Kari had met the previous morning. "You know what they say—winning is the best revenge."

After she left, the two friends stared after her.

"Are most kennel club shows like this?" Kari asked faintly.

"No, thank goodness," Suz said. "This one has really gone to the dogs."

Kari slugged her on the shoulder.

Kari walked back to the sanctuary's tent to make sure that everything was under control. Naturally, it was. Sara and Bryn were both there, and having a blast as far as she could tell.

Sara was explaining to a prospective volunteer how the shelter worked, and making it sound as though cleaning out litter boxes was the world's most satisfying job. Bryn was showing a young married couple a pair of two-month-old kittens, one black and the other gray with the most adorable white spot on its nose. When Kari walked in, Bryn was in the midst of persuading the couple that even though they'd only been looking for one cat, they would be so much happier with two. From the expressions on their faces, it seemed as though the siblings would get to stay together.

Clearly they didn't need her, so Kari decided to take a break for lunch. It was barely eleven thirty, but she'd only had that muffin for breakfast, and that had been a long time ago. Besides, she had been able to smell the aromas from the food trucks as she'd been making her way back to the tent, and they had definitely been calling her name.

Taking advantage of a rare moment when no one wanted anything from her, Kari took a meandering route back to the edge of the grassy area where the food trucks were parked. The campus was unusually pretty in the summer sunshine, and she caught a glimpse of the river shimmering in the distance. Everywhere she looked there were dogs—stately elders and frisky puppies, long haired, short haired, and everything in between.

The thing she loved the most was how happy everyone seemed to be. Yes, here and there she could see the signs of stress in someone fussing over an animal whose fur didn't want to cooperate or, once, a male dog who got a little too distracted by a passing female. But for the most part, the atmosphere was festive and everyone seemed to be having a good time.

It was hard to believe there had been a murder there just the day before, but Kari was glad it hadn't dampened people's enjoyment of the event. She still intended to help the police get to the truth and make sure that Suz wasn't unfairly accused of something she hadn't done, but so many kennel club members had worked so hard to make these three days a success, it cheered Kari up to see it moving forward anyway.

"Hey there," a welcome voice said as Angus came up next to her while she was stopped for a moment watching the herding dogs do their thing. Her particular favorite was the border collie who was running circles around the opposition, its black ears pricked up with joy.

"Hey there," she said, a smile spreading across her face. "I was wondering if I was going to see you today."

"They've been keeping me busy," he admitted. "But I

finally have a break and I was going to get something to eat. I don't suppose you have a few minutes to join me." The sunlight turned his red hair to burnished copper and made his green eyes seem to glow.

Kari told herself her heart was only beating faster because her blood sugar was low. Yup, that was it. "I was actually on my way to grab something myself," she said. "I didn't really get breakfast and I've been on my feet since early this morning, helping Suz and dealing with the cops."

"I'm not going to have to bail you out, am I?" Angus teased. "Should I buy you a last meal as a free woman?"

"I don't think it is that bad," Kari said, grinning at him. "But I should probably keep my strength up just in case."

"I agree," he said. "So how about if I treat you to a cheeseburger and fries? You know, for the sake of your health? We wouldn't want you to get weak and pass out."

Queenie popped her head up at the word *cheeseburger*. Clearly she approved of this plan.

"No fries for you, young lady," Angus said to the kitten sternly. "But I might be persuaded to share a tiny bit of my burger."

Loud purring began to emanate from the direction of the tote bag.

"Now you've done it," Kari said. But since she'd also planned to sneak a bit of her lunch to Queenie, she really couldn't give him too hard a time.

They stood in line at Barney's Burger Bus, which was one of the most popular food trucks, even that early in the day. Barney, who was middle-aged, balding, and had a belly that indicated he ate plenty of his own wares, sold delicious burgers made from locally raised beef, hot dogs, fries, and various drinks.

He also had a menu item called "Doggie Delight," which

turned out to be a small bowl of unseasoned cooked ground beef, made especially for the dogs. Kari thought that was the most brilliant piece of marketing she'd ever seen and decided to buy one for Queenie, figuring if it was good enough for the spoiled canines, it was good enough for one very spoiled kitten.

Kari wasn't sure if it was the fresh air—which always seemed to make food smell better—or the lack of breakfast, but the aromas coming off the truck were enough to make her practically sit up and beg by the time they got to the front of the line. Sizzling fat, crispy potatoes, and grilled meat all combined into a heady scent that made her stomach growl in anticipation. Since Queenie was getting her own dish, that left Kari free to squeeze abundant amounts of ketchup onto her cheeseburger from the bottle at the edge of the window.

True to his word, Angus insisted on paying, and they grabbed a wad of napkins each and two bottles of ice-cold water and made their way down to the edge of the river at the side of the campus. Kari nodded at a few people she knew as they walked down the path, but they had the bank overlooking the river to themselves, since most other folks had chosen to stick closer to the action.

There were a few picnic tables scattered about, but Kari and Angus decided to sit on the grass under the spreading branches of an oak so large, they could both lean against it if they didn't mind their shoulders touching. Kari decided she didn't mind at all. The sun glinted off the river as it flowed past and the water provided a background murmur and burble of sound that soothed her spirit.

A cool breeze caressed her skin and the first bite of juicy burger and creamy melted cheese tasted like heaven on a plate. She let out a sigh, feeling herself relax for the first time since she'd found Francine Carver's body the day before.

"Are you okay?" Angus asked. His kind face was creased with concern. "I know this dog show hasn't exactly gone the way you expected it to."

"You could say that again," Kari said, feeding a bit of beef to Queenie, who was happily ensconced on the ground between the two of them. "I can't believe I'm involved in another murder."

Angus shook his head. "Me either. But on the bright side, at least this time you're not the prime suspect."

He had a point. When Kari had been on the top of the sheriff's list for the murder of the former dog warden, it hadn't been a pleasant experience, to say the least.

Still, there were worse things than being suspect number one. Like having your best friend in that position.

"I'm worried that Richardson thinks Suz did it," Kari admitted, after swallowing a large mouthful of burger. "A pair of her scissors was the murder weapon. And she'd argued with Francine earlier in the day because the woman was mistreating Olivia's dog. It doesn't look great."

Angus raised one red eyebrow. "Suz's scissors were the murder weapon?"

Oops. "Uh, I don't think that's supposed to be common knowledge," Kari said. "I'm guessing the sheriff isn't releasing that information in case they have to question someone and figure out if they knew that or not."

"I'll pretend I didn't hear you, then," Angus said, feeding Queenie another tidbit. Unlike Kari's other cats, she had very good manners, waiting to be given a treat instead of grabbing it for herself. Of course, like the royalty she was named after, she had no doubt that said treat would be coming her way. "But really, someone used a pair of Suz's

grooming scissors to kill this woman? How did the murderer get them?"

Kari was grateful Angus didn't seem to even consider
the possibility that Suz might have done it. But even so, her
burger suddenly tasted like sawdust, and she put it back
down on the paper plate.

"We don't know," she said. "But Suz's tent was empty
for much of the day while she was running around trying
to deal with show stuff, and she had a bunch of grooming
clients in between, so she didn't bother to lock up her tools.
Anyone could have taken them."

"Wouldn't someone have noticed if a suspicious person
was in her tent when Suz was gone?" he asked, swiping a
couple of fries through a pile of ketchup and popping them
in his mouth.

Kari shrugged. "Apparently no one did. And honestly, if
one of the dog show people had been found in there, they
probably would have just said they were looking for Suz. It
wasn't much of a risk."

"Hmmm." Angus thought for a minute, absently feeding
Queenie another bit of Doggie Delight. "But surely the
cops don't think that Suz would be stupid enough to stab
Francine with her own scissors and then just leave them
behind. Unless they think she could claim the scissors belonged to someone else. There must be plenty of people
with grooming tools at the show."

"Oh, undoubtedly," Kari said. "But no one else with specialty shears with Suz's trademark lavender handles.
They're definitely hers, and she told the cops as much. As
to whether or not they really believe she'd be that dumb,
apparently the local police are leaning toward the 'lost her
head in the heat of the moment' theory." She rolled her

eyes. "I'm not sure what Richardson thinks. He's nearly impossible to get a read on."

"I've never dealt with him in his official capacity," Angus said. "But he brings his dog in to the veterinary office, and he seems like a nice enough guy."

Sure. A nice enough guy who might put her best friend in jail. "Maybe he is," Kari said. "But he's going to do his job based on the evidence he has. And if they can't find the person who really committed the murder, I'm afraid they're going to decide it was Suz by default."

"I'm sure that's not going to happen," Angus said, patting her arm reassuringly.

Kari set her jaw. "It's definitely not," she said. Because if they didn't figure out who did it, she would.

🐈 Twelve

Angus walked her back in the direction of the Serenity Sanctuary tent after lunch, with Queenie tucked safely back into Kari's bag, purring quietly and smelling faintly of ground beef. As they passed by the supply tent where she and Suz had found Francine's body, Kari noticed a couple sitting at what she now secretly thought of as the Picnic Table of Doom. Both Kent and Clark were seated at the table across from them, and Richardson was standing next to it, not exactly looming, but doing a close impression.

The two people the cops were talking to looked more belligerent than worried. The man was almost cadaverously skinny, with thinning light brown hair peppered with gray. He was wearing a SHAFFT tee shirt that was a little too large for his narrow frame in a bright orange color that did nothing for his pale complexion, blue jeans, and a sullen expression. The woman next to him was almost his mirror image, and Kari would have bet they were one of those couples who had been together so long that they started to look like each other.

The sheriff glanced up as Kari and Angus were walking by and waved her over with a commanding gesture.

"Hello, Sheriff," she said, approaching the table. "Is there something I can do for you?"

He nodded, a brief dip of the head. "This is Shawn Mahoney and his wife, Minnie. Can you tell me if he is the man you saw threatening Francine Carver yesterday?"

For a second, Kari wasn't sure. After all, she hadn't been that close, and she'd mostly been paying attention to the yelling, not to the man doing it.

Then Shawn said loudly, "I didn't threaten anyone," and Kari recognized the booming voice, so surprising coming from such a skinny body. He sounded like an old-fashioned fire-and-brimstone preacher.

"Yes, that's him," she said. "I'd know that voice anywhere. He's the one who told Francine she should be killed for the good of all dogs. Which doesn't even make sense."

"I wasn't threatening anyone," Shawn insisted adamantly. "I have the right to free speech."

"Shut up, Shawn," his wife hissed at him. "Don't say another word until we get our lawyer here." She held up a cell phone and pointed it at the sheriff as if it was a weapon. "I have a lawyer on speed dial, and I'm not afraid to push that button. I know how you people like to pin things on innocent animal lovers like us."

Richardson raised an eyebrow. "Your husband told a woman she should be killed, and then she ended up dead that same day. Doesn't sound very innocent to me."

"Dead? That lady is dead?" Mahoney's voice went up about an octave and a half, and he rose part of the way off the bench before his wife tugged him back down again. "I'm telling you, I didn't have anything to do with that. I didn't mean anything personal by what I said. I didn't even know her."

"You tell a lot of people you don't know that you think they should be killed?" Kent asked, leaning forward. He looked like he was ready to slap the cuffs on the SHAFFT protester right then and there. Kari kind of hoped he would.

"All I meant was that people who breed purebred dogs are directly responsible for the deaths of mutt dogs who then go unadopted in high kill shelters. People like her have blood on their hands, and if we don't tell them that, who will? Not the people shelling out thousands of dollars for inbred animals with delicate constitutions, no sir. It's up to folks like us, the ones who really care. So yeah, I might have gotten a little carried away with my rhetoric, but that doesn't mean I killed her."

Kari's bag began to wiggle, and before she could prevent it, Queenie jumped out and onto the top of the picnic table. "Queenie, get back here," Kari hissed, sending an apologetic look in Richardson's direction. But the kitten scooted out from underneath her hands and sauntered over to stand in front of Shawn, where she proceeded to stand on her hind legs and sniff at a small red stain on his shirt.

"Hey, what the heck! Get this thing away from me!" the thin man said.

"That 'thing,' as you called her, is named Queenie," Kari said. "And she'd not going to hurt you, you big baby. I thought you liked animals."

"Of course I do," he muttered. "Just not on me."

Kari leaned over the table and grabbed Queenie. "What's that she's licking at?"

Richardson peered down at Shawn. "Is that dried blood?" he asked in a quiet voice.

"Blood? No, of course not," Mahoney sputtered. "It's probably just something from my lunch."

The sheriff looked at his watch. Although Kari had just

eaten, it was pretty early for most people. "You've already eaten lunch?"

"Well, not today's lunch," Mahoney said in a grumpy tone. "I wore this shirt yesterday too. My other SHAFFT tee shirt is in the wash." He glared at his wife. "It was supposed to be done for this weekend, but it wasn't."

She rolled her eyes. "I'm sorry I was too busy cleaning the house, organizing the rally, and making your dinner to be able to do the laundry as well. You could have gotten off your butt and done it yourself. Last I checked, you knew where the machines were and neither of your hands were broken."

Richardson cleared his throat. "Yes, well. So you could have gotten that stain yesterday, is what you are saying?"

"Well, uh, yes, I suppose so," Shawn said sullenly. "Obviously I didn't notice it before this."

"Maybe it's ketchup," Kari said, trying to be helpful. She pointed at a similar stain on her own jeans. "I had a burger for my lunch and managed to get some on me even though I was trying to be careful."

"We are *vegans*," Minnie said, her thin chest puffing out indignantly. "We don't eat burgers. Or any living creatures. It must be from something else. Maybe he cut himself shaving." She curled her lip at her husband. "He's a little clumsy."

"I see," the sheriff said. "And were you with the rest of the SHAFFT folks from four to six yesterday, Mr. Mahoney?"

"Uh, sure," Shawn said quickly. "We were together all day."

Minnie's sparse brows drew together. "No, we weren't. Don't you remember, Shawn? We ran out of leaflets to hand out around four, and you went to the Office Everything shop to get more printed. You didn't get back until almost five, when we were packing up to leave for the day. You said they were having problems with their copier." She narrowed her eyes at the cops, who had perked up at this. "He wasn't anywhere near here when that woman was murdered. He'd gone down the road to the store."

"Is that so?" Kent said, staring hard at Mahoney. "That's rather convenient. Will anyone at the store remember you being there?"

"Of course they will," Shawn blustered. "And I have a receipt to prove it. Hang on." He pulled out his wallet and rooted around for a minute, then held up a slip of paper triumphantly. "Here, see? One receipt for five hundred SHAFFT flyers. Would you believe they charge extra to do them at short notice? It's outrageous."

"I'm sure it is," Richardson said, reaching out to pluck the receipt from Mahoney's fingers. "I'll take that, thank you."

"HEY," Mahoney said. "I need that for my accountant. Not-for-profits have to account for every darn penny, or the IRS comes down on us like jackbooted thugs."

The sheriff let out the smallest of sighs. Kari wasn't sure anyone but her caught it.

"I'll be happy to give it back to you when our investigation is over, Mr. Mahoney," he said. "But I'm afraid that in the meanwhile, we're also going to need your shirt."

"My what?" Mahoney said, his mouth gaping. "You want my shirt?"

Richardson nodded and held a hand out. "Yes, sir, if you don't mind. We're going to need to get that stain tested, just in case." He turned to Kent. "Please make a note saying we've taken possession of these two pieces of evidence."

Mahoney stood up and stripped off his shirt, glaring at Queenie as he did it. The kitten appeared completely unmoved, yawning in his general direction. Kari was relieved to see that the SHAFFT protester wore a sleeveless white undershirt under the tee. She wasn't sure the world was ready for the sight of a half-naked Shawn Mahoney. She knew she wasn't.

"Our lawyer is going to be hearing about this," Minnie said, standing up from the picnic table bench. "And you will be hearing from him bright and early Monday morning." She leaned in and said to Kari in a confiding tone, "He charges extra on the weekend. And really, it's just a ratty old shirt." She hauled her husband off with a surprisingly forceful grip. Neither of them looked back.

Clark shook his head. "If I was going to peg one of them for a murderer, it wouldn't be him," he said.

Richardson ignored the comment, although he didn't look as though he disagreed. "Check this in to evidence," he said, handing the orange tee shirt to Clark. "And have someone in the lab examine that stain as soon as possible." He gave the store receipt to Kent. "You go to Office Everything and see if anyone remembers seeing Mahoney or printing up those flyers. I want to know whether or not he really has an alibi for the time of the murders."

He turned to Kari, who was holding Queenie in her arms (in the no doubt futile hope that she could keep the kitten from getting into even more trouble).

"Thank you for the assist, I think," he said with a wry smile. "I didn't even notice that stain until your cat pointed it out." Kari wasn't sure if he was talking to her or to Queenie.

He shifted to address Angus. "Hey, Doc, since you're here, maybe you can come with us to check the microchips on the dogs out at Francine Carver's kennel. We're following up on a lead, although it isn't something that is really likely to go anywhere. Still, I like to be thorough." He gave the two younger cops a pointed look, as if making sure they were paying attention.

Angus smiled apologetically. "I'm sorry, Sheriff. But the kennel club rules say there has to be a vet available during the show. I can't really leave the grounds until the end of the day. I'd be happy to go with you later, if you can wait until the last dog has left."

This time Richardson's sigh was definitely audible. "No, that won't be necessary. Ms. Stuart has offered to help us out. I was just hoping not to involve someone with a vested interest in the case."

"I'm afraid I'm rather partial to Suz too," Angus said with a grin. "In fact, I suspect you'd be hard-pressed to find anyone around here who *doesn't* have a vested interest in proving her innocent."

"Hmmph," Richardson said. "I suppose you have a point there. Very well." He swiveled back to face Kari. "In that case, if your offer still stands, Ms. Stuart, do you think you could get one of your people to bring the scanner from the shelter to the campus and meet me back here in about an hour?"

"I expect so," she said. "But in that case, I'd better get back to the sanctuary tent and see if I can relieve one of the volunteers so they can run and pick it up."

She smiled at Angus. "Thanks for lunch," she said. Queenie meowed in agreement. "Hopefully I'll see you around later."

"I heard there is an ice cream truck," Angus said, a mischievous look in his eyes.

"Then I'll definitely see you later," Kari said, and set out to accomplish her mission so she could do just that.

Sara agreed to drive to the shelter and pick up the scanner, on the condition that Kari waited until she got back to give Bryn the latest update.

"This is better than a soap opera," Sara said as she grabbed her purse and car keys.

"Other than the fact that Suz might end up in jail," Kari pointed out.

"Not going to happen," Bryn said, her jaw set in a stubborn manner that boded ill for anyone who disagreed with her. "We're not going to let it."

"No, we're not," Kari said decisively. "That's one of the reasons I want to go to Francine's house. Not only do I want to help the sheriff look for Miriam's dog, which, by the way, I doubt is actually there, but I also want to see if I can find any other clues as to why someone would want to kill the woman."

"Hold that thought," Sara said, lifting a hand in the air. "I'm going to get the chip scanner and I will be right back."

She nodded in the direction of a little girl and her father, who were clearly entranced by a half-grown yellow kitten in the cage on one of the tables. The kitten had lost one eye to an infection when it was only a few weeks old, but it was still as adorable as could be.

"Go convince those folks that imperfect kitties make the best pets," Sara commanded, much the way she had told multiple generations of English students to hand in their papers on time, or else. "I'll be back in two shakes of a cat's tail."

True to her word, Sara made it back in a surprisingly short amount of time. Kari decided it was best not to ask the older woman if she'd broken any speed limits. After all, they knew where most of the cops were.

Sara handed over the scanner, smiling approvingly when she saw that the yellow kitten was gone. "Good job," she said. "He was one of my favorites."

Kari tried not to laugh. Every cat was one of Sara's favorites. "Luckily, they were already on our preapproved list for adoption, so they didn't have to wait to take him home."

"Okay," Sara said. "Now spill. What have you learned that might help Suz?"

"Well, remember I told you about that SHAFFT guy who yelled at Francine when he saw the sign for her kennel on the side of her SUV? It turns out that he had some kind of red stain on his shirt." She kissed the kitten on the top of her head, and Queenie preened and purred, jumping back up to her usual spot on Kari's shoulder. "Queenie was actually the one who spotted it."

Sara fished a treat out of one of her many pockets and gave it to the kitten. "Good job, sweetie. You are such a clever girl." The purr grew louder.

"So was it blood?" Bryn asked. "That would be great!" She bit her lip. "I mean, not great that Francine is dead, but great if they found the killer and Suz was off the hook."

"I knew what you meant," Kari said. "And they don't know yet. The cops confiscated the shirt so they could send it to the lab."

"Wow," Bryn said. "Does that mean he doesn't have an alibi?"

Kari wrinkled her nose. "Yes and no. At first he said he was with all the other protesters, but then it turned out he'd gone to get more flyers made. He had a receipt from the store, but I guess Richardson is going to look into it."

She thought back over the entire conversation for a minute. "You know, I am pretty sure he was lying about something, but I can't see him killing Francine just because she bred purebred dogs. I mean, why her specifically? There are plenty of breeders at the dog show. It's not as though she was the only one."

"You never know with fanatics," Sara said. "Although I agree, it seems like a stretch as a motive." She tapped her fingers on the table they were sitting at. "I have to admit, I sometimes have qualms about people buying purebred animals for a lot of money instead of just rescuing one of the thousands of cats and dogs who can't find homes." She sighed. "It breaks my heart to see some of our longtime residents at the shelter waiting for the right person to come along who can see past their imperfections to the loving animal inside."

"Me too," Bryn said. "But I can also see the appeal of some of the fancy breeds. Bichons, for instance, are hypoallergenic, so people who are allergic to other dogs can sometimes have one of those. Plus, there are some breeds, like the French bulldog, that I just think are incredibly cute. I have to admit, I'd love to have one of those, although I'd probably try and find one through a rescue organization."

"I can see both sides," Kari said. "And the truth is, even if there were fewer purebred dogs available, that doesn't guarantee that people would adopt one from a shelter." She reached up and patted the kitten sitting on her shoulder. "Can you believe that some people won't take home a black cat? Apparently they are the hardest to get adopted. I don't understand it."

As much as she loved her other animals, she couldn't imagine her life without that tiny black face staring back at her every morning. Heck, Queenie had led to Kari buying the Serenity Sanctuary in the first place, so finding the little stray had completely changed Kari's life.

"I guess I am a fan of the animals that need me the most," she said in summary. "No matter whether they are purebred or not."

Sara gave her a blinding smile. "And that's why I love you, dear. So what's our next step?"

"I guess I take the scanner and go to Francine's house, and hope to find something there that points at someone other than Suz," Kari said. "There was definitely something kind of creepy about that guy Herman Blue who lives on the property. I hope the sheriff is looking into his story."

She plucked Queenie off of her shoulder and popped her into the special cage they'd brought for her, complete with one of her own cushions from home. "Sorry, baby, but we're going to be dealing with a lot of dogs up close and personal," she said to the kitten. "You're going to have to stay here and supervise."

The kitten yawned, showing lots of white teeth, curled up on the cushion, and immediately fell asleep.

"Way to keep an eye on things," Kari said with a laugh. Then she picked up the scanner, stuck it in her bag, and set off on her mission. Suz was depending on her, and there was no way Kari was going to let her down.

✦ Thirteen

When she arrived back at the Picnic Table of Doom, the sheriff was pacing back and forth and looking at his watch, a sturdy, old-fashioned Timex with a wide black leather strap. No fancy electronic step counter for him, apparently.

"I'm sorry, am I late?" she asked. They hadn't set a specific time for her to get back that she was aware of.

He shook his head. "Not you. I was waiting for Miriam Rosebaum. I have a few more questions for her, and she was going to go along with us to see if she could identify the dog she formerly owned that she believes Ms. Carver supposedly has in her kennel." He glanced at his watch again, scowling. "Mrs. Rosebaum was supposed to be here a half an hour ago."

He tapped his pen on his notebook. "Plus, I tried to call Herman Blue to warn him that we would be coming out, but there is no answer at the kennel, which is the contact number on all of Ms. Carver's paperwork, and I failed to get a number for him when we were there last night."

Ah, now she got it. He was more frustrated with himself than anything else. She knew that feeling.

"Is he listed in the phonebook?" she asked.

"He's not listed *anywhere*, as far as I can tell," the sheriff growled. "In fact, I'm not sure the man actually has a phone." He looked at his watch again. "I guess we'll just go without Mrs. Rosebaum."

Swiveling on one booted heel, he turned to Kent, who was sitting at the table typing notes into a tablet with one finger, his forehead wrinkled in concentration.

"If Mrs. Rosebaum shows up, you have the list of questions I wanted to ask her. I'm hoping to be back within the hour." Richardson gestured to Kari. "Come on, let's go. The sooner we finish this fool's errand, the sooner I can get back to interviewing half the known universe and their dogs."

They took his car and drove the short distance down scenic back roads to the kennels. Kari tried to make small talk for a minute but gave up after getting nothing but grunts. Apparently his attempts to formulate any kind of a timeline for Francine Carver's last couple of hours had only been partially successful. From the little he did say, Kari gathered that most of the folks he'd talked to were more aware of where their dogs were supposed to be at any given moment than they were of other people.

She figured that laughing was probably not a helpful response, although based on what she'd seen at the show so far, she couldn't say she was surprised.

They pulled into the driveway at Francine's house and went inside. As with their last visit, the front door was unlocked, which made the sheriff mutter under his breath about fools who think everyone who lives in the country is honest.

But he was suddenly all business when they entered the living room to discover a large bald man going through Francine's things. He was in his mid-forties, dressed neatly enough in tan pants and a polo shirt, but his nose had clearly been broken more than once and he looked like he'd know his way around a barroom brawl.

He had obviously been there for a while. Drawers were pulled out and papers strewn across the floor. The couch cushions were tossed around, and a picture of a bichon hung crooked on the wall, as if he had been looking behind it. For what, Kari didn't know. A safe, maybe? Or did that only happen in the movies?

Her heart stuttered in her chest and then started racing, and she was suddenly glad for the equally large and infinitely more comforting bulk of the sheriff, who was now standing in front of her with his gun drawn and aimed at the stranger.

Except he wasn't exactly a stranger.

"Sheriff," Kari hissed. "That's the man I saw Francine arguing with yesterday."

"Is it?" Richardson said, sounding as though his day had just improved. He raised his voice. "Spectacular. If you would kindly put your hands up, sir, and step away from that desk, I would very much appreciate it."

The big man put his hands about halfway up, narrowing his eyes at Richardson's uniform. "I think there has been some kind of misunderstanding, Officer. I have every right to be here."

"Sheriff," Richardson corrected. "I'm Sheriff Dan Richardson, and I'm pretty sure that breaking and entering is still a crime." He thought for a minute, probably considering the unlocked door. "Trespassing too. Unless you live here, which I don't believe you do."

"No, I don't," the man said. "But my wife does, so it isn't exactly trespassing. Can I lower my hands now?"

Richardson put his gun down but not, Kari noticed, away. "Fine. But no sudden moves, if you please. Do you have any identification to prove you are who you say you are?"

The man reached slowly into his back pocket and pulled out a wallet, from which he took a driver's license. Richardson gestured at Kari to stay put and stepped close enough to pluck it out of the man's meaty fingers.

"This says Anthony Keller," the sheriff said. "Francine's last name was Carver."

"You can call me Tony," the bald man said. And then he laughed, although it had a bitter undertone. "And her name was never Francine Carver. It's Lois Keller. Two years ago she emptied our bank accounts and took off. I've been looking for her ever since. The private detective I hired finally tracked her down here."

Kari's mouth dropped open. "Holy crap," she said. "Miriam was right after all."

The sheriff looked almost as stunned as she did. "I don't usually find someone's husband ransacking her house. Do you have any proof to back up your story?"

Keller pulled a worn picture out of his wallet. It was a younger version of him, already bald and even more muscular, with his bulky arm around a woman who was thinner than Francine, with brown hair and eyes, but still recognizably the same woman. "This was us in happier days," he said. "Mind you, I thought we were pretty happy right up until I came home to find half our stuff gone, but there you are. Marriage. Bah."

"So is it true that Francine, I mean Lois, falsified breeding papers and was kicked out of the AKC?" Kari asked.

Wow, she really owed Miriam Rosebaum an apology the next time she saw her.

Tony rolled his eyes, which were deep-set under heavy black brows that seemed to be trying to make up for the lack of hair on his head. "Yeah, so what? I don't know why they made such a big deal about it. So some fancy purebred dog didn't have the father she said it did. Who cares?" He gave a laugh. "You should have seen the kids in my neighborhood when I was growing up. I'll bet half of them didn't have the father it said on their birth certificates."

The smile slid away from his face. "If that stupid organization hadn't raised such a stink, all those people wouldn't have sued her, and she wouldn't have taken off like she did. I'd like to get a few of those jerks into a boxing ring and see if they're so smug then."

"You're a boxer, Mr. Keller?" the sheriff said. Kari thought that explained the nose, and probably the physique.

"Retired," Keller said shortly. He clearly wasn't in the mood to reminisce. "When Lois left, she took most of my life savings with her. I'm forty-six years old—too old to get back into the ring. I took a lot of abuse for that money, and I want it back."

The sheriff raised an eyebrow. "And you thought you were going to find it in a drawer in the living room?" His tone made it clear that he thought such a thing was highly unlikely.

Tony shrugged massive shoulders. "We had a bunch of bonds in a safe-deposit box at the bank, and she cleaned it out. That's what I'm looking for. Plus I want Lois's signature on divorce papers."

Richardson glanced at Kari, as if checking that she was there to provide emotional support if Keller took the news badly.

"I'm sorry to tell you this, Mr. Keller, but your wife is dead. She was killed yesterday," Richardson said.

"Dead," Tony repeated flatly. "Huh. Well, that's damned inconvenient."

Kari could feel her jaw drop in astonishment. "'Inconvenient'?" she repeated. Yes, the man had been abandoned and had come looking for a divorce, but she would have expected him to be at least a little broken up. Apparently not.

"Well, she can't exactly tell me where she hid my money if she's dead, now, can she?" Keller said, giving Kari a look of annoyance. "So yeah, I'd say it is inconvenient as hell." He cheered up a little. "But at least I don't have to pay any lawyer's fees to get the divorce now, so I suppose that's something."

"You don't seem very surprised, Mr. Keller," the sheriff said. "Maybe you already knew that your wife was dead?" His eyes gazed piercingly in Tony's direction. "Can you tell me where you were yesterday between four and five o'clock in the afternoon?"

Tony scowled, which only had the effect of making him look even more menacing. "After I tried to talk to Lois at the dog show and she blew me off, I waited out in the parking lot for her to come out." He rubbed a large hand over a slightly stubbly chin. "I can be a very patient man when I want something bad enough.

"I only knew she was in the area, not her exact address. The detective was able to track her down through the kennel, but it only had a post office box, and he wasn't able to find out where the kennel itself was located. Nothing else was in her name, either her real one or the one she is using now. She'd done a good job of keeping a low profile in the area until she came out for this stupid show. So I was going to wait for her to leave for the day and then follow her home."

That didn't sound ominous at all, Kari thought, suppressing a shudder. Based on the grim look on the sheriff's face, he'd gotten the same impression. But his voice when he spoke was meticulously neutral.

"So what did you do when you actually saw her?" Richardson asked.

"Nothing," Keller said. "She never came out. And when I saw cops arrive, I gave up for the day and went out to dinner at some local restaurant, then back to the motel I'm staying at."

Richardson obviously knew exactly what time he and the other policemen arrived, and that it was well after the time of the murder. "So you don't have anyone who can place you in the parking lot, where you were supposedly waiting patiently to accost your former wife?"

Keller narrowed his eyes. "No," he said. "I was sitting in my car, parked under a shady spot with a good view of the entrance to the show. People walked past me when they were leaving, but I doubt anyone paid much attention to me."

"I see," Richardson said, drawing out the words slowly. "And would you by any chance happen to know anything about Francine's SUV getting broken into in that same parking lot?

Keller let out a loud sigh. "Yeah, yeah. I probably left my fingerprints all over the thing. I admit it. I came back early this morning, because I was determined not to miss her again. When I got there, I saw her car sitting at the far end of the lot with that kennel sign on it—I would have seen it yesterday if I'd parked closer to that side, or if there hadn't been a bunch of other cars in the way."

He rubbed his hand over his chin again, as if it were a habitual motion that helped him focus. "There was no one else around yet, so I smashed the window with a rock. I wanted to get to the insurance papers in the glove compartment, because I knew they'd have her address on them." He didn't sound even remotely remorseful. "Then I walked around the show for a while looking for her, but when I didn't find her again, I gave up and came here looking for my money."

There was a muffled sound from the end of the room and they all turned to see Herman Blue standing in the doorway, wearing what looked like the same sunglasses and cap as the last time Kari had been there. From what Kari could see, beneath those, he also wore a slightly indignant expression.

"What are you doing back here?" Herman asked the sheriff, ignoring the others for the moment. Maybe he assumed that Tony was another cop and they'd been searching the room for some reason. "I answered all your questions."

"It turns out I have quite a few more, Mr. Blue," the sheriff said in what Kari had come to recognize as his dangerously mild tone. "I did try to reach you but I neglected to get your number the last time I was here." He finally slid his gun back into its holster and pulled out his notebook instead.

"Oh, ah, I don't actually have a cell phone," Herman said. "There is no one I have any interest in talking to. I do most of my business through the Internet, and if I need to make a call, I simply use the house phone. My handler set it up for me, so the number isn't readily available."

"I'll take that one," Richardson said, and kept his pen poised in the air until Herman muttered the numerals reluctantly.

"Now that we have that resolved," the sheriff said, "can you confirm for me that Francine was actually married?"

Herman made a face that pulled at his scars in a disturbing manner. "She had a husband, if you want to call him that. I never met the guy, but from what she told me, he was much older than her, a loser who didn't deserve her and treated her lousy. That's why she had to turn to me for help. She knew I would never let her down."

Tony stared at him and then burst out laughing. "Oh man. You're that guy. The one who had such a huge crush on her in college. Lois used to laugh about you. Said you followed her around like a big puppy. Talk about a loser. No wonder she ran away to you. I'll bet she was taking you for every penny she could get. I ought to know. I was married to her, and she did that to me."

"You? How dare you!" Herman shouted, his face turning red. "You took her for granted. You never appreciated her like I did. You shouldn't even be allowed to speak her name!"

He lunged at Tony, who took a swing at him and missed. Herman's sunglasses went flying, along with his cap, and Kari could see that the scarring on his face got even worse when it got higher. The skin around his left eye was puckered and drawn, so the eyelid was permanently pulled halfway over the eye. The hair around his left temple and the edge of his hairline was gone too, leaving only a mass of scar tissue. No wonder the poor man hid behind glasses and a hat and rarely left his own property.

But it didn't seem to have slowed him down any. Tony might have been tougher and stronger, but the former mob accountant was filled with righteous indignation, and fast on his feet. Before she even knew what was happening, the two of them were going at it hot and heavy, punches flying and curses turning the air blue.

"CUT IT OUT!" the sheriff bellowed, pulling his gun

out again and aiming it at the battling duo. "Back away from each other or I will shoot, and I really don't care which one of you I hit."

Kari was pretty sure he was bluffing, but she wouldn't have wanted to put it to the test. Fortunately, apparently neither Herman nor Tony did either, since they each took a step back and then stayed there, breathing hard. Herman had a cut above his good eye that was dripping blood onto the floor and looked as though it would develop into one heck of a shiner before too long. Tony didn't look much better, with a rip in his shirt and a rapidly developing bruise on his squared-off chin.

"What the heck is wrong with you two?" Richardson asked indignantly. "Do you not even see me standing here?"

Herman dabbed at his eye with a formerly pristine white handkerchief, sputtering. "But, Sheriff, he said—"

"I don't care if he called your mother a donkey," Richardson said, putting his gun away again with a noticeable show of reluctance. "A woman has died. A woman who each of you was close to at one point, I might add. I am attempting to solve her murder and the two of you are still fighting over her. It's insulting both to her memory and to me. Now do yourselves a favor and get a grip before I arrest you both for interfering in a police investigation."

Kari wanted to applaud. She had never been so impressed. But she knew the sheriff well enough to know he wouldn't appreciate it, so she just kept quiet. She didn't want to give him a reason to threaten to arrest her too.

Tony wiped blood off a swollen lip. "You're a fool," he said to Herman in a quieter tone. "If Lois had been found out again, she would have left you too, just like she did me, without a backward glance."

"No," Herman said, blotting his cut. "You're wrong. Yes,

she called me yesterday from the dog show, all upset about some woman who recognized her, and she talked about packing her bags and leaving. But it was just talk, that's all. I calmed her down. Told her that she'd built a whole new life and a successful business here. We were happy. I promised her we would figure it out together. She wouldn't have left."

He finally got a good look at the room and gave Tony a stare so filled with hatred, Kari actually took a step back, even though it wasn't aimed at her. If Queenie had been there, she would have been hiding in the bottom of Kari's bag by now.

"What the heck have you been doing in here?" he said to Tony through clenched teeth.

"Looking for what belongs to me," Tony shot back. "And she was still my wife, so if this place was hers, it's technically mine too. You have nothing to say about it."

Herman smiled triumphantly through a bleeding mouth, something that didn't improve his appearance at all. "Ha," he said. "That's where you're wrong. This is my house, and my land. I was just letting Lois live here. So you are trespassing on my property, not to mention trashing the place." He turned to Richardson. "Sheriff, I want this man arrested."

Richardson's eyes gleamed. "With pleasure," he said, twisting the large man around and placing handcuffs on him. "Anthony Keller, I am arresting you for trespassing, destruction of private property, breaking into the victim's car, and whatever other charges I add on later. You have the right to remain silent. Anything you say can be used against you in court. You have the right to talk to a lawyer for advice before we ask you any questions. You have the right to have a lawyer with you during questioning. If you cannot afford a lawyer, one will be appointed for you before any questioning if you wish. If you decide to answer questions now without a lawyer present, you have the right to stop answering at any time. Do you understand your rights as I have told them to you?"

"Yeah, yeah, yeah," Keller muttered. "Whatever." He glared at Herman Blue. "You're not fooling me. I might be under arrest right now, but you're next. I'm betting you killed Lois because she didn't return your obsessive love and was about to leave you. You murdered her, didn't you?"

Herman gazed at him sullenly. "Don't be ridiculous. We lived together in the middle of nowhere on a property with sixty acres. If I were going to kill the woman I loved, I would have done it at home and buried her where she would never be found, not murdered her in the middle of a dog show."

Kari tried not to stare at him. She thought it sounded as though he had given the whole thing a little bit too much thought. Mind you, he wasn't wrong. Tony Keller, on the other hand, seemed like the kind of guy who would strike out in anger without considering the consequences. Although she wasn't sure how either one of them would have gotten Suz's grooming scissors. Still, she was glad the sheriff now had two more viable suspects. Suspects that weren't her friend.

Fourteen

Richardson called one of his deputies to come and collect Tony Keller, and once he'd been taken away, Herman gave the sheriff grudging permission to check the dogs in the kennel.

"I still don't see how this is going to help solve her murder," he said for about the fourth time as he led them out there. "But if it will get you out of my hair once and for all, I'll allow it." He was holding an ice pack on the cut over his eye, which had at least stopped bleeding once Kari had taped it with a bandage from a first-aid kit he'd fetched from the bathroom. The cap was firmly back on his head, but he'd had to leave the sunglasses off.

"I could come back with a warrant if that would make you feel any better," the sheriff said. As usual, his expression didn't reveal whether he was bluffing, joking, or anything in between.

"Nah," Herman said. "I don't care. I never cared about the dogs or the business. Just about Lois. Now that she's gone, I guess I'll sell them or something."

"We'd prefer you not remove any of the animals until this case is settled, Mr. Blue," Richardson said. "Some or all of them might be evidence. Not to mention that until the victim's will is found, if she had one, the ownership of the dogs is still in question. If she didn't have a will, I suspect they will end up going to her husband, as next of kin."

Herman rolled his eyes, wincing as the movement pulled at the one he was holding the ice pack on. "Whatever," he said. He opened the door to the kennel and gestured them in. "Here you go. There are six adults, including two females with puppies. I don't think the puppies have microchips yet, but the others should have them."

Kari looked around the main room with interest. It was neat and professional looking, with plain white walls and a vinyl floor in a checkerboard pattern. A row of gray metal filing cabinets sat along one wall, with a black glass-topped desk in the opposite corner.

Atop the desk sat some papers, a computer, a printer/copier, and an answering machine that blinked every couple of seconds, to show it had messages waiting for a woman who would never hear them. Another wall held dog supplies, including bins filled with dry food, shelves stacked with cans of dog and puppy wet food, medications and vitamins, harnesses, and a row of leashes hanging neatly at the end.

One three-drawer white plastic cabinet on wheels held various grooming supplies, and Kari pulled open the top drawer eagerly. But all the shears and combs were simple stainless steel and looked like standard off-the-rack equipment. No fancy lavender handles. She held one up to show the sheriff, who nodded in acknowledgment.

"The dogs are through here," Herman said, opening a door opposite the one they'd come in.

They trooped through into another room, this one filled with large wire kennel areas, six of which held nearly identical small dogs with curling white hair and black button eyes. The bichons were adorable, and they seemed to be well taken care of, as far as Kari could tell. Each kennel had plenty of space to move around in, and each dog had a soft bed, dishes filled with water and food, and a few toys.

But Kari couldn't help thinking it was a sad life, spending most of their time in cages, no matter how large or luxurious they might be. Hopefully when Francine—Kari had to try and remember to call her Lois—had been around, she'd let them out into the runs Kari could see out the window. But even having more space wouldn't make up for their not living in a house with someone who loved them. The glimpse she'd gotten of Francine with Olivia's dog hadn't exactly suggested that Lois was warm and affectionate, but maybe she had been different with the animals that belonged to her.

The sheriff glanced around and shook his head. "Doesn't look very homey," he said. "Are all professional kennels this Spartan?"

Kari shrugged. "It really varies. Some people have a lot of dogs and use spaces much like this, although I have to admit, they usually make more of an effort to make them a bit cozier." She sniffed the air. "On the bright side, it is very clean and airy, and the dogs look like they are well taken care of."

She walked over to a cage where a mother dog was nursing three tiny fluffy white puppies. Their little paws kneaded at mama's belly, and one of them gazed up at Kari with such a sweet expression on its diminutive face that she had to remind herself that the last thing she needed was another dog.

"Ah, let me take a look," she said, clearing her throat. There was a plaque over the cage door that said *Blue Skies Honey Belle*, then another smaller one underneath that said *Bella*. "This tells us the mother's name," she told Richardson.

"That's a pretty strange name," he said, peering up at it. "And why are there two different ones?"

"Usually there is the official name for registered pure-breds, which includes the kennel where they were born, and two names that are connected in some way to the sire and the mother. In this case, Blue Skies tells us that she was born here at this kennel. The shorter name underneath is probably the name she is actually called every day, since, let's face it, you don't want to be saying, 'Here, Blue Skies Honey Belle!'"

"So when you read her chip, it will tell us her name?" he said.

"Oh, no," Kari said. "The chip itself just has a number on it. I'll have to go to a chip registry website and put the number in, and then it will tell me the information associated with it, which is usually the dog's name, sex, birth date, owner, and contact information."

She shook her head ruefully. "These chips are great for reuniting people with their lost pets, but it only works if the owner remembers to keep their address and phone number up to date. Of course, with these dogs, in theory the chip should simply tell us that they are registered to Francine." She looked at Herman and winced. "Sorry, Lois."

Richardson glanced at his watch and opened the latch on the cage door. "Okay. Why don't you scan each dog, and I'll write down their names and the numbers on their chips. Then, with Mr. Blue's permission, we can use the computer in the other room to do a quick check and be out of his hair."

"Sounds like a plan," Kari said. She was as eager to get back as the sheriff was, although in her case it was because she knew that Suz would be running around trying to do everything on her own.

"Hi there, Bella," she said in a soft voice, kneeling down by the nursing dog. "I'm sorry to interrupt, but I just need to wave this machine over your back, and I'll be out of your way in a minute."

She ran the scanner across the dog's neck and upper back, and a low beeping signaled that she'd found the chip. She read the number off the screen and patted Bella on the top of her silky head before getting back up. "That's one," she said.

Kari worked her way through the six cages, taking a moment to pet each dog and call it by name. They might be in a hurry to get back to the show, but these poor babies had lost their person and didn't even know it. She could spare a few minutes to give them a little affection.

Once she was done, they went back into the main room, and Herman fired up the computer. Kari thought it was interesting that he knew the password by heart, but she wasn't sure if that was important or not. Let Richardson worry about that stuff. She had bigger fish to fry. Now that they knew Miriam had been right about Francine's real identity, Kari was curious to see what else, if anything, the elderly woman had been correct about.

It didn't take Kari long to find out. She put in the numbers she'd gotten off the dogs' chips and then wrote down the information she found online on a piece of paper. When she was done, she swiveled the desk chair around to face the sheriff, who was standing not far away. Herman was leaning against the door to the outside, still holding a dripping ice pack to his head, and looking completely indifferent. She suspected he already knew what she was going to say.

"Two of the numbers match the names of the dogs in the kennels," Kari said, her voice sounding grim even to her own ears. "CH Twin Oaks Treasured Snowflake and Fallow Acres Mighty Whitey are both registered to this kennel, with Francine Carver listed as the owner. She must have gotten them after she moved here, so they still have their original kennels as part of their names."

"What the heck is wrong with Fido and Spot?" the sheriff muttered, looking as though he was getting a headache. "And what kind of name is 'CH'?"

"That's a designation that means the dog is a champion," Kari explained. "It is added to the animal's existing name after he or she has won a championship show. But you're missing the important part."

"Of the dog's name?" Richardson asked. "Because honestly, I don't care."

"No," Kari said. "Two of the dogs have chips that fit the names on their cages, and undoubtedly whatever information is given out to prospective buyers for either the dogs themselves or any puppies bred from them. That means that four of the dogs do not. Three of the male dogs and one of the females have microchips that don't match the names Lois had them under."

"Huh," Richardson said. "What exactly does that mean? Other than the fact that I apparently owe Mrs. Rosebaum an apology when she finally shows up."

"It's hard to say for sure, other than the obvious—Lois was up to her old tricks, and almost certainly selling dogs with fake pedigrees," Kari said. "I suspect that the information on the dogs' true identities is somewhere, either in this computer or somewhere in these files." She gestured across the room. "Lois would have had to have kept track of whom she was mating to whom, or risk dangerous inbreeding. But it might take an expert to track it down, unless she was foolish enough to label the files in some obvious way."

Herman, who had been remarkably silent during all of this, gave a coughing laugh. "Lois was a lot of things," he said. "But she wasn't foolish."

"I don't suppose you know the key to finding the information," the sheriff said. "And would be willing to help us get it. It might lead us to someone motivated enough to commit murder."

"That doesn't seem likely," Herman said. "They're just dogs."

"In a business worth multiple thousands of dollars a year," Kari added in a dry tone. She pushed away from the computer and stood up to face the sheriff. "I can't tell you who most of these animals really are, but I might be able to help you with one in particular."

"Oh?" Richardson said. "How's that?"

"Well, Miriam never told us the name of the dog she gave back to Lois, but she did tell us that it had progressive retinal atrophy," Kari said, feeling sad.

"When I was checking them out, I noticed that one of the male dogs was almost completely blind, although he seemed healthy enough otherwise. I suspect Lois was still using him as a stud, despite the hereditary blindness issues he could have passed on to any puppies he sired.

"We'll have to find Miriam and get her to look up the microchip number for her dog. The information for owner name and address could have been changed by Lois in the registry once she took the dog back, but not the number itself. But I'm betting we've found the poor boy, just as Miriam suspected we would."

"It would have been helpful if she'd shown up to come with us," Richardson said in a disgruntled voice. "Considering we're out here because of her in the first place. Presumably she would have recognized the dog and saved us a lot of trouble."

He scowled at Herman Blue. "Mr. Blue, I'm going to have to ask you not to touch anything in this room except whatever is necessary to care for the animals. I'll be sending officers over later to confiscate the computer and all the paperwork. They are obviously evidence in a crime— whether that is murder or simply fraud, I don't yet know. You can continue to feed the dogs and walk them, but other than that, I don't want you in this building at all. Is that clear?"

"Clear enough," Herman said with a sigh. "I already told you, the dogs were Lois's passion, not mine. I had nothing to do with the business, and whatever schemes she was working on, I didn't know or care." He gave them a wry look. "Mind you, I would have helped her if she'd asked me. She just never did."

Kari had wandered over to look at the shelves of supplies while the two men were talking, idly picking up the bottles of medicine and putting them down again. She used many of the same things at the shelter and had been curious to see if any of the dogs here had issues that would require ongoing medical attention she'd need to alert Herman or the sheriff to.

Something caught her eye and she took a closer look at the vial of ear drops she'd been about to replace on the shelf. Then she checked another couple of bottles of pills.

"Sheriff, we may have a problem," she said in as neutral a voice as she could manage.

"Oh?" Richardson said, not sounding very interested.

Most of his attention was on his cell phone, which he'd pulled out of his pocket, probably to call the sheriff's department to send a deputy to pick up a massive load of files that someone would be stuck sorting through.

But she noticed Herman had swiveled his head around, suddenly seeming more alert than he had been since they'd come out here. She had a feeling she knew why.

"Sheriff," she said again, a little more forcefully. "I think I've found something."

"What's that?" he asked. "Was she giving them some kind of illegal drugs?"

"Not that I know of," Kari said. "But I've got a bunch of prescriptions with names that don't match any of the dogs in this kennel. I think there are other dogs here somewhere that we haven't seen yet."

♟ Fifteen

O ther dogs?" the sheriff said, looking around as if they would suddenly appear from underneath the desk. "What do you mean, other dogs?"

"I mean," Kari said, "that I have found at least five different medications labeled with the names of dogs that don't match any of the ones in this kennel. They all have current dates. And interestingly enough, they are from a number of different vets, including one over an hour away." She stared at Herman. "That could suggest there is an additional kennel space somewhere on this property. One that maybe wasn't being shown to inspectors. Would you happen to know anything about that, Mr. Blue?"

The scarred man gazed at the ceiling, avoiding her eyes. "Like I said, I didn't have anything to do with the business. That was all Lois's territory."

"Is that so?" Richardson said. He walked through the main room and back through the area where the dogs were kept. At the far end, there was a door that led to the outside.

He opened it and exited the building, Kari on his heels, and Herman not far behind her. She spotted what he was looking at right away. He must have noticed it through the window while she was checking the dogs earlier.

Two dirt and stone paths led away from the kennel, veering off in different directions into a more wooded section of the property. There was no indication as to their purpose or destination.

"Can you tell me where these paths lead, Mr. Blue?" the sheriff asked. He walked a little ways down each one and peered into the distance, then returned.

"The one on the left goes to my house," Herman said, his hands twitching restlessly at his sides. "The other one is just a walking route for the dogs. It's important they get plenty of exercise, you know."

Kari and Richardson exchanged glances. His said, *Are you sure about this?* and hers replied, *You bet I am.* He gave her a small nod.

"You're so right about that," Kari said to Herman in her best fake-perky voice. "I'll tell you what. Why don't I go get one of the dogs and take him for a quick walk? That will save you doing it later."

Before he could argue, she popped back inside, grabbed a leash, clipped it onto the collar of Twin Oaks Treasured Snowflake, and led the bouncing white ball of fur back outside.

"Let's go for a walk, Snowy," she said to the eager dog, and let him trot happily down the right-hand path. The other two men followed her, Richardson as inscrutable as ever and Herman looking pained and uncomfortable. Of course, that could have just been his head, but somehow she didn't think so. It was a pleasant enough trail, winding through the aromatic boughs of pine trees that cast cooling shadows overhead, filled with flitting birds and the occasional squirrel that made Snowy strain at his leash.

They hadn't gone very far when Snowy started barking. At least a dozen canine voices answered him back, and Kari gave Richardson a grim glance. As they came around a curve in the path, another building came into view. This one wasn't nearly the showplace the first one had been. Long and low, it had peeling gray paint under a battered black shingle roof that had clearly been patched more than once. One of the windows appeared to be held together with duct tape.

"Want to explain this?" Richardson asked in a gravelly voice.

Herman just sighed and shrugged, clearly giving in to the inevitable, then led them up to the front door, which creaked as he opened it, reached in, and turned on a light switch. The sound seemed to set the dogs off even more, since the noise level ratcheted up to rival that of a jet engine taking off.

"QUIET!" Kari said in a firm tone, and things died down to at least a bearable level. She'd learned a few things at the shelter over the last few months. She tied Snowy up to a post outside and then popped back inside.

Then she looked around and put one hand over her mouth and nose. In part to keep out the stench of too many dogs in too small a space, and in part so she could hold in the curse words that were threatening to tumble out at the sight in front of her.

"Dear God," Richardson said in a quiet voice. "What the heck *is* this?"

"It's a nightmare," Kari said. "Francine was running a puppy mill, hidden back here where no one official would think to look for it." Her stomach did slow flip-flops as she looked around the room, and it was all she could do not to cry from the sheer horror of it.

The building had probably been some kind of shed or garage. It was one long room, with only a few narrow windows set up high, in which fans whirred and clacked tunelessly, and no other source of ventilation that Kari could see. That probably accounted for some of the smell, although the obvious lack of basic hygiene more than explained the rest.

A quick count told Kari that there were over two dozen cages in the room, all of them much smaller than the spacious professional kennels they'd seen in the other space. Almost every cage was occupied, most of them with females with puppies in different stages of development. Some of the puppies were so young their eyes still hadn't opened, and some were tumbling over their mother and siblings as they played the best they could in the enclosed spaces. Kari didn't see any youngsters older than about six or seven weeks old, which almost certainly meant that the puppies were being taken away from their mothers too early and adopted out to people who didn't know (or care) that for this breed twelve weeks was much more optimal. Every single one was a fluffy white bichon frise, and they did, as Angus had said, look remarkably alike.

Shredded newspapers in the corners of each cages sent up the ammonia reek of dog urine, which told her the animals weren't being walked often enough, if at all, and while she would have liked to have blamed Herman for not keeping up with them, she suspected this was more likely to be a normal state of affairs.

"A puppy mill," the sheriff repeated in an unhappy tone. "I've heard of them, of course, but I've never seen one. Is this typical?" He shook his head in disgust as he glanced around the room.

Kari sighed. "Pretty much, from what I've read, but like you, this is the first one I've ever been to in person. Although I've seen pictures that would make you ill."

"*This* makes me ill," Richardson said. He gave Herman a hard stare. "I'd like an explanation, and I'd like it now. And don't give me any of that crap about you not knowing anything about the business. I don't believe for a minute that you didn't know this was happening on your own property."

Herman stared back at him briefly, then dropped his eyes. "Fine, fine," he said, raising one shoulder in a halfhearted shrug. "Yes, Lois was running a puppy mill. It's not as bad as you make it out to be. The puppies end up with good homes and she put some extra money in her pockets. Miss Nosy here saw the medication bottles," he said, glaring at Kari. "Lois took better care of these dogs than most people in this trade do."

Kari pointed at one particularly crowded cage. "You call this taking good care of them? I'll bet she only came down once a day to give them food and water. Did they even get out of this building?"

"Periodically," was his only answer. "When she had time. The animals in the main kennel took up most of her attention." Kari got the feeling, not for the first time, that Herman was one of those people who lacked a sense of right or wrong, or the ability to empathize. Something about him wasn't quite normal, just *off*. Of course, that didn't make him a murderer.

The sheriff didn't let his gaze waver. "How did it work?"

Herman subsided onto a stool near the door, which had

been left open for fresh air, and dropped his now-melted ice pack at his feet.

"After she got burned by the AKC, Lois steered clear of professional dog people," he explained. "The dogs from the official kennel got sold to rich folks, mostly in New York City, which is close enough to make it easy for Lois to deliver the animals. We didn't like anyone coming here, if we could avoid it." He reached one hand up to touch his scars, probably not even aware he was doing it.

"Didn't they want to see the animals first?" Kari asked. She had always ended up with her pets because she met them and fell in love with them or, as in Queenie's case, was adopted by the animal. Of course, a lot of times pure-bred puppies were actually reserved before they were even born, so she guessed it wasn't as strange as it seemed that the folks buying dogs from Lois didn't expect to come to the kennel in person.

"Pffft," Herman said derisively, rolling his eyes and then wincing. Kari thought it served him right.

"Those kind of people aren't looking for a dog to love," he said. "They're looking for something they could show off to their friends and brag about its championship background. One woman actually wanted one that was the exact same shade as her couch, and we had to send a clipping of the puppy's fur so she could make sure it matched her room."

"Good grief," Richardson muttered.

"Yeah," Herman agreed. "Crazy. But they paid extra for us to deliver them, so it worked out just fine."

Kari noticed that *her* had changed to *us*. She guessed he was done denying he'd been involved in the business. She suspected Richardson had noticed too, since not much escaped him. She wasn't sure if this meant that Herman wasn't worried about being prosecuted for helping to run a puppy mill, or if he knew, as she did, that there were rarely any substantial legal penalties beyond fines, which he could clearly afford.

"What about these dogs?" the sheriff asked, jerking his head in the direction of the cages lining the walls. "Did they get sold to wealthy collectors in the city too?"

"Oh, heck no," Herman said. "These ones went to pet stores or got sold online using craigslist and such. By spending less on their upkeep and breeding the mothers a lot more often, Lois could make extra money by selling quantity instead of quality. So to speak." He laughed. "It's kind of ironic, since she used the same male dogs as sires for both sets. You could say that the people who bought these puppies were actually getting a bargain."

Kari heard a sound like growling come out of her mouth and she didn't even care. She glared at the scarred man. "That's appalling. If Lois wasn't already dead, I'd be tempted to kill her myself."

Richardson snorted. "You know, that might not be the best thing to say in front of an officer of the law." But he didn't look as though he was going to argue with her. He gazed around the room and then back at Kari. "What the heck do we do with them now that we know they're here?"

"Well, they can't stay in this place," Kari said, putting her hands on her hips. "Some of the animals are in pretty bad shape, and they all need more space and better care."

"Hey!" Herman protested. "These dogs are Lois's property. You can't just take them."

"You had better tread carefully, Mr. Blue," Richardson said, fingering the handcuffs hanging from his belt in a meaningful manner. "You are still a suspect in the murder, not to mention a possible accomplice to fraud and animal abuse. If I were you, I would try and be a little more cooperative."

He turned to Kari. "I don't suppose you have room for all of these dogs at your shelter." He grimaced as he said it, looking around at all the full cages.

"I don't," Kari said, wishing that she did, even with the extra work these animals would entail. Truth be told, she wanted to take them all home with her and give them hugs every day for a week, and all the treats they could eat. Sadly, their systems would probably rebel at that last approach. Transitioning them to healthier diets and exercise would take time and a lot of effort. But at least they'd found them now and could make sure they were given the best of care to make up for their rough starts.

"I'll figure out something," she promised. "I can call some of the other local shelters and see if we can spread the dogs out so no one place gets overwhelmed." She thought for a moment. "Is it okay if I call Dr. McCoy, the vet, and tell him about this? I think he'd be willing to help."

"Go right ahead," Richardson said, a trifle grimly. "I don't expect to be able to keep this under wraps for long, although it is going to complicate our investigation into Ms. Carver's murder."

He gazed around the room. "This gives us some whole new motives to consider. Those SHAFFT people, for instance. Or maybe someone who thought they'd gotten a champion and found out they'd been ripped off." He sighed. "You weren't kidding when you called this a nightmare. But yeah, go ahead and reach out to the doc. We're going to need all the help we can get."

Kari pulled out her cell phone and called Angus. After she had explained the situation to him and listened to some angry squawking from the other end of the line, she got him to agree to come to the shelter and check out the worst cases once the dog show closed down for the night. Just knowing that he was on board made her feel better, for reasons she didn't have the time to analyze right this very minute.

"It looks like we're done here for now," Richardson said to Kari. "Unless there is anything else you can think of, we'd better get back to the campus. I have more people to interview, and apparently I'm going to need to talk to Shawn Mahoney again and see if he actually knew about this puppy mill or was just making random accusations." He didn't sound terribly grateful to have been given new leads, although under the circumstances, Kari couldn't exactly blame him.

After escorting Herman Blue (and Snowy, who was the only one of them still in a good mood) back out to the house and telling him not to leave town, the sheriff drove Kari back to the dog show.

"If you can arrange for those animals to be picked up, I'll place a deputy on-site to make sure there is no trouble with the transfer," he said. "And if you see Miriam Rosebaum, you tell her I want to see her ASAP so she can confirm her former dog's identification." He slammed the car door after he got out, for emphasis.

"It isn't as though we don't have plenty of evidence that Lois was up to no good, but every fact helps. Obviously we can't prosecute a dead woman for her crimes, but at the very least we might be able to clean up some of the mess she left behind." With that, he stomped off in the direction of the Picnic Table of Doom, leaving Kari free to go to the Serenity Sanctuary tent to check on how things had been going in her absence.

*   *   *

When she got there, Kari found Queenie being adorable for visitors. Not exactly a stretch for the naturally cute kitten, but in this instance she was demonstrating her ability to chase her own tail without ever catching it, which even Kari found endlessly entertaining.

Bryn was taking advantage of the distraction to refold tee shirts in a pile that had clearly been rummaged through, and Sara was trying to convince the couple who were admiring Queenie that they would be equally charmed by a pair of black brothers currently at the shelter.

"But we want this one," the woman said, pointing at Queenie, who, having spotted Kari approaching the table, immediately did her mysterious cage-opening trick, launched herself onto Kari's shoulder, and started purring loudly.

"Sorry," Kari said with a laugh, giving the kitten a kiss on the top of her soft, furry head. "This little monkey is all mine. But I promise, Casper and Jasper are the sweetest things ever, and if you go meet them, I think you'll fall madly in love."

She brought up a video on her phone of the two kittens roughhousing together, and a few minutes later the woman was dragging her husband out of the tent in the direction of the parking lot completely ignoring his protests that they'd come to look at dogs, not cats.

"Nice job," she said to Queenie, who purred even louder, especially once she'd been given a couple of treats.

"Yes, nice job," Sara said. "I was hoping those brothers would get to go home together, and something tells me they are going to. Now that there's no one else in the tent, tell us what happened at Francine's house. Did the chip reader give you any answers?"

"Did it ever," Kari said. "But can the interrogation wait until I've had a cup of coffee and something sweet to take the nasty taste out of my mouth?"

Bryn's jaw dropped. "That bad?"

"Worse," Kari said. "For one thing, it turns out Miriam Rosebaum was right. Francine's real name was Lois Keller, and under her previous identity she was kicked out of the AKC for falsifying breeding records."

"No!" Bryn breathed. "That's wild."

"It gets wilder," Kari said grimly.

"Hang on," Sara said, and popped behind the table with the stacks of paperwork and Serenity Sanctuary merchandise and came up with a thermos and a plate with half a gigantic piece of fried dough on it, like some kind of culinary magician.

"Ta-da!" she said. "The coffee is still hot. The fried dough isn't, but it should still be pretty tasty. We saved you some." She poured the coffee from the thermos into a cup and set the plate in front of Kari. "Of course, if you'd rather have a fresh one, I could run and get it."

Kari inhaled the heavenly scents of fat, carbs, and sugar. "Oh, heck no. This will do just fine." She took a slightly too-large bite, almost choking as she breathed in a bit of powdered sugar. It was still the happiest she'd been all day.

Bryn gave her a chance to finish chewing—barely—and then said eagerly, "So what's the second thing? Did the scanner turn up Miriam's dog?"

Kari washed the fried dough down with a swig of Sara's fabulous coffee and wiped her mouth off with the back of her hand. "We're not sure, because Miriam never showed up. She was supposed to come with me and the sheriff, and you'd better believe he wasn't happy when she stood him up.

The scanner did prove that some of Francine's dogs weren't who she said they were. But that's not the big surprise."

"You found something worse than that?" Sara said, raising one gray eyebrow. "This I have to hear."

"Francine, I mean Lois, was running a puppy mill," Kari said with a grimace. "It is hidden out behind her legitimate kennel, farther back on the property. There are dozens of female bichons there, many of them with litters of puppies. The noise and the smell—well, you had to be there." She shook her head and took another big bite of her dessert, as if its sweetness could erase the bitterness left by what she'd seen.

"What? That's terrible!" Sara said. "I can't believe it." She thought for a moment. "Well, of course I can. Greed and lack of ethics aren't exactly unusual. But still, that it was going on in our area and no one knew . . . that's awful."

"It is," Kari agreed. She told them all the grim details, and everything they'd found out about the dogs.

"I hope the sheriff throws the book at her," Bryn said, a furious expression on her normally pleasant face. "Oh, wait. Darn."

"Yeah, hard to prosecute a dead woman," Kari said. "Although I think the sheriff is going to be looking into this guy Herman Blue that lives on and owns the property where the puppy mill is located."

"Does the sheriff think the puppy mill had anything to do with Francine's murder?' Sara asked. She shook her head. "Or are we supposed to start calling her Lois, now that we know that was her real name? Argh. This is too confusing."

"I suggest we stick with Francine, since that's how we knew her," Kari said. "And as for a motive, Richardson seems to think it is a possibility. That kind of widens the suspect field, which isn't a great thing, as far as he's concerned."

"But it's good for Suz, isn't it?" Bryn asked a little anxiously. She and Suz had been spending a lot of time together since Kari had bought the shelter. Despite a twelve-year age difference, the two had a surprising amount in common, and Kari was beginning to wonder if there were sparks there, although they both denied it.

"Oh, I should think so," Kari said. "Plus there is the husband to consider now. I think the sheriff moved him way up the list when we got to Francine's house and found him ransacking it, supposedly looking for some bonds she'd taken from their safe-deposit box when she left him to move here."

"Wait—Francine had a husband?" Bryn said. Her eyes got even wider than they had when she heard about the puppy mill.

Kari gave a short laugh, spraying bits of powdered sugar over her jeans. She brushed at them ineffectually as she answered. "Well, technically, Lois had a husband. His name is Tony Keller. He's the big bald guy we saw arguing with Francine yesterday. According to him, after the AKC banned Lois and people started suing her for selling them dogs with fake papers, she took off, taking the contents of their bank account and half the stuff in the house with her. He *says* he's here because he finally tracked her down using a private eye and he came to get his money back."

She turned to Bryn. "Get this—he's the one who broke into Francine's car early this morning."

"No way!" Bryn said.

"He says he got here early looking for her, saw the car

in the lot, and smashed in the window so he could get her address off her insurance papers in the glove box."

"You know," Sara said, looking thoughtful, "there's something odd about all this."

Kari blinked. "Ya think? I'd say there are a bunch of odd things."

Sara waved one hand through the air. "Well, sure, but they all make sense, if you look at them from a certain point of view. But there's one thing that doesn't fit."

Queenie jumped from Kari's shoulder to Sara's, as if to say, *Go on* . . . Then the kitten started playing with the turquoise streak in Sara's hair, which now had shiny strands of thread wrapped around it, courtesy of one of the booths at the show.

"What?" Kari asked. "The ex-husband?"

"No, no," Sara said with a slight frown. "They turn up all the time, usually when you least expect them. I'm talking about Francine. She was so careful not to let her old life cross with her new one. And yet she ended up coming to this event, where she did in fact end up meeting someone from her old life, who recognized her despite the changes she'd made in her appearance. That just doesn't make sense. Why would she risk it?"

"Hmmm," Kari said. "That is a little odd. But let's face it, we all know from experience how hard Olivia can be to say no to. I'm guessing that when she asked Francine to handle Snowball, Francine tried to say no, and Olivia just bulldozed over all of Francine's objections, like she's done with everyone else involved in the show. Look at everything she's got poor Suz doing."

"Yeah," Bryn said. And then hopped up from the stool she was sitting on and said, "SUZ!"

Kari spun around in her seat expecting to see her friend standing behind her, but there was no one there. "What are you shouting about?" she asked Bryn.

Bryn looked aghast and appalled. "We forgot about Suz," she said. "She's never going to forgive us."

❦ Sixteen

What?" Kari said. Then she glanced at her watch. "Oh,
crap! It's almost time for Suz to show her dog in the
agility trials, isn't it?" She turned to Sara. "Do you know if
she thought she was going to be able to find the time to do
it after all?"

Agility trials were a test of an animal's skill, and the
dogs who took part didn't have to be purebred, just have a
special registration with the AKC. Suz's dog Jazz, a gangly
black-and-white hound and border collie mix who was all
legs and long nose, was getting pretty good at going over
and around the obstacles on the course. Suz had been really
looking forward to showing him this year, but of course,
that was before things had gotten so crazy.

"She did, last time I saw her," Sara said. She got up and
shoved the other two toward the entrance to the tent. "The
agility competition is in Ring Three. I think you can make
it if you hurry. Go on, go on. I'll take care of things here."

Kari grabbed her bag, and Queenie dived into it. Then
they and Bryn took off at a fast trot to Ring Three, which

wasn't that far from the shelter's tent, Kari holding the bag in her arms so the kitten wouldn't get too jostled.

They arrived just in time, skidding to a halt at the edge of the ring, joining the circle of spectators who were there to watch friends or family, or just to cheer on whichever dog struck their fancy. Agility was a popular event, because it was always fun to watch the dogs trying to run up and down A-frames, jump through tire rings, and weave in and out between sets of poles.

Suz and Jazz were standing on the opposite side waiting to take their turn as a golden retriever trotted around with stately grace and streaming ears. Unfortunately, he also had a tendency to skip the obstacles he didn't like, much to the dismay of the towheaded teenage boy who was running around the course with him. They both still got a big round of applause when they finished, and a tall, rawboned blond woman with a long braid down her back ran over and gave them both big hugs.

Suz spotted Kari and Bryn as they arrived, only slightly out of breath, and sent a wave and a big grin in their direction, accompanied by an energetic fist pump. Queenie jumped up onto Kari's shoulder as if she wanted to watch too, which wouldn't have surprised Kari one little bit.

When it was their turn, Suz and Jazz ran the course as if they had practiced it a hundred times, which was probably pretty close to the truth. Jazz barely needed Suz's encouragement as he ran through a tunnel, jumped over a series of hurdles, raced over the other obstacles, and then finished up with a grand leap through the hanging circle of the tire.

The entire audience burst into applause, with Bryn and Kari clapping the loudest of all. Kari clapped so hard, her hands were still tingling as they greeted Suz after she had claimed her first-prize ribbon. The tall lavender-haired groomer was grinning from ear to ear, Jazz panting happily at her side. Suz's tee shirt was edged with sweat and her cheeks were pink, but Kari had never seen her look happier.

"Good job, Jazz!" Kari said, leaning down to give him a treat. Then she hugged her friend, sweat and all. "You did great, Suz. I'm so proud of you both." Queenie gave an extra-deep purr before reluctantly being persuaded to crawl back into the tote bag.

"I can't believe it," Suz said. "There were a lot of other really good dogs there, and I was afraid that all the stress from the last couple of days would throw me off, but Jazz really came through, didn't you, boy?" She bent down to scratch behind his silky ears, then gratefully accepted the cold bottle of water Bryn handed to her. "This day is really looking up."

"Suz!" one of the other volunteers from the local kennel club hailed her as he trotted across the grass. "I'm so glad I found you. There's a problem with one of the Porta Potties. Can you go and deal with it? No one else is free right now."

"Well, that didn't last long," Suz said, rolling her eyes. "What's the problem, Chuck?"

"Apparently a couple of women were standing around one of the more remote sets of Porta Potties chatting," Chuck explained. "And seriously, who stands around those things talking? These ones are pretty clean, but they still stink."

"Chuck," Suz said warningly.

"Right. Anyway, after a while, they realized that no one had come out while they'd been there, even though one of the doors was in the locked/occupied position," Chuck went on. "They got worried someone was sick in there, so they knocked, but no one answered."

"It's probably just a faulty lock or something," Suz said

with a sigh. "But it's better to be safe and check. Someone could have gotten dehydrated from the heat and passed out or, heaven forbid, had a heart attack. I'll take care of it. Thanks for letting me know."

Chuck nodded and walked away after giving Suz directions, looking relieved to have handed the problem off to someone else.

Kari choked back a laugh. Trust a Porta Potty problem to take the shine off of Suz's big moment. "Well, on the bright side, I have some interesting updates for you. I'll tell you along the way."

"Seriously," Bryn said. "You're not going to believe it."

They all set off across the lawn, past the tents belonging to participants and vendors, the rings full of dogs and their proud owners, and plenty of people just wandering around and enjoying the day. The temperature had warmed up into the mid-eighties, but a slight breeze helped to keep things reasonably comfortable. Jazz, tired from his endeavors, trotted along at Suz's heel without showing much interest in any of the goings-on.

The Porta Potties, when they finally reached them, were set in a stand of trees that provided a nice bit of shade and kept the narrow plastic boxes from getting too warm. They were on the farthest side of the show, away from much of the activity, but there was a set of picnic tables under the same trees, which might have explained why whoever was in charge had chosen to place them nearby, though at opposite ends of the clearing.

A trio of middle-aged women sat at one of the tables with paper cups of coffee that had probably cooled off long ago, but they rose as Suz and her friends entered the clearing and walked over to meet them.

"Hi," one of the women said. "I hope you're someone official."

Suz smiled at her and shrugged. "As official as it gets, I guess. I'm Suzanne Holden from the local club. Are you the ladies who reported the issue?"

The woman nodded. She had short black hair with a few strands of gray in it and clever eyes behind wire-rimmed glasses. She and her companions all wore blue tee shirts with matching logos that identified them as members of the Chenango Valley Kennel Club.

"Mimi," she said. "And this is Roz and Bev. I'm sorry to drag you away from whatever you were doing, but I was concerned that someone might have gotten ill." She made a face. "When we hosted an event at home last year, a man had a stroke and we almost missed it because everyone thought he'd just fallen asleep on his lawn chair."

She gave a small shudder. "It turned out okay, but I've been a little paranoid ever since. And when we realized that no one has come out of that locked toilet the whole time we've been here, I decided we should alert someone, just in case."

"Very sensible," Suz said. "I take it you still haven't seen or heard anything?"

"Not a peep," Mimi said, and her friends nodded their heads in agreement.

"Okay," Suz said, squaring her broad shoulders. "Let's take a look." She, Kari, and Bryn walked over to stand in front of the potty on the left, where the red "occupied" sign could clearly be seen. She knocked briskly and called out, "Anyone in there? Are you okay?" but there was no answer. Jazz barked once, then rubbed a paw over his nose. Kari couldn't tell if he smelled something suspicious or just didn't like the scent from the potties.

Queenie popped her head out of Kari's tote bag and reached one small black paw out to play with a string that was dangling from the edge of the door.

"Queenie, leave that alone," Kari said, leaning down to peer at it, then wrinkling her nose at the pungent odor wafting out. "Suz, is that a piece of twine?"

Suz bent down to look over Kari's shoulder. "Huh. That's odd. You don't suppose someone tied a string to the door latch and then slid it shut from the outside, do you?" She made a face. "If this is someone's idea of a funny prank, I am not going to be very amused. Unfortunately, I don't know how to find out for sure. I guess we're going to have to call the company we rented them from."

"Don't waste your time," Bryn said with a chuckle. "It's really easy to open those locks from the outside if you know the trick to it. My younger brother got stuck in one when he was little and we were camping in a state park. I saw what the ranger did to get it open. It's pretty simple."

She glanced around the clearing. "Can anyone spot a small stick or some other kind of stiff, pointed object?"

Suz plucked the pen off of the clipboard she'd been carrying everywhere. "Will this do?"

"Sure," Bryn said, smiling shyly as their hands brushed together when she took it. "That should work."

The three women from out of town crowded in behind them and watched avidly as Bryn stuck the tip of the pen into a small hole at the side of the sliding lock and slid it to the left until the green *Empty* sign was visible. Kari was amazed by how easy it was, but she expected that people did occasionally get locked inside, so the things must have been designed that way on purpose.

"There you go," Bryn said, then stepped out of the way so Suz could knock one more time.

"Hello? We're going to open the door now," she said, just in case there actually was someone in there, and pulled it ajar just a crack. When they still didn't hear anything, Suz exchanged glances with Kari, shrugged, and pulled it open the whole way.

One of the women behind them screamed, a loud and piercing sound in the otherwise quiet clearing.

"Crap," Suz said with feeling, the pun no doubt unintentional. But Kari had to agree wholeheartedly with the sentiment.

They'd apparently discovered the reason why Miriam Rosebaum had never shown up to meet the sheriff. The diminutive elderly woman was propped up on the (thankfully closed) seat of the portable bathroom. She was clearly dead, eyes bulging and staring at nothing, white hair gleaming eerily in the dim interior. A lavender-colored leash was cinched tightly around her neck.

"*Crap*," Bryn whispered in an unconscious echo, glancing from the leash digging into Miriam's flesh to the one Jazz was currently straining against, whimpering quietly. "Isn't that one of yours, Suz?"

"It sure as heck looks like it," Suz said. "So much for my day getting better. Although it looks like poor Miriam is having a worse one."

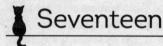# Seventeen

After Suz had calmed Mimi and her friends down and persuaded them to go back and sit at the picnic table again, Kari could see her swallow hard and brace herself before she lifted a walkie-talkie to her mouth.

"Hey, Frankie," Suz said to whoever was on the other end. "Are you still over by the old supply tent area, where the cops are questioning people?" The crackling answer she got was apparently in the affirmative. "Great. Uh, I'm at the farthest relaxation station, past Ring One and the tent where the woman is selling those weird crocheted dog-bed cozies. You know the place I mean?"

More crackling, accompanied by something that sounded like Russian but almost certainly wasn't. The walkie-talkies were annoying, but cell service could be spotty at certain points on the campus, so apparently the dog show folks had been relying on this more primitive method of communication for years. Under the circumstances, Kari was glad they had it.

"Okay," Suz said. "Could you do me a favor and tell the

sheriff that Kari and I found something important here that he needs to see right away. Emphasize the 'right away,' please. Thanks, that's great." She clicked off the handheld set and stared at the ghastly tableau inside the portable toilet, her face drawn and pale.

"I didn't want to start a panic, or any rumors, by mentioning another dead body," she explained to Kari and Bryn.

Kari was seriously regretting the few bites of fried dough she'd had, not to mention the coffee, as the mingled odors of bodily waste and overly-scented sanitizer combined with the gruesome sight in front of her to cause acid to rise into her throat.

"No, I think you're right," she said to Suz. "It's going to be bad enough when this gets out. I mean, one murder at the dog show is bad enough, but two?" She shook her head. "We'll be lucky if the whole thing doesn't get shut down. Might as well put that off as long as you can."

"Besides," Bryn put in, "I'm guessing the sheriff wouldn't have been happy to have you broadcasting it over a walkie-talkie channel that anyone working the show could overhear."

"Gah," Suz said. "Definitely not."

The gentleman in question strode into the clearing five minutes later, looking less than pleased. Clark trailed along right at his heels in a way that reminded Kari of Jazz following Suz. Kari suspected she would have found the sight amusing under different circumstances.

"This had better be important," Richardson thundered in his sternest voice. "I was in the middle of questioning Shawn Mahoney and his wife, and I'm not looking forward to trying to drag them away from their picket line yet again."

He looked around the clearing, taking note of Roz at the

picnic table, quietly crying into a blue bandana and being comforted by Mimi and Bev, and Kari and her friends clustered in front of the Porta Potties. "You brought me here to look at toilets? If you called me away because someone drew rude graffiti in one of those things, you are going to be very sorry."

"I wish," Suz said, and the three of them stepped to the side so the sheriff and his companion could see into the interior.

"What the hell? Is that Miriam Rosebaum?" Richardson asked, although he stepped forward quickly enough that it was undoubtedly a rhetorical question. "What on earth is that around her neck?"

Suz bit her lip. "It's a dog leash," she said. She held up the end of Jazz's identical leash, which she still held in one hand. Thankfully, after an initial deep sniff that made him snort, Jazz had shown little interest in the body. "Like this one."

Richardson glanced from her leash to the one wrapped around Miriam's neck like a macabre necklace. "They're both lavender," he said slowly. "Like your scissors."

She nodded. "Yes, they are."

Kari could practically see the wheels turning inside Richardson's head, and she didn't like the direction they were going.

"Sheriff—" she started to say.

He held up one finger. "Clark," he said, turning around and then nearly jumping out of his shoes when he found the young officer standing directly behind him, looking over the sheriff's shoulder with his mouth hanging open.

"Jeez," Richardson said. "Stop doing that. And close your mouth. You look like a guppy." He shook his head. Then he pulled out his cell phone, looked at the complete lack of bars, and shook it again. "Clark!" he said in a louder voice.

The officer snapped to attention, pulling his gaze away from what might well have been the second dead body he'd ever seen. "Yes, sheriff?"

"There's no cell service in this spot. We're going to need more officers, the coroner, an ambulance, and some crime scene tape and evidence bags. Go back to where we're set up and make some calls, then grab Kent and get back up here." When the officer didn't move fast enough, Richardson added, "Sometime this century, Clark?" and the younger man hustled off back in the direction they'd come from.

Richardson stood there for a minute without saying another word to anyone. He peered inside the Porta Potty at Miriam's body, hands behind his back so he wouldn't touch anything accidentally. He gazed from the distinctive leash wrapped tightly around the elderly woman's neck to the identical one more conventionally attached to Jazz's collar.

Finally he straightened up and stared at Suz, his posture rigid and his face as hard to read as ever. Kari had no idea what he was thinking. But she had a feeling they weren't going to like it, whatever it was.

"So you admit that this item, which appears to be the murder weapon, belongs to you, Ms. Holden," he said.

"Maybe you should call a lawyer, Suz," Bryn said in a nervous voice. "You know, before you say anything."

Suz pressed her lips together and shook her head. "I'm not guilty of anything," she said. "Unless you count having a slightly obsessive attraction to the color purple. I'm happy to cooperate with the sheriff if it means finding whoever did this and bringing them to justice." She met his gaze without flinching.

"Yes, Sheriff, it would appear that the leash is one of

mine," Suz said. Kari put one hand on her friend's arm for support, but didn't interrupt. "But I am telling you, I had nothing to do with this crime."

"I see," Richardson said. "And I suppose you expect me to believe that you were there when both bodies were found, and they were both killed with tools belonging to you—which, by the way, you don't deny—and that is just a coincidence?"

Kari could feel her blood beginning to boil. "You know Suz, Sheriff. She is not a stupid woman. Why on earth would she use her own things to murder two people and then just leave her stuff behind, knowing they would tie her to the killings?" She crossed her arms across her chest and glared at the lawman. As if in support, Queenie popped her head out of the tote bag and stared in his direction too.

He didn't seem particularly intimidated by either of them, not surprisingly. "Maybe they were both impulsive crimes of passion and someone came along before Ms. Holden could remove the incriminating objects."

Suz snorted. "I'm not that passionate," she said in a dry voice.

Next to her, Bryn blushed. The sheriff ignored both of them too.

"Fine," he said. "So maybe you were just being tricky and trying to make us think you wouldn't be that stupid, to throw us off. A smart person might think that was clever."

"I'm not that tricky either," Suz said, in the tone of someone who doesn't expect to be believed. Kari could see Suz's shoulders starting to sag.

"What about motive?" Kari demanded. "Suz and Miriam only knew each other in passing, and they got along fine. Suz had no reason to kill her."

Richardson shrugged. "Ms. Holden is a groomer. Maybe

she was working with Francine Carver on the breeding scheme. After all, someone had to have been grooming all those dogs. Maybe the two of them had a falling-out over money. Then maybe Mrs. Rosebaum found out about it and threatened to tell the authorities. So Ms. Holden killed her too."

"And maybe the moon is made of green cheese," Suz said with a grimace. "Lots of breeders groom their own dogs. Plus I would never be involved with a puppy mill. I think they're despicable. I never even met the woman before yesterday. You're really reaching, Sheriff."

"Fine," Richardson said. "Then you won't mind telling me where you were this afternoon."

Suz rolled her eyes. "The same places I was yesterday when Francine was killed. I was all over the show. I just got out of the competition ring before we came here, but before that I was either in my tent grooming or running around dealing with issues."

She leaned down to pat Jazz, who was whining slightly, no doubt concerned about the tension in his mistress's voice. Suz might have seemed calm to anyone who didn't know her, but Kari could see the slight tremor in Suz's hand and knew her friend was taking as much comfort from touching her dog as he was from being touched.

"I'm going to need you to come down to the sheriff's department and give me a list of everywhere you went and anyone who can corroborate that you were there when you said you were," Richardson said. "Now."

"I can't do that!" Suz said in a shocked voice. "I have too many things to do to shut the dog show down for the day, and I'll have to tell the people from the Saratoga Kennel Club about Miriam's death. I can't just let them hear about it from some random stranger or on the news."

"I will be taking care of notifying the Saratoga contingent," the sheriff said. "I need to talk to them anyway to find out if any of them knows of a connection between her and you or has more information about this issue she had with Francine Carver when she was still Lois Keller."

He set his jaw. "And there is no way I am going to let you go around and talk to people and get them to back up your story. You can tell me where you were all afternoon and then I will check those details before you speak to anyone. That's the way this portion of the program works."

Kari could tell he was in full-on sheriff mode and there was going to be no arguing with him. She'd dealt with that herself more than once when he'd suspected her of killing the local dog warden a few months ago. No doubt that stubborn determination was what made him a good lawman, but hoo boy, it was pretty unpleasant to be on the other side of it.

"Don't worry about the show," she said, plucking Suz's clipboard out of her friend's clenched fingers. "I walked around with you last night when it was time to shut everything down. I know what to do, and if I don't, your notes will tell me."

"I'll help her," Bryn said, glaring at the sheriff as if he'd kicked a puppy. "I'll take Jazz too. He can stay at the sanctuary tent until we're done for the day."

"Yes, and if for some reason you're not back by then, he can come home with me," Kari said, trying not to think about the reasons her friend might not be able to pick up her dog. Like if she was locked in jail. Luckily, Jazz visited Kari's house every once in a while when Suz came over, and he got along fine with Kari's dog, Fred. Her two older cats would probably stalk off to the bedroom in a snit, but she could placate them with treats if necessary.

"Thanks, you two," Suz said, blinking back tears. "You're the best."

Kari bit her lip, trying not to upset Suz even more by getting emotional. It was just questioning. Kari had been through it herself, and it had all turned out okay.

Just then Clark drove up in his squad car, accompanied by Kent and two other officers who were equally young.

"Is nobody in that department over the age of twenty?" Richardson muttered to himself. "My mother has jam in her pantry older than this bunch."

He stalked off to direct the newcomers, sending one to interview the three women from the visiting club and instructing Clark and Kent to put up crime scene tape and take pictures. The last of the four was apparently instructed to stand by the entrance to the clearing and turn away anyone other than the coroner and EMTs, who were expected to arrive at any minute.

Then Richardson and Suz left, the groomer looking a bit like a bedraggled peacock. Before they went, Richardson told Kari and Bryn that since he'd gotten their accounts of how they'd come to find the body, they were free to go for now but to expect to be questioned in more detail tomorrow.

"Oh goody," Kari said, watching him walk away. "Something to look forward to."

She and Bryn walked around the show, which was slowly shutting down for the day. There was one last event finishing up in Ring Five, but everyone else seemed to have completed their competitions. The vendors were closing up their tents, and the food trucks had fastened metal sides over the service windows that were normally open to the public. The campus was slowly emptying of both people and dogs as participants and spectators headed en masse for the parking lot.

"Look on the bright side," Kari said to Bryn as they walked around with Jazz, checking things off Suz's list. "At least by the time we get done with this, the crowds will be gone and there won't be any traffic going home."

"Yeah," Bryn said, trying to muster up a smile and failing miserably. She twisted one of her tiny braids between two fingers. "Do you think Suz will be all right?"

"Of course she will be," Kari said, hoping her smile was at least marginally more convincing. "She's Suz. Besides, she didn't do anything wrong. The sheriff may be a little heavy-handed sometimes, but he isn't going to arrest someone who didn't actually commit the crime. Crimes." She winced, thinking that two murders was somehow a lot worse than one. The papers were going to have a field day. She could see it now: *Lottery Winner Involved with Spate of Murders at Dog Show!* Or *Local Groomer Prime Suspect in Murder Spree!*

"Maybe we should call a lawyer for her," Bryn said. "Or would that just make it look like we think she's guilty?"

Kari shook her head. "Suz is perfectly capable of calling her own lawyer if she needs one. Hopefully she has one as a grooming client, since I don't know about you, but the only lawyers I've met are the one who handled the closing when I bought the shelter and the one who dealt with my divorce years ago. I'm pretty sure that neither a real estate lawyer nor a divorce lawyer would be all that helpful in these circumstances."

"I've never met one at all," Bryn said glumly. "I guess we could look in the phone book."

"If we get to the point of really needing one," Kari said, "I'll ask around the diner. Someone there will know who to call. But for now I think the best thing we can do for Suz is make sure everything here is taken care of and ready to go for tomorrow." *Assuming the cops didn't shut down the entire dog show, since it was now the scene of two murders.*

"Kari Stuart," a piercing voice said. Kari and Bryn twitched in unison.

"Ah, Mrs. Weiner," Kari said, turning around and plastering a pleasant expression on her face. "We thought you'd left with everyone else."

"I never leave until I am sure a job is done," Olivia said, chin in the air. "Besides, my husband was supposed to pick me up, and he is late." Snowball danced at her feet, apparently unconcerned by their tardy chauffeur.

Olivia looked around. "Speaking of jobs, where is Suzanne? I expected to see her checking that the tents are all closed up and tidying the show rings."

"Uh, Suz had to leave early," Kari said. "But Bryn and I are handling things."

"Leave early?" Olivia's voice rose, and Kari saw Queenie duck down farther into her bag. She would have liked to have joined the kitten. Sadly, that would have required a much larger bag. "What on earth could be so important that she would abandon her duties at this dog show? I have half a mind to speak to the show committee and have her banned from next year's event."

"You can't do that, Mrs. Weiner!" Bryn said, practically quaking with indignation. "It's not her fault the sheriff made her go down to the department and answer questions. She wanted to clean up everything here first and go down afterward, but he wouldn't let her!"

Kari tried to make subtle shushing motions, but it was too late.

"What do you mean, she had to go to the sheriff's department and answer questions?" Olivia asked. She scooped up Snowball and clutched him close, as if some villain from a melodrama was suddenly going to swoop in from offstage and tie him to a railroad track. "Has something else happened?"

"There's been another murder," Bryn said. Then she suddenly caught sight of Kari's signals and said, "Uh, I'm not sure if I was supposed to mention that. But I suppose it will be all over the news tomorrow anyway."

Olivia clutched at the pearls around her neck. Kari had heard the expression, but she'd never actually seen anyone do it.

"Another murder?" Olivia said. "Who?"

Bryn gazed at Kari as if looking for guidance. Kari just sighed. "Miriam Rosebaum," she said. "We found her stuffed into a Porta Potty on the far side of the show site. She'd been strangled with a leash."

"Dear me," Olivia said. "Not poor Miriam. The woman was a ninny, but she didn't deserve that fate. And in a Porta Potty. How distasteful." She looked as though she was trying to appear sympathetic, but either Botox or her general personality thwarted the attempt.

A shadow crossed her face as something occurred to her. "Wait. You said the police took Suzanne away for questioning?"

Kari wasn't about to tell Olivia that it had been Suz's leash that had been used to kill Miriam. "It's just routine," she said instead. "Nothing to worry about."

"They don't haul someone down to the sheriff's department for 'routine,' Ms. Stuart," Olivia said. "Clearly they believe she is guilty of something." She gasped. "Oh dear. She must have killed poor Francine too. They did have that awful fight yesterday morning. This is dreadful. Just dreadful. Think of what it is going to do to the reputation of our show! No one will ever attend again. What will the AKC say?"

The AKC was the least of Kari's worries, although she wasn't stupid enough to say that out loud.

"The sheriff hasn't accused Suz of anything," she said instead, in as calming a voice as she could manage under the circumstances. Honestly, she thought, if anyone was going to commit a crime of passion, it might be her, right here and now. She couldn't believe that after everything Suz had done for the show, Olivia was willing to assume she was guilty of two murders without even hearing her side of the story. "He just needed her to answer some questions."

"It's a disgrace," Olivia said, completely ignoring Kari's words. "I'm going to have to call all the board members. Then I'm going to have to call Charlie Cooper at the *Daily Standard* and see if I can convince him to downplay the kennel club's involvement in this whole debacle." She shook her head. "Thank goodness the paper doesn't come out on Sundays. At least by the time the story hits on Monday, the show will be over."

She pulled out her cell phone, the most recent model with all the bells and whistles and a Swarovski crystal–embossed case. Unfortunately, neither of those things seemed to make a cell signal magically appear, so she stalked off in the direction of the main section, where you could usually find one at least eighty percent of the time.

"You two had better finish up all of Suzanne's tasks," Olivia said over her shoulder as she hustled away. "Since there doesn't seem to be anyone else to do it. I will come in early in the morning and double-check to make sure you didn't mess it up."

Bryn scowled after her. "Oh, no, don't thank us," she said loudly. "It's our pleasure." She shook her head. "What a witch."

"Tut-tut," Kari said.

"Hey, I said witch, not the other word," Bryn protested.

"Yes," Kari said. "But I happen to know some witches, and they are perfectly lovely women. I'd just as soon you didn't insult them by comparing them to Olivia Weiner."

"Point taken," Bryn said. "Come on. The sooner we get this dealt with, the sooner we can figure out what to do next."

☙ Eighteen

By the time Kari finally made it back home, it was well after six. Unfortunately, it would be a while before she could put her feet up, since there were still the dogs they'd rescued from Francine's kennels to deal with. She got a quick text from Suz saying she was done at the police station and heading home. That was a relief, at least. Kari made a mental note to check in with her friend later in the evening.

Kari dropped Queenie and Jazz off at her house, quickly fed dinner to them and the rest of her animals (Robert and Westley decided to ignore Jazz's presence as long as there was food involved), and then raced down the path that connected her little farmhouse to the shelter.

Bryn was already there, having come directly from the dog show despite Kari's insistence that the young woman had already done enough for the day. Bryn had just responded with, "You've done the same amount as me or more, and you're not quitting yet. Why should I?" It was hard to argue with that.

Plus, despite the fact that Kari was nominally Bryn's boss, both Bryn and Sara had so much more experience with the shelter than Kari did—having volunteered there for years before Kari ever bought the place—that Kari tended to just let them do whatever they thought was best. Other than organizing the schedule of paid workers and volunteers, Kari's "boss" duties tended to revolve around dealing with paperwork and paying bills more than they did actually telling anyone what to do. The rest of the time she just pitched in to help with the work, the same as everyone else.

The shelter closed at five on Saturdays, but despite the late hour, the place was bustling. All the lights were on, and the sound of barking could be heard even before she reached the door. When she opened it and walked in, at first it seemed as though the place was overrun with dogs. As she looked around, the seeming chaos resolved itself into a more organized effort, although there really were a *lot* of dogs.

Normally the only animals in the front room were kittens, some still with their mothers, and the few cats who for some reason or another couldn't be left loose in the adult feline room with the others, although there were a few resident cats and dogs who were so well behaved, they were allowed to wander around at will.

Tripod, the three-legged yellow cat, had his own bed at the top of a fancy cat condo, although he was just as likely to be found sleeping on top of the front desk or on a stack of papers on Kari's desk at the back of the room. At the moment he was up on his perch, looking vaguely disgusted by all the commotion. Kari couldn't blame him.

There were at least a dozen large dog carriers scattered around the room. Kari could tell they'd all been placed as far away from the cat cages as possible, no doubt to try and minimize the stress on the current residents. They were used to dogs coming in and out, but never in this overwhelming an amount. Thankfully, one of the carriers was taken out back as she walked in, so it looked like the situation was only temporary.

Sara was in the midst of everything, taking notes and directing the activity, and a few of the other volunteers had either stayed late or come in when they'd heard about the crisis. Kari took a moment to allow herself to feel immense gratitude for the fabulous people she worked with, all of whom gave of their time and efforts far beyond what most others would consider reasonable. Their dedication to the animals made her impulsive purchase of a run-down, failing shelter seem well worth it.

Her gratitude swelled even larger when she spotted a familiar mop of red hair attached to a lanky body currently bent over one of the occupants of one of the carriers.

"Angus!" she said as she hurried across the room, greeting the others as she made her way over to where the veterinarian was crouched down, a small white puppy looking even tinier in his large, capable hands. "I didn't know you were here already."

"Hey, Kari," he said, giving her a crooked grin that did funny things to her insides, as usual. "Yeah, I came as soon as the show was officially over for the day. I've been working my way through the dogs and doing a kind of triage."

"How's that going?" Kari asked. To her eyes, the puppy he was holding looked too thin, and its eyes seemed red and inflamed. She'd bet anything it was from the puppy mill kennel, not the official one.

Angus shook his head, his face darkening with anger. "I can't believe anyone would treat poor innocent animals this way. Most of the mothers and puppies from the primary kennel were in great shape, but these others . . ." His voice trailed off.

He went on. "At the very least, a couple of the smallest puppies are going to have a fight ahead of them. Some of the mothers have untreated mastitis, which should clear up with antibiotics. They all need better nutrition and a lot more exercise." He looked down at the puppy in his hands. "This little guy and the rest of his litter all have an upper respiratory illness and will need antibiotics too."

Kari knelt down next to him and stroked the puppy's head with one gentle finger. "They are awfully cute. Do you think they're going to be okay?"

"I think so," Angus said. "I'll help out as much as I can, and your staff is experienced at dealing with problem cases, which helps." He bit his lip. "I hope you won't mind, but I sent the healthier animals on to the couple of other local shelters who offered to take in some of the seized dogs. I know it makes more work for you, but I figured it would be easier to keep all the more urgent cases here, where I knew I could check in on them more readily."

"That makes sense," Kari said, thinking not for the first time what a good man he was. "We'll handle it. How many does that leave us?"

Sara came over and handed her a cup of coffee. Decaf, because of the hour. "We've got five adult females and a total of twenty-three puppies. I know it seems like a lot, but we've made room, and I contacted a bichon frise rescue organization that will be able to take most of them as soon as we get the sheriff's okay to move them and Dr. McCoy says they are healthy enough to leave."

Kari tried not to flinch. That many new dogs at one time would really put a strain on their resources, especially since the majority had health issues that would have to be dealt with too. Still, that was why she'd bought the Serenity Sanctuary in the first place, to make sure there was somewhere that could take in the animals that didn't have anywhere else to go. She foresaw a lot of early mornings and late nights in her future, though. On the bright side, some of them would be spent with Angus, so that was a perk.

He tucked the puppy back into the carrier with its mother and siblings and closed the door. "Mark this one as number six," he said to Sara. "And make a note that all the puppies need to be treated with antibiotics for ten days."

He bent over a bag full of supplies and wrote brief instructions on the side of a small box before straightening up and handing it to Sara. "The dosage is on there. I'll check on them tomorrow, but for now they can be put in one of the spaces you've got set up in the back. Try and keep this bunch separate from the others, if you can."

"We took a couple of the larger kennels at the far end and turned them into a temporary ward for some of the sicker moms and pups," Sara told Kari. "Thankfully, they're all small dogs, so we can fit quite a few into just a couple of the big dog kennels. We've got some of those folding metal pens we occasionally use to let puppies play outside while still safely contained, and we're using those to keep them separate from each other while still in the same space. I think it will work out okay, and it will make it easier for both the volunteers and the doctor to get in and out."

"Plus they won't be as restricted as they were in those small kennels they were housed in at Francine's place," Angus added. "It will be a good way to help gradually transition them to larger spaces. Sara has already attached clipboards to each pen with the names of the dogs, any physical issues, and instructions for their care so those tending them won't get confused and can write down when any medicines are given. Remarkably organized, your Sara."

Kari beamed. "Yes, she is. I don't know what I'd do without her."

The older woman brushed her hair back out of her face, looking both embarrassed and pleased by the praise. "Oh, piffle. It's nothing compared to dealing with four classrooms of ninth graders. I could do this in my sleep."

She probably could too.

"Well, I still appreciate what you and everyone else did here tonight. It really is above and beyond the call of duty. I feel bad about keeping you all from your homes and dinners."

"Oh, Dr. McCoy took care of that," Sara said, giving him a fond glance. "He showed up with a stack of pizzas and soda for everyone."

"Speaking of which," Angus said sternly to Kari. "I don't suppose you managed to get anything to eat tonight."

Kari tried to remember the last time she'd eaten anything. "Uh, no?"

"I knew it," he said. "Let me wash my hands and I'll take a break and join you. I think I've gotten a look at all of my new patients. I'll stop by in the morning before I head over to the campus and check in on the worst cases. We'll have to see if the sheriff can find us any records Francine might have kept that will give us better ideas of ages and whether or not any of them have been dewormed or vaccinated, but for now, I think we've got it as under control as possible."

"But I just got here," Kari said. "I should help."

"You should eat," Sara said in her official Teacher Voice, which no one in their right mind argued with. "And let us get on with it."

"Yes ma'am," Kari said. She knew when she was beaten. She settled onto one of the stools behind the L-shaped front desk and absently petted Tripod when he strolled over to say hello.

A couple of minutes later, Angus plopped down on the other stool and put a paper plate down in front of her with a slice of pizza so large it overflowed the sides. He had a matching one in his other hand. The smell of melted cheese, tomato sauce, and garlic made her salivate, and she bit off the point at the end—her favorite part.

"I can't possibly eat this whole thing," she said with her mouth full. But not long afterward, she was gazing at the ragged remnants of crust and feeling stuffed, but a lot less like she was going to fall on her face.

"Thanks," she said to Angus. "I really needed that. And I appreciate you bringing enough to feed the whole crew. It was really considerate."

He was going to respond when there was a brief knock on the door, which then swung open to reveal the stocky figure of Jack Falco, the new dog warden. He and Kari had initially gotten off on the wrong foot, in part because of her bad experience with the previous dog warden, but lately they'd been getting along a lot better. After all, they both cared about the welfare of the animals they were responsible for. So they had that in common, at least. He'd turned out not to be a bad guy after all.

"Hey, Kari," he said, sticking his head inside the door. "I saw the lights on as I was passing and thought I'd take the opportunity to check in on the dogs you rescued, if it's not too late. The sheriff's department called and notified me about the situation."

"Come on in," she said. "We've already sent some of the dogs on to other shelters, but Sara has a complete list of who is where and what their conditions are, if that would help." Kari wiped her hands on her third napkin and got up to walk around the desk.

"That would be spectacular," Jack said, sounding relieved. "The sheriff said the woman who ran the puppy mill was killed, so I'm not even sure if there is anyone left to prosecute for this, but I've got to have official notes for the case anyway."

"Do you want a slice of pizza?" Kari asked. "Angus brought enough for a small army."

Jack looked around the room. "It kind of looks like you have a small army," he said. "And I've already eaten, but thank you."

He nodded at Angus, who nodded back coolly. Sara, who was passing by collecting used plates, whispered in Kari's ear, "Ah, I love the smell of testosterone in the evening," and walked off chuckling.

Kari rolled her eyes. Somehow the older woman had gotten the crazy idea that both men were interested in Kari and viewed each other as rivals. As far as Kari could tell, there was nothing to that theory. She was pretty sure Sara just read way too many romance novels.

"I've checked all the dogs over," Angus said. "Some of the youngsters from the puppy mill don't have names that we've been able to find as yet. The tags on their kennels just had the mother's name, a date that we assume was the date of birth, and a brief note."

Sara came back with photocopies of all of her lists. Angus hadn't been exaggerating about how efficient she was. She handed them to Jack and pointed at a page. "See, here there is a mother with four pups. The note just said 'two female, two male.'"

"That's not terribly helpful," Jack said. "Normally you

could at least tell them apart by markings, like spots or coloring, but when every single one is completely white, that doesn't work. And you'd have to give them names in order to register them with the AKC. With these mass-market puppies, I suppose the breeder didn't see any point in bothering with that kind of nicety." He and Angus both scowled, united at least in their disgust over the abuses of puppy mills.

"We're going to put collars on the ones that are big enough to wear them and give them names for now," Bryn said, coming over to join them. She had, of all things, a basket full of nail polish bottles in one hand.

"That's good," Jack said. "But, uh, surely you don't plan to paint their nails. I mean, these aren't show dogs."

"Suz stopped by on her way home to drop off these special dog polishes she sometimes uses while grooming," Bryn said. "She figured we could use them to help keep track of the littlest puppies."

"Oh, I see," Angus said, his expression lighting up. "You take a particular litter and put blue polish on the first puppy, red on the second, and so on. That way you can identify which ones are sick, whether they've been medicated, and so on. Very clever."

"She is," Bryn said, beaming. "Now I'm going to take care of it so we can move the rest of these poor babies into the back. Maybe then it will be quiet enough to hear ourselves think." She and Sara moved off to the carriers still up against the back wall, Sara's handy notebook at the ready.

Jack looked slightly stunned, and a lot impressed. "Wow," he said. "You're all doing an amazing job. I guess I have everything I need for now. I'll stop back in a few days and get an update, if that's all right."

"Of course," Kari said. "We're hoping to get official permission to hand some of them off to a bichon rescue soon. I'll keep you posted."

"Appreciate that," he said with a nod, and headed out the door.

"I should probably take off too," Angus said. "My cat is probably chewing the furniture to punish me for being late with her dinner. I'll be back in the morning to make sure all my patients are doing okay."

"Sounds good," Kari said. "We're usually here by seven to start with the feeding and cleaning, so you can come any time after that. Someone will be around to let you in. Thanks for taking care of all these dogs. I really appreciate it. The pizza too."

"It's my pleasure," he said. "Anything for you." He grinned at her, then picked up his bag and left.

"Told you so," Sara said, materializing at Kari's shoulder.

"Oh hush, you," Kari said. But she was pretty sure she was blushing.

Nineteen

Once all the dogs were moved back into either the kennel area or, in a couple of cases, the medical quarantine room, Kari sent all the volunteers home with leftover pizza and her profound thanks. Jim, one of the few paid workers, offered to come in early in the morning to help deal with the extra workload, even though Sunday was supposed to be his day off. Kari made a mental note to add a bonus to his paycheck.

Finally, around eight thirty, it was just her, Sara, and Bryn, all sitting around the front desk and drooping from the stress and the long day. Kari had exchanged a couple of text messages with Suz, who swore she was fine, but Kari could tell from the looks on the faces across from her that none of the others were completely convinced.

"I can't believe there was a second murder," Sara said, playing idly with the turquoise streak in her hair, a mug of decaf slowly cooling on the counter in front of her. "That's just crazy. This is normally such a safe area."

"They have to be connected somehow," Bryn said.

"There's no way there were two random murders at the same dog show."

"No, that would be a little bit of a stretch," Kari agreed. "But who would want to kill both Francine and Miriam? From what I can see, most of the suspects in Francine's murder didn't have any connection to Miriam at all."

"At least that we know of," Sara said. "I'm worried that the sheriff is going to settle on Suz as the guilty party, simply because she had public run-ins with both of them and both the murder weapons belonged to her." Worry made her normally ageless face suddenly seem older. "We really need to figure out who did it. Surely if we all put our heads together, we can at least come up with someone for the sheriff to look at more closely."

"Well, on the bright side, I think we can eliminate Miriam as a suspect in Francine's murder," Kari said, trying to lighten the mood. "Not that I ever really thought she was a likely prospect, despite her belligerent confrontation with Francine earlier in the day."

"What about that SHAFFT guy?" Bryn asked. "What was his name?"

"Shawn Mahoney," Kari said. "He hated Francine for being a dog breeder, and if he actually knew that she ran a puppy mill and wasn't just spouting off empty accusations, he had motive. Supposedly he has an alibi, but I'm not sure how strong it is."

"He'd definitely be my first choice for Francine's killer," Bryn said with a shudder. "Fanatics do all sorts of crazy things in the name of the cause they believe in. But why would he kill Miriam too?"

"Maybe she saw something she shouldn't have?" Sara said in a dubious tone. She had pulled out her trusty notebook and was jotting down the conversation. "I wonder if the sheriff has asked Mahoney if he had an alibi for the time of the second murder."

"I think the sheriff was planning to interview a bunch of people again tomorrow morning, so I'm guessing that's one of the questions he'll be asking," Kari said. She petted Tripod, who had somehow ended up on her lap.

"What about Francine's husband? I mean, Lois's husband." Kari shook her head. "I still can't believe the woman had completely changed her name and identity. I wish I could apologize to Miriam for doubting her."

"Anthony Keller certainly seemed angry enough about Francine running off with all their money, assuming he was telling the truth about that," Bryn said. "He's a scary-looking character, and as a former boxer, I'm sure he's strong enough to have stabbed Francine and strangled an elderly woman and dragged her into a Porta Potty." She scrunched up her face in disgust at the thought.

"Plus he smashed the window to Francine's car and broke into her house and tossed the place," Kari added. "So he clearly doesn't care about breaking the law. Although burglary and trespassing aren't exactly on the same level as murder."

"Not to mention that if Francine really did hide assets that belonged to both of them, he would have had a better chance of finding out where she hid them if she was still alive," Sara pointed out.

"Yes," Bryn countered. "But it could have been a crime of passion. Maybe he confronted her and she refused to tell him where the money was, or sign the divorce papers, so he lost his temper and killed her. Then he had to go looking for the money on his own, which is consistent with his later actions."

"He didn't have an alibi," Kari said. "On the other hand,

while I could definitely see him murdering his former wife in a fit of anger, what would have been his motive for killing Miriam? She didn't have anything to do with any of that."

"Maybe he knew Miriam from Francine's previous life as Lois?" Sara suggested, tilting her head to the side as she thought and looking like a quizzical bird. "Since Miriam had purchased a dog from Lois, it's possible they crossed paths back then."

"What if Miriam spotted him the first day and threatened to warn Francine he was there, and he killed her for that?" Bryn said, leaning forward eagerly.

Sara shook her head. "That would have made sense if Miriam was killed that day, but once Francine was already dead, it wouldn't have been much of a threat."

"Oh," Bryn said, her face falling. But then she perked up. "Maybe Miriam realized he was the murderer, and he killed her to keep her from telling the police!"

Kari thought about that one for a minute. "Maybe," she said slowly. "But by the time Miriam was killed, the cops already knew Keller was there. They'd even caught him rifling Francine's house. So it wouldn't have been much of a threat."

"Unless she was killed before you and the sheriff found Keller at Francine's place," Sara said. "Do you know if they have figured out the time of death yet?"

"Believe it or not," Kari said wryly, "the sheriff does not exactly keep me apprised of every development on the case. But I'll see if I can find out anything in the morning. Richardson said he'd want to talk to me again, so maybe I can get some information in return."

"What about Herman Blue?" Bryn asked. "He lived with Francine, didn't he?"

"Sort of," Kari said. "It is kind of an odd situation. In fact, he's kind of a strange guy."

"So were they a couple or weren't they?" Bryn asked.

Kari wrinkled her nose. "Honestly, it's hard to say. If I had to guess, I'd say they weren't, but he wished they were. From something Francine's husband said, it sounds like Herman had had a crush on Francine since they were in college together, and she took advantage of that to get a free place to live and monetary help setting up her new kennels."

"Ouch," Sara said. "So she was just using him?"

"Only two people know that for sure, and one of them is dead," Kari said. She stifled a yawn. It wasn't that the topic wasn't riveting, but it had been a really long day. "From what I gathered, Herman let her live in the main house and he was happy to move to a smaller, even more private residence toward the rear of the property. He also gave her the outbuildings to use for her kennels. It sounds like a pretty sweet deal."

"Maybe he got tired of being a sugar daddy and not getting anything in return," Sara suggested. "But that doesn't explain Miriam's death."

Kari thought about it for a minute. "Francine's husband told Herman that she would have run off if the truth came out, just like she did when it happened the first time. Herman said that she'd mentioned leaving after her run-in with Miriam, but he'd talked her out of it. What if he hadn't?"

"So she told him she was going to pack up and go before Miriam revealed her real identity, and Herman killed the woman he loved so she couldn't leave him?" Sara said. "That doesn't make sense."

"Obsessive relationships often don't," Kari said grimly. "They're often more about control than love. Maybe he would rather have had her dead than off living her life happily without him."

"And he murdered Miriam because he blamed her for making Francine want to leave?" Bryn considered this possibility, twirling one of her braids around her fingers. "That actually makes sense."

Sara tapped her fingers on the counter. "You know, that is probably the most likely scenario of all the ones we've come up with. After all, we know that Suz didn't do it. But that leaves the question of why Herman Blue would choose to use a pair of Suz's scissors to kill Francine and then follow up by murdering Miriam with one of Suz's leashes."

Kari yawned again and Sara gave her a stern look. "Sorry," Kari said. "Long day."

"Of course it has been," Sara said, patting Kari's hand. "And we're probably all too tired to think of anything else useful tonight. I suggest you go home, have a glass of wine, and curl up with your animals. Maybe one of us will have a brilliant idea during the night."

Kari had a feeling that the only thing she was going to have during the night was nightmares about finding dead bodies, but Sara wasn't wrong about the rest of it.

"I'll shut things up here," Bryn said. "I'm not scheduled to be at the shelter tent until noon, so I can come in and help with the new puppies before I go over." She sounded ridiculously happy about the prospect of extra work, and Kari had a feeling that Bryn's aunt was going to be hearing impassioned pleas to allow *just one tiny white puppy* into her house sometime in the near future.

"Okay," Kari said, pushing herself off the stool with arms that felt like wet noodles. She didn't have the energy to argue. "I'll see you two in the morning. Thanks for everything you did today."

Bryn came around the desk and gave her a hug, the first time she'd ever done that. "Don't worry," she said in a quiet, assured voice. "We're going to figure this out and Suz will be just fine."

Kari really, really hoped she was right.

Early the next morning, after a hurried breakfast of granola, yogurt, and fresh blueberries from a farm down the road, Kari popped in to the sanctuary to check on everything before heading out to the last day of the dog show. She had to admit, if only to herself, that she'd be seriously relieved when the event was over and behind them. She wasn't sure what she'd expected from her first dog show, but two murders, the discovery of a puppy mill, and her best friend in danger of being arrested definitely hadn't been on the list.

She'd tried persuading Queenie that it might be a good idea to stay home just this once, but not surprisingly, the kitten had other ideas. Kari wasn't sure at what point she'd completely lost control of the little black fuzzball, but it was clear which one of them was in charge about ninety percent of the time.

When Kari arrived at the campus, the parking lot was already starting to fill up. This was the day the local kennel club was hosting, so friends and neighbors had apparently turned out in even greater numbers than they had the first two days. Luckily, she and Suz had arranged to meet up at the entrance to the campus, so at least they didn't have to search for each other.

Queenie spotted the groomer first, popping her pointed ears and inquisitive nose out of the top of Kari's tote bag and letting out a loud meow.

"Hi to you too, Queenie," Suz said with a smile. Kari thought Suz looked tired and frazzled, but admired the ef-

fort she'd taken to appear as bright and vivacious as usual.
Her short lavender hair was as perky as ever, and she wore
a row of stud earrings in various matching shades from
light to dark purple. Suz was even wearing bright purple
laces in her sneakers, although Kari didn't have the heart to
tell her she'd somehow put on two different colored socks.

"How are you doing this morning?" Kari asked, allowing Queenie to crawl out of the bag long enough to give Suz
a purring head butt before tucking the kitten back inside
out of harm's way. "Did you get any sleep last night?"

"Some," Suz said. "I'll be fine once I get another cup of
coffee inside me." They made a beeline for the nearest food
truck, from which floated the delicious scents of fresh coffee and, if Kari's nose didn't deceive her, cinnamon donuts.
It was a good thing she'd had a healthy breakfast.

Duly fortified, the two women headed toward the Picnic
Table of Doom. Before they started in on the tasks for the
final setup, Suz wanted to check in with the sheriff to make
sure they were really going to be allowed to proceed with
the day's events, despite everything that had happened.

Kari figured that Richardson would have let Olivia
know if the show had been canceled and Olivia would have
told Suz, but at this point, who the heck knew what was
going on. It couldn't hurt to make sure.

As they approached the table, they could see Richardson
sitting opposite the guy from SHAFFT, Shawn Maloney,
and his wife, Minnie. Clark and Kent were standing behind
the couple like twin crew cut dark and blond Ken dolls.

Mahoney was gesturing wildly with his hands, his face
a warring arena of guilt and righteous indignation. Minnie
just looked annoyed, but somehow Kari suspected that was
more of a habitual expression than anything to do with the
sheriff's current line of questioning.

Kari and Suz stopped a few feet away from the group, but Richardson gestured them closer with an impatient hand motion.

"Can I help you ladies with something?" he asked.

"We don't mean to interrupt, Sheriff," Suz said. "I just wanted to check with you and make sure you hadn't decided to cancel the show for today. We can wait until you're done."

"The show must go on," Richardson said in a wry tone. "Hopefully no one will decide to make it three for three." Something about his attitude made Kari wonder if he was tempted to add at least one of the people sitting in front of him to the list.

"You might be interested in this, actually," the sheriff said. "It turns out that Mr. Maloney's alibi didn't check out after all."

"What?" Kari said. "He's the killer?" She tried not to jump up and down for joy, since that would have been completely inappropriate. She'd do it later, in private.

"What?" Minnie Maloney said. "He went to the office shop to get flyers made. We showed you the receipt. We even showed you the stack of flyers!"

"What?" Mahoney said, but his protestation lacked much conviction.

"Cool," Kent said, reaching for his belt. "Should I cuff him? Is the wife in on it? Should I cuff her too?" He turned to his partner. "Clark, can I borrow your cuffs? I only have the one pair."

Richardson sighed loudly. "Nobody is getting cuffed," he said. "Yet." He gazed up at Kari, an innocent look on his face, and she realized he was up to something. Hey, as long as they got to find out what was going on, she was willing to play along. "Would you like to know what's wrong with Mr. Mahoney's alibi, Ms. Stuart?"

"I would," she said. "Did he not go to the office store at all?"

"Oh, he went," Richardson said. "Mrs. Mahoney is quite correct about the receipt and the existence of the flyers. But when we checked with the clerk who was working that afternoon, he remembered Mr. Mahoney quite clearly, because he seemed to be in such a rush. Said that Mr. Mahoney dropped off the flyers to be printed and then came back a half an hour later to pick them up."

"Is that so?" Kari said. She wasn't sure if she was playing good cop or bad cop, but she was kind of enjoying it. "And where did he go in the meanwhile?" She thought about it for a minute and some of her humor seeped away. "You know, it doesn't seem like a half an hour would be enough time to get back here and murder Francine. Maybe if he drove really fast?"

"Hard to say," Richardson said, his face serious. He reached into a box next to him and pulled out an evidence bag with a folded tee shirt inside. "Do you happen to remember this shirt, Mr. Mahoney?"

"Of course I remember it," Shawn said, puffing his chest out with a bravado that perhaps seemed a little strained around the edges. "You made me strip down to my undershirt to take it. I'm not an idiot."

"That remains to be seen," the sheriff muttered. In a louder voice, he pointed at a section of the shirt with one strong finger. "In that case, you'll certainly remember that we spotted a suspicious stain on this shirt."

Queenie popped her head up and gave a loud meow.

Richardson bit his lip to hide a smile. "Sorry. That the *kitten* spotted a suspicious stain on this shirt."

Suz snickered, but subsided when Minnie glared at her.

"I told you then, there is no way that stain is blood,"

Mahoney's wife said. "My husband would never take a life."

"As it turns out," the sheriff said, "you're correct about the stain. It's not blood. It is, in fact"—and here he turned the full force of his basilisk stare on Shawn Mahoney—"barbecue sauce."

"What?" Kari said. She hadn't seen that one coming.

Apparently neither had Minnie. "Barbecue sauce!" she shrieked. "That's impossible. I told you, we're vegans."

Her husband hung his head, revealing the beginnings of a bald spot, and mumbled something indistinct.

"What was that, Mr. Mahoney?" Richardson said, sounding almost cheerful. "You purposely lied to us and wasted police time? We tend to frown on that, you know."

"Well, I uh, I didn't exactly *lie*," he said, glancing at his wife with something akin to panic is his close-set eyes. "I really did go to the office store. I just got hungry and ran out for a quick bite of something while I was waiting for them to finish printing the flyers. I swear, I had nothing to do with that woman's death."

Kari tended to believe him, albeit reluctantly. She suspected the sheriff did too.

"A quick bite of what, exactly?" Minnie said through clenched teeth. "What could you possibly have found to eat that came with barbecue sauce on it?"

"There is a great little restaurant right down the street from that shop," Kent said helpfully, leaning over to point at the stain. "They have the best ribs in the county. I should have recognized that stain when I saw it. Heaven knows I've gotten enough of them on my own shirts. Impossible to eat those things without dripping sauce everywhere, but man, are they worth it."

"You ate *ribs*?" Minnie said, in the same tone one might

use to accuse someone of cannibalism. "And then lied to me about it?"

"I think lying to the police is a little bit more important, ma'am," Clark said.

"You've clearly never been married," Richardson said. "But you do have a point."

Minnie ignored both of them and turned on her husband with a glare so furious, Kari was afraid they were going to witness another murder right on the spot.

"You ate ribs, and you lied to me," Minnie said, poking Mahoney in the middle of his thin chest with each word for emphasis. "You *hypocrite*. I am never painting a picket sign for you ever again. Disgusting." She picked up her purse and stomped off in the direction of the parking lot, probably to out Mahoney to the rest of their SHAFFT cohorts.

"Aw, crap," he said, his shoulders drooping. "It's going to take her months to get over being mad. I snuck a hotdog in nineteen ninety-four, and she didn't speak to me for a week."

"A week's not so bad," Clark said sympathetically.

"We were on our honeymoon," Mahoney said.

Suz nearly choked on her coffee.

"Look on the bright side," the sheriff said. "You're off the hook for the murder. Plus, as peeved as I am with you for lying to me, which I tend to get downright cranky about, I suspect you're about to get kicked out of SHAFFT and have to sleep on the couch for quite a while, so I'm just going to let it slide this time."

He handed the evidence bag to the despondent man. "Take your shirt and get out of here. Clear your people off too. I've got enough on my plate without dealing with all that noise and commotion." He chuckled. "Maybe go picket that barbecue place. Big Phil who owns it has quite the temper, I hear."

Mahoney grabbed his shirt, gave the sheriff a half-hearted glare that lacked most of the force he'd shown before, and slunk off after his wife.

"Well, that was amusing, Sheriff," Kari said. "But if he didn't do it, where does that leave us?"

Richardson stared at Suz meaningfully. "With the same batch of suspects we had before, minus one."

"Great." Suz said. "Not only am I still on the suspect list, but now I have a craving for ribs."

🐈 Twenty

For a moment, Kari was caught up in a daydream about barbecue, but she was rudely snapped back to reality by the arrival of Olivia Weiner, who bustled up with the air of a woman who has much more important places to be. Olivia slapped her designer purse down onto the top of the picnic table and said to the sheriff, "One of your men said you wished to speak to me? I can't imagine why."

Before he could answer her, Olivia's attention was caught by the sight of Kari and Suz, whose presence she apparently hadn't noticed in her laser focus on Richardson.

"Suzanne Holden," she said in a tone full of venom. "What are you still doing here?"

Suz took an involuntary step back. "Excuse me? I was just checking with the sheriff about the show before going around and making sure everything was ready to go for the day."

"'Going around'?" Olivia said, her voice rising. "'Going *around*'? Where everyone can see you, and think that you still represent our local kennel club, with its years of proud history? I think not."

"I beg your pardon?" Suz said, stiffening her spine. "No one said anything to me about not being here. Is there some kind of a problem?"

"Well, I don't know about you," Olivia said, glaring at Suz, "but I consider it a problem that you have practically been accused of murder. Everyone is talking about it. It's a huge embarrassment."

She turned to Richardson. "Sheriff, I want this woman thrown off the grounds. She is no longer associated with my show. Frankly, if she stays, I'm afraid I am going to be the next victim. Either lock her up or make her leave, your choice."

"You have *got* to be kidding me," Kari said, springing to Suz's defense. "Suz hasn't been accused of a crime. Since this show started, she's been doing all the work with nothing but criticism from you. You should be ashamed of yourself."

"You stay out of this, Kari Stuart," Olivia said, curling her lip. "You're not even a member of this kennel club. The matter has nothing to do with you."

Kari's jaw dropped open. "You mean other than the fact that I've been helping out all weekend? And that you're being unfair to my best friend?"

Suz blinked rapidly a couple of times and put a hand on Kari's arm. "It's okay, Kari. I don't need to stay where I'm not wanted."

Richardson shook his head. "Mrs. Weiner has no legal right to kick you out, Ms. Holden," he said, not unsympathetically. "What happens within your group is outside of my authority, but I can tell you that this event is open to the public, and as such, you are entitled to be here as much as any other attendee."

"Thank you, Sheriff," Suz said. "I appreciate the support. But if Olivia feels my presence will be disruptive and distract from the show, I'm not going to ruin things for the people who have worked so hard to get to this day. I assume my tent and supplies aren't evidence of any kind?"

"No, they're not." Richardson said. "Just the two murder weapons we already have." He gave her a small nod. "I assume I can reach you by phone if I have any further questions?"

"Certainly, Sheriff," Suz said. "I'm not planning to leave town, if that's what you mean." She turned and started walking away without so much as glancing at Olivia again, and Kari quickly followed. Queenie stuck her head out of the bag and growled quietly.

"You tell her, Queenie," Kari said, racing to keep up. "I'm so sorry, Suz. That woman is just horrible. I'm sure the other people in the kennel club don't feel that way."

"I hope not," Suz said. "And hey, it will serve Olivia right to have to do all the things she had me doing." She was silent for a minute. "Although if I know her, she'll just find another sucker to step into my shoes."

Suz was walking so fast, and her legs were so much longer, Kari could barely stay even with her. Kari could tell Suz was really upset, even though her friend was putting on a brave face. When they got back to Suz's tent, they started packing up all the things she'd brought, a task made easier by the tools still being locked in their cabinet.

Kari put her tote bag down on the top of a card table Suz had been using for paperwork and other odds and ends. "Stay here, and keep out of the way, please," she said sternly to Queenie. "We have to fold up Auntie Suz's grooming table, and I wouldn't want you to get your cute little toes pinched."

They made short work of collapsing the portable table, then stacked it, with its attachable arm for tying the dogs to, against the cabinet filled with clippers and scissors.

"You know, I am really confused by something about these murders," Suz said as they started tossing decorative bows into a box.

Kari raised an eyebrow. "Just one thing?" she said. "I'm baffled by a whole bunch of stuff, including but not limited to why on earth anyone would kill a harmless old woman like Miriam and then stuff her in a portable outhouse." She rescued a stray pink ribbon that had tried to flutter away on the breeze. "But go ahead, what are you confused about?"

"Why me?" Suz said.

"Huh?" Kari felt like she was missing something.

"Why use my tools to commit the murders?" Suz asked. "I mean once, that might be a coincidence. Somehow someone ended up with my scissors accidentally—although really, I don't see how that could happen. But say it did, and they had my scissors in a pocket or purse when they got into a confrontation with Francine, pulled them out in a fit of rage, and stabbed her with them."

"Okay," Kari said slowly, not really following.

"But then the second time, this same murderer just happens to also have one of my leashes?" Suz scowled at a bow she'd just shredded without realizing it and tossed it into the garbage with a sigh. "Doesn't it seem a bit far-fetched to you that the killer would accidentally use something that belonged to me twice in a row? It just seems unlikely."

Kari stopped what she was doing and stared at Suz. "Are you suggesting that someone is purposely setting you up to take the fall for these deaths?" It wasn't as though the thought hadn't crossed her mind before, but she'd dismissed it as paranoia. Now that Suz had said it out loud, though, it was a little harder to ignore.

"Why would anyone do that?" Kari asked.

Suz made a face and shrugged. "Honestly, I don't know. That's why I haven't said anything to the sheriff. He'd just think I was trying to convince him I wasn't guilty. But you and I know I had nothing to do with these killings. So I have to ask myself, why use *my* tools as murder weapons?"

"Could it just be a coincidence?" Kari asked. "I mean, yes, it seems unlikely, but so do two murders of completely different people at a perfectly lovely dog show."

Suz sighed. "Maybe. I just don't know. That's why I agreed to leave. Maybe if I pack up and get out, no one else will end up dead."

"I thought you gave in a little too easily," Kari said, standing up and putting her hands on her hips. "You can't really think any of this is your fault, Suz. Some crazy person is out there murdering people. You can't be held responsible for that."

There was a soft *thud* from across the tent, and they both turned to look at the table in the far corner where Queenie was sitting, looking benignly innocent in that way only a misbehaving kitten can. On the grass below her, one of the thick dog show programs fluttered in the breeze.

"Queenie," Kari scolded. "We're trying to clean up here, not make more of a mess." She crossed the tent and picked the program up, putting it back on the table before turning back to help Suz pack the rest of the ribbons.

Thud.

Kari swiveled around. The program was on the ground again, and Queenie was licking one black paw and gazing expectantly in Kari's direction.

"This is not a fun game," Kari grumbled, going back to pick up the program. But as she bent down, she realized that the booklet was opened to the same page it had been the first time.

"Huh," she said. "That's odd."

"What's odd?" Suz asked, coming over to join her. "If you mean your kitten, that's not exactly news."

Kari laughed. She had to admit her friend was right about that. Queenie had always been an unusual kitten in more ways than one, including her somewhat inexplicable tendency to point out clues in the last murder Kari had found herself involved in.

"I can't argue with that," Kari said. "But in this case, I was talking about something I spotted on the page this program was opened to. Here," she said, pointing her finger at one particular section. "Check this out."

Suz took the book from her, a quizzical expression on her face. "It's a list of the dogs who are participating in the show, in order by breed. So what?"

"Not just any dogs," Kari said, tapping her finger on the page. "This page lists the bichons. Including Olivia's dog. Notice anything strange about the information in the listing?"

Suz looked at the page, frowned, and took a second look. "That doesn't make any sense," she said. "You're talking about the formal name, right? And the breeder information? That can't be right."

As they had explained to the sheriff, show dogs were registered with the AKC under elaborate names that reflected their kennel of origin, and often their parentage, although no one actually called their dogs by this complicated name in daily life. But that was the name listed in the show booklet, along with the breeder, the sire and the mother, and the owner of the dog.

Under *Bichon Frise*, there was a listing that read *Blue Skies Boule de Neige*, followed by the AKC registration number and the dog's date of birth. After that, it said *Breeder, F. Carver, by CH Twin Oaks Treasured Snowflake—Twin Oaks Silver Angel. Owner, Olivia Weiner.*

"That's impossible," Suz said again. "Olivia told us, and the sheriff, more than once that she was glad her dog had come from a different breeder. But this says that Snowball came from Francine's kennel and lists her as the breeder of record." She scratched her head, causing one lock of lavender hair to stand out from the rest as if it had taken a wrong turn at Albuquerque. "Could they have listed the wrong dog by mistake?"

Kari peered at the book again. "I don't think so. My high school French is pretty rusty, but I'm nearly positive *Boule de Neige* is French for Snowball. Besides, the sire's name sounds really familiar."

"Familiar? How is that possible?" Suz asked.

"I think 'CH Twin Oaks Treasured Snowflake' was one of the dogs we found at Francine's kennel." Kari frowned. "We need to get another look at the paperwork at the kennel to see if there is anything that says what the name of Francine's previous kennel was."

"If the kennel was called Twin Oaks, that would confirm that both of Snowball's parents came from Francine's earlier business, but that doesn't necessarily mean that one of them was the dog Miriam had to give up." Suz's brow was scrunched up in frustration. "I feel like this is telling us something, but I'm not sure what."

"Well, it tells us that Olivia lied about where her dog came from," Kari pointed out.

"That's true," Suz agreed. "But we both know how proud Olivia is. Maybe she just didn't want her name associated with someone who was murdered. Heck, she kicked me out of the show just for being a suspect."

Kari pressed her lips together, since any comment she had about that particular choice was bound to be less than helpful. "Mmm," she said. "I guess the question is, did Olivia know about Francine's previous issues with the AKC when she bought a dog from her, or not?"

"She'd certainly not going to tell either of us," Suz said, sounding only slightly bitter.

Kari thought for a minute. "Hang on a second, I might have an idea," she said, and stepped out of the tent to make first one phone call, then another. "I might be able to get us the answer to that," she said, coming back in. "Although I'm not sure if it helps us at all, other than to prove Olivia was lying. But we need to meet my source at the Picnic Table of Doom in a half an hour."

Suz raised an eyebrow but didn't ask any questions. They'd been friends for long enough that she knew there wasn't much point.

"Okay," she said. "In that case, let's get this stuff loaded in the car in the meanwhile, so I can leave right afterward. I'm ready to be done with this whole show."

"I don't blame you," Kari said, narrowing her eyes at Queenie before tucking the kitten back into her tote bag and slinging it over her shoulder. It would make carrying boxes a little more awkward, but she wasn't about to leave the little black menace on her own while they ran back and forth to Suz's car.

Kari still wasn't convinced that it had been an accident when the kitten pushed the show booklet onto the ground, although how she could possibly have known there was something important in it was a complete mystery.

They made three trips back and forth from the tent to

the parking lot, which seemed to get farther away every time. Kari consoled herself with the knowledge that at least she wouldn't have to worry about getting her steps in that day.

Each time, they ran into at least one member of the local kennel club who bemoaned the fact that Suz was leaving. Most of the folks they met commiserated with them about how unreasonable Olivia was and asked Suz to stay, which was some consolation to the miserable groomer. One woman practically burst into tears when she realized that Suz wouldn't be there to give her dog a final touch-up before he went into the ring, and Suz had to spend ten minutes persuading her that the dog really did look spectacular just as he was.

Talking to all these people really slowed them down, so they still hadn't made it back to take down the tent itself when Kari glanced at her watch and realized they were already late to meet her secret weapon.

"Are you sure there is any point in this?" a reluctant Suz said as they headed to the area where the cops were still trying to catch up with the dog show participants they hadn't been able to talk to the day before. "It's just a trivial misunderstanding."

"I'm not so sure," Kari said, and the kitten meowed in possible agreement from where she was looking out of the top of Kari's tote bag. Of course, Queenie might have just been complaining about them walking so fast that the tote bag bumped up against Kari's side.

"Ah, there you are," the sheriff said, standing up to greet them when they got to the site of the first murder. "I have someone here who says he has come to see you. He implied he might have information pertaining to the case but wouldn't say any more until you got here." He didn't sound very pleased by this.

Herman Blue stood up from the other side of the picnic table and nodded in their direction. He looked a little shaky to Kari's eyes, and she wondered how long it had been since he'd left the relative isolation of his hermit-like retreat and gone out in public among other human beings besides Francine. The usual baseball cap and large sunglasses hid most of his face, but his scars were still glaringly visible.

To be honest, she hadn't been sure he would show up. But she'd hoped that his desire to find Francine's killer would be stronger than his need to stay out of sight, and apparently she'd been right.

"Thank you for coming," she said quietly. "I know it can't have been easy."

"Probably past time I got over it," he said, although he pulled his cap down a little as he spoke. He gave her a crooked smile. "No one has started screaming or run away yet, so that's something."

"These are dog show people," Kari said with a laugh. "If you don't have four legs and fur, they don't even notice you."

"She's not kidding," Richardson said to Herman. "I've actually had to flash my badge in some people's faces to get them to look up from admiring someone else's animal. Usually being a cop makes you stand out in a crowd and attracts attention you don't want. I'm finding the opposite to be somewhat annoying."

He turned to Clark, who had been standing nearby typing notes into his phone with one finger. "Speaking of annoying, go fetch that Weiner woman for me, will you? Tell her I need to speak to her now, and don't take no for an answer."

Clark made a face. "Can't you send Kent?" he asked plaintively. "The last time I had to go ask her something, she threatened to sue me for police brutality because I interrupted her lunch."

Kari snickered, then hid her grin behind one hand as Clark glared at her.

"Just do what I tell you for once," Richardson said with a sigh. "I know it seems like I'm a really sweet guy, but believe me, you should be more afraid of me than you are of her. Now scoot."

Clark scooted.

Less than three minutes later, he came back with an extremely indignant Olivia in tow. She must have been at one of the show rings nearby watching a competition. Snowball pranced merrily at her feet, seemingly oblivious to his mistress's sour mood.

"What was so important that you had to send one of your overzealous minions to drag me away from watching someone in our club win a first prize?" Olivia asked. As the president of the kennel club putting on that day's events, she couldn't enter her own dog into any of the competitions, but apparently she'd decided to put her energy into gloating on others' behalves.

"I have a few more questions for you, Mrs. Weiner," Richardson said smoothly. "They won't take long." He gestured in Herman's direction. "I'm not sure if you've met Mr. Blue, Francine Carver's friend."

Olivia recoiled slightly and turned pale, but Kari couldn't tell if it was because the woman actually knew Herman and hadn't expected to see him there or if she was just startled by his scars. It was obvious, though, that she wasn't happy to see Kari and Suz.

"What are *you* still doing here?" she asked Suz, chin in

the air. "I thought we'd agreed it was best for everyone if you left."

Suz shrugged. "I'm packed and ready to go. I just have to take my tent down," she said. "But Kari had a crazy idea. I've learned from experience that when that happens, it is easier to just get out of her way and let 'er rip."

Kari snorted. Suz had been aiding and abetting Kari's crazy ideas for years, including the one that led to Kari buying the Serenity Sanctuary animal shelter, not to mention adopting Queenie. Suz didn't so much get out of the way as give a good shove from behind. And Kari thought it might be time to give Olivia a good shove. Preferably off a cliff of her own making.

"Maybe it would help if you showed the sheriff what we found in the program booklet," Kari suggested to Suz.

If anything, Olivia went a shade whiter. "I don't think either of you are in a position to show anyone anything," she said. "Sheriff, I'm a very busy woman, and my husband is an extremely important man. In fact, I believe he contributed a substantial sum to your last campaign. If you know what's good for you, you'll drop this nonsense now, stop wasting my time, and let me get on with my day."

"I ran unopposed," Richardson pointed out in a bland voice. "So I doubt your husband had anything to do with my still being in office." He quirked an eyebrow. "But even if he did, I certainly wouldn't let that stand in the way of getting to the bottom of this or any case. As for being busy, I have a great deal of sympathy for that, so if you let me get on with my job, I'm sure we will both be able to return to our very important tasks that much sooner."

He turned to Kari and Suz. "Now, what is this crucial information you feel I need to have?" Kari couldn't tell if he was just humoring them or if the conversation he'd been

having with Herman Blue when they'd arrived had actually
convinced him there was something for him to know.

Suz bit her lip and glanced at Kari, who nodded encour-
agingly. She could have told the cops as easily as Suz could,
of course, but she thought it was important for her friend to
have a hand in clearing her own name. Assuming it worked,
of course. Not everything went as smoothly in real life as it
did on episodes of *Murder, She Wrote*. Surreptitiously, Kari
crossed her fingers behind her back.

"So, we told you about the way show dogs are named,"
Suz said, folding the copy of the program book back to the
page they'd been looking at before.

"Yeah," Richardson said. "It confused the heck out of
me. Still seems like it is way more complicated than it
needs to be."

"I can't argue with you there," Suz said. "But in this
particular case, the name of a dog turns out to be pretty
important." She pointed at Snowball, who was sitting at
Olivia's feet, panting happily. "That dog, actually."

"Shut up, Suzanne," Olivia said through clenched teeth.
"You don't know what you're talking about."

"I do, actually, Olivia," Suz said almost cheerfully. "You
made such a big deal out of how crucial it was that I be
versed in every aspect of kennel club rules and regulations,
I've been studying for weeks leading up to the show."

Olivia rolled her eyes, but stopped interrupting. For the
moment.

"This is the name of Olivia's dog," Suz said, pointing
out the relevant lines on the page. "You can see that his
formal name is *Blue Skies Boule de Neige*, which means
'Snowball' in French."

"See?" Richardson said, sounding exasperated. "Why
not just call the darn dog Snowball in the first place?"

"It's an American Kennel Club thing," Kari said. "Now, are you going to listen?"

Richardson sighed, but nodded. "Do go on, Ms. Holden. Explain to me why the dog's fancy name is important enough to drag Mr. Blue out of his house and me away from my interviews."

"Because the first part of an animal's formal name is the name of the kennel where he or she was born. In this case, Blue Skies," Suz said.

The sheriff's bushy eyebrows shot up. "Is that so?" He turned to Olivia. "Mrs. Weiner, I could swear that you told me that your dog most definitely did *not* come from Ms. Carver's kennel. In fact, I believe you said you only hired her to handle your dog because you knew she raised bichons, and therefore, you thought she would be the best one qualified for the job, but that you had barely spoken to her before the show began."

Olivia waved one hand dismissively through the air. "You must have misunderstood me, Sheriff Richardson."

"Really?" he said in a flat voice, staring into her eyes.

She pursed her lips. "Oh, very well," she said, her unnaturally firm chin high in the air. "So I was embarrassed to be associated with a woman who had had the bad taste to be murdered on the hallowed grounds of a historically tasteful kennel club dog show, and I told a tiny little white lie. You caught me." She held her wrists out in front of her dramatically and added, "Are you going to clap me in irons for telling a harmless fib, or can I get back to work? With Suzanne leaving, all the thankless tasks of running this show are now falling on *my* shoulders."

Kari almost choked. She loved the way Olivia made it sound as though Suz had deserted her in her hour of need instead of being forced to leave at a moment's notice.

Suz took a deep breath and let it out. Kari recognized the move from long experience and knew her friend was counting to ten so she didn't lose her temper.

When she was done, Suz said in a pleasant tone, "Actually, there's more, Sheriff."

"Fabulous," he said. "Do tell."

"The rest of the information that follows the dog's name includes not only the breeder—which is clearly stated to be one F. Carver—but also the names of the animal's father and mother. In this case, the father is listed as *CH Twin Oaks Treasured Snowflake*."

"What the heck kind of name is that?" Richardson said. "Treasured Snowflake? Ack."

Suz grinned. "I know, it's awful, but after a while it gets hard to come up with new names. Only thirty-seven dogs in any given breed can have the same name, and there are a *lot* of dogs registered with the AKC at any given time. They register about a million new dogs every year, believe it or not."

The sheriff blinked. "Wow. I had no idea. Sorry, you were saying?"

Kari was watching Olivia out of the corner of her eye, and saw the woman tense as Suz went on.

"So the 'CH' at the beginning of the father's name means he was a championship dog. They're the most desired for breeding, because it is assumed that their progeny will be superior," Suz said.

"Like with racehorses," Clark said, starting to look interested. "When a horse wins a major race, like the Preakness or the Belmont, the charge for breeding a mare to him goes way up. The few winners of the Triple Crown—all three big races in one year—can get up to sixty thousand dollars per stud fee. It's huge money." He noticed the sheriff staring at him and shrugged. "I love the horse races. Kent and I go to the racetrack at Saratoga every year."

"Good to know," Richardson said dryly. "I assume championship dogs aren't in the same league, though."

"No, they're not," Suz said. "Although people definitely pay larger sums to get puppies from championship blood-lines. As Olivia undoubtedly did to get her dog." She gestured at the booklet again. "My point, however, is the name of Snowball's sire, which has the kennel of origin listed as Twin Oaks. It occurred to Kari and me to wonder if that was actually Francine's original kennel, when she was still Lois Keller."

"Shut up, Suzanne," Olivia hissed. "You are going to ruin everything."

Kari ignored her. "I didn't know how to find out that information, so that was when I called you to ask for Mr. Blue's phone number. I called the kennel office, and thank-fully he was there. I explained what I wanted to know, and why, and he was intrigued enough to agree to come talk to us."

Richardson looked both curious and confused. "I see. Or rather, I don't. Perhaps Mr. Blue could explain it to me. *Was* that the name of Ms. Keller's old kennel?"

Twenty-One

"It was," Herman said, nodding his head. "She called it that because there were two large oak trees on the property. She told me once they were the only thing she missed about the place." A shadow crossed his scarred face, but he pulled himself together and went on. "But Mrs. Weiner didn't know anything about that when she bought the dog."

"You see?" Olivia cried. "I told you this whole thing was a big mistake."

"Yeah, and you made it, lady," Herman said. "Snooty, greedy bitch. My Lois sure saw you coming."

"I beg your pardon," Olivia said, putting one hand to her chest. "I don't know what you're talking about. And I will not be spoken to in that manner." She started to turn as if she was going to leave, but Richardson tilted his head at Clark, who took a step to block her.

"It was your own damn fault," Herman said, going on as if she hadn't spoken. "Lois went to the vet's right after she moved here," he explained to the cops. "Brought the dogs from Blue Skies Kennel to get their rabies shots and such under her new name, since she'd need that paperwork to sell them to the city people, and while she was sitting in the waiting room, this woman comes up and starts talking to her." He tilted his head in Olivia's direction.

"Lois came home and told me all about it. She said this pushy woman overheard her checking in at the front desk and saying she had a professional kennel operation. The woman, Olivia here, insisted that she knew superior breeding when she saw it and demanded to come out and see the dogs because they were so adorable."

"Well, I was right, wasn't I?" Olivia said, sounding proud of herself. She indicated Snowball, who was now licking his butt, one leg pointing up into the air. "Snowball is well on his way to being one in a million."

"Yes, he's very impressive," Richardson said. "Go on with your story, Mr. Blue. So Mrs. Weiner was interested in buying a dog from Ms. Carver, as she was known by then?"

Herman nodded, tugging his cap back into place when it slipped. "Oh yeah," he said. "Especially when she saw the bloodlines of the sire Lois was supposedly using. She demanded to be allowed to buy a puppy. Lois told Olivia that all the puppies were usually claimed years before they were born and that she had a waiting list of exclusive New York City buyers, but someone had just canceled on a puppy."

"She told me I was lucky," Olivia said, shaking her head. "My timing was perfect, because she hadn't called the next person on the list yet. She let me persuade her to sell me the puppy, at a premium price, of course. Then I paid her extra—a lot extra, I'll have you know—for the promise that she wouldn't sell to anyone else in the area. I just knew I had a champion in my hands at last, and I didn't want any competition."

Herman snorted. "But the laugh was on you, lady. You were so insistent that no one else nearby would get a dog from that same championship sire. Lois was only too happy to comply, since she had no intention of selling to anyone local. She'd learned her lesson about that the first time. She wouldn't even have sold to you if you'd given her any choice. But since you didn't, she made you pay through the nose for the privilege."

"It was worth it, though," Olivia said, her back straight and her head held high. Kari thought she looked a bit like a purebred dog herself, overly groomed and slightly high-strung.

"Snowball did well from the very beginning. He won all his competitions from the time he was old enough to compete. The wall in my study is covered with first-place ribbons and Best in Show awards. My husband finally stopped complaining about how much money I was spending on my 'hobby' and threatening to cut me off." She tried a sneer, although it would have worked better if her face had been a little more flexible.

"Would you believe that Jack made me stop showing my bulldog because he said Majestic Saint Michael was too ugly to be in his stupid car ads?" Olivia leaned down to pet Snowball. "He said that if he was going to be spending all that money, the least I could do was get a dog that was cute enough to use in his commercials. That's why when I met Francine, she was like an answer to a prayer. Jack would get an adorable fluffy white puppy to help persuade people to buy his cars, and I would finally have the champion dog I have been waiting for all these years. I worked hard for this. I deserve it."

She gave a small smile, a faraway, dreamy look on her face. "I could just see it in my mind's eye, us competing at

Westminster and the sound system reverberating with the words: 'Blue Skies Boule de Neige, Best in Show!'"

"So what went wrong?" Kari asked quietly. "I saw Snowball in the ring, and he was great."

"He was great," Olivia said. "He is great." Her shoulders sagged. "But then I found out something dreadful. Devastating, even."

"Oh dear," Suz said. "Is he sick?"

Olivia shook herself, as if coming back to the present. "What? No, of course he's not sick. He's in perfect health. Absolutely perfect from head to toe to tail." The tail in question wagged enthusiastically, as if Snowball could tell he was the focus of the conversation.

"So what happened?" Kari asked. By now, they were all riveted by the story. Richardson had one foot up on the bench of the picnic table, and Clark and Kent were both leaning in to listen. Kari and Suz had slid onto the seat on the other side, leaving Herman and Olivia standing facing each other at the far ends.

"Success happened, that's what," Olivia said bitterly. "Who knew that getting what I wanted could turn into such a nightmare?" She glared at Herman, who glared right back, as far as Kari could tell through the sunglasses he wore.

"I was so proud of Snowball's success, and my husband was still nagging me about how much money it cost to maintain a dog of this level and travel to shows and such. So I started breeding Snowball, to recoup some of the expenses." She stood up even straighter. "He was quite in demand, as you might expect, because he was such a rising star."

"Ah," Suz said. "The breeding rule."

Kari blinked at her. Obviously this part of the tale meant something to her friend that it didn't mean to her. From the blank expressions around her, she wasn't the only one who had lost the thread.

"Breeding rule?" Richardson asked. "What's that, and what the heck does it have to do with Francine's murder? That is still what we're talking about, isn't it?"

Olivia just sneered at him, as if anyone who didn't speak "professional dog" wasn't worth paying attention to. So Suz answered the question.

"The AKC has a lot of rules. One of them is that any dog who is bred more than three times in one year has to be DNA tested," she said. She gazed at Olivia with something almost like pity in her eyes. "I'm guessing the tests showed something unexpected. Something that would have an impact on his future career."

"Unexpected?" Olivia's lips twisted. "You could say that. The DNA test showed that the dog Francine had sworn was the puppy's father wasn't a match for the DNA I sent in. All this time I'd been bragging about his championship lineage, and it turns out his sire could have been *anyone*."

"I assume you confronted her when you learned of this," Richardson said. "What did Mrs. Carver have to say?"

"Francine insisted it must have been some kind of mix-up," Olivia said. "'These things happen,' she said, 'when you are breeding so many dogs. Such a pity.'"

"That doesn't sound so bad," Kent said. "I mean, yeah, the dog's father wasn't who you thought, but the dog itself turned out pretty good, so you could still just keep going on his merits, right?"

"If that had been the only issue, perhaps I could have just let it go," Olivia said. "But the DNA tests also showed that Snowball has the gene for progressive retinal atrophy. I wouldn't be able to breed him anymore if anyone found out, and eventually he'd go blind. It was a disaster. My heart was completely broken." She gazed down at the dog at her feet, looking about as heartbroken as a tree stump. "Not to mention that my husband would never have let me hear the end of it, paying all that money for a faulty purebred."

Kari and Suz stared at each other in shock as the other shoe dropped.

"Miriam's dog!" Kari said. "The one she returned to Lois, who promised she wouldn't breed it again. He had PRA. And championship bloodlines. The temptation to keep using him as a sire must have been too much."

Suz looked thoughtful. "Miriam swore she heard a dog with a bark just like her old dog. I wonder if Snowball inherited his father's unusual deep bark along with his catastrophic genetic disorder."

"I wondered where Mrs. Rosebaum came into this," the sheriff muttered. "The plot thickens." He turned back to Olivia. "So what did Ms. Carver say when you told her about the disease? Did she offer to give you your money back?"

"I didn't want my money back!" Olivia said, as if he was an idiot to even suggest it. "I wanted the dog I thought I had. I wanted to go on winning." She shook her head, although not one hair dared to move out of its assigned spot. "Francine suggested I simply stop showing the dog, or admit to people that his sire wasn't who I had been claiming him to be. I told her that was out of the question."

"And . . . ?" The sheriff let the word just hang in the air.

"And she had the temerity to blackmail me," Olivia snarled. "After putting me in this impossible situation, selling me a dog whose parentage she'd lied about and setting me up to become the laughingstock of the dog show community, she had the nerve to suggest I pay her to keep her mouth shut about it all."

Kari couldn't believe Olivia was telling them all this, but at this point, the woman had built up such a head of steam, it would probably have taken a concrete wall to stop her. And Kari wouldn't have bet on the wall.

Olivia went on, frothing over with indignation and fury. "Five hundred dollars a month she wanted. She said it was petty cash for someone like me, that I'd paid more than that for the shoes I was wearing." Olivia glanced down at her feet, which were currently clad in inappropriate stilettos whose brand Kari couldn't identify, but which probably had cost at least that much.

"Well," Kari said.

"That wasn't the point," Olivia said, practically spitting. "It was bad enough that I wouldn't be able to breed the dog anymore and I'd have to come up with some kind of excuse to explain it, but I didn't trust Francine not to keep raising the price. In fact, I started to wonder if she'd played me all along, selling me a dog she knew had tainted bloodlines."

Herman made a tiny noise that sounded slightly like a snicker, although he immediately hid it behind one hand. Olivia swung her head in his direction. "You think this is funny?" she yelled. "This is my life we're talking about."

"Oh, come on," Herman said. "You still had the dog. So you were out a little money. Like Lois said, you can afford it."

"Actually, I can't," Olivia said through tight lips. "I have no money of my own. It all comes from my husband, who begrudges every penny. There was no way I could come up with the kind of money Francine wanted month after month without Jack finding out about it. If he had figured out I'd been ripped off and paid too much money for this dog, plus I was paying some crooked breeder to keep quiet about it, he probably would have cut off my funds altogether. It would have been the end of my dog show days. The end of everything."

She paled at the thought, shaking from fear or fury, or both. "I was finally about to realize my lifelong dream of having a champion dog and winning at Westminster, and Francine was going to take it all away from me." Olivia took a deep breath, then let it out in a put-upon sigh. "I just couldn't let that happen."

"YOU," Herman bellowed. "You killed Lois! You killed the woman I loved!" He lunged at her, hands out as though he was trying to wrap them around Olivia's neck. Kent and Clark jumped on him, each grabbing an arm, and wrestled with him until they brought him to a halt halfway around the table. In the process, his cap fell off, leaving his scarred face looking strangely naked.

"Not so funny now, is it?" Olivia said in a low, nasty voice, apparently not even aware that she'd just confessed to murder. Kari had to wonder if the woman was completely sane, since once the cops had control of Herman Blue, Olivia seemed bizarrely calm.

"Mrs. Weiner," the sheriff said, getting to his feet slowly. "Are you telling me that you are responsible for the death of Francine Carver, also known as Lois Keller?"

Olivia gave him the kind of look one bestowed upon a not very bright child. "She was blackmailing me, Sheriff Richardson. Not to mention that she'd sold me a dog that was not what she'd claimed it to be. She was a criminal. You might actually say I was doing a public service by ridding the dog show community of a bad element."

"A public service," Richardson repeated, taking a couple of subtle steps in Olivia's direction. "You know, I hadn't actually thought of it that way."

"Well, there you are," Olivia said. "It was really her own

fault, for lying to me and being so greedy. She brought it on herself."

Kari could feel her jaw hanging open and forced herself to close it. Then she opened it again to ask, "But what about Miriam? She hadn't done anything to you."

"Oh really, Kari," Olivia said. "I should think it would be obvious even to someone who used to be a *waitress*." She said the word as though it tasted bad in her mouth, and Kari had to bite her tongue to keep from saying something rude. But the pointed stare Richardson aimed in her direction made it clear he wanted Olivia to keep talking.

"I'm sorry, Olivia," Kari said, gritting her teeth. "All the fumes from the deep fryer probably lowered my IQ. Maybe you could explain it to me."

"Miriam was insisting on having all the dogs from Francine's kennel DNA tested," Olivia said in a patient tone. "All Francine's current dogs, and all the dogs she'd sold since she'd opened her business here. Everything would have come out into the open."

She shook her head. "I asked Miriam to meet me in that clearing, because hardly anyone went there, and I tried to persuade her to change her mind. Told her she was imagining the barking she'd heard, that there was no way Francine was Lois."

"She wouldn't agree?" Kari said.

"Worse," Olivia said. "She *laughed* at me. That stupid old woman in her ugly track suit laughed at me. She said she couldn't believe I'd never heard of the scandal when Lois was expelled from the AKC. Told me it was my own fault, that if I ever actually socialized with other people in the kennel club, instead of thinking I was above them, I would have known about Lois and to watch out for a breeder selling bichons.

"I couldn't believe she had the nerve to criticize me for not listening to gossip," Olivia said. "I tried telling her Snowball was my last chance at greatness, but she insisted that the AKC had to be told about all the puppies Francine sold under false papers. Kept yammering on about the integrity of the breed." Olivia sighed. "I'd already come too far. She left me no choice."

Kari would have felt a little more sympathetic—although not much—if it wasn't clear that Olivia had gone in on both occasions prepared to kill. With tools belonging to Suz, no less.

"I understand why you felt both women had to die," Kari said as gently as she could manage, although she had to clench her hands together behind her back so tightly her knuckles hurt. "But why use Suz's scissors and leash?"

Olivia shrugged, as if they were talking about who was going to bring the scones for tea. "Well, someone had to take the fall for Francine's murder," Olivia said. "I certainly wasn't going to. And to be honest, I've never really approved of Suzanne."

"I beg your pardon?" Suz said, staring at the other woman in disbelief. "You framed me for murder because you don't *approve* of me?" Kari put a hand on Suz's arm and jumped up from the bench, standing up next to her, a little worried the cops would have to wrestle her friend down next.

Olivia pressed her lips together. "Really, Suzanne, you're not exactly kennel club material, are you? You have a dubious lifestyle, an altogether too flamboyant appearance, and your dogs aren't even purebred. If it had been up to me, you would never have been allowed into the kennel club at all, regardless of how willing you are to do all the hard work."

From the depths of Kari's bag, Queenie let out a hiss. The kitten had been so quiet, Kari had almost forgotten she was in there. Kari reached in and pulled the little black ball of fur out and hugged her for comfort. Besides, as silly as it seemed, they never would have figured it out without Queenie, and it felt only right that she was a witness at the end.

"How did you get my scissors?" Suz asked. "Did you sneak into my tent when I was out?"

Olivia gave a short, sharp laugh. "I didn't need to. You were standing right there when I took them."

Kari cast her mind back to that first day. "You knocked over that bunch of tools and then helped pick them up! You must have pocketed the scissors then." She narrowed her eyes. "So it was no accident. Very clever. But that would mean you were already planning to kill Francine when you came into Suz's tent."

"Unlike some people, I am not impulsive." She stared at the kitten in Kari's arms and curled her lip. "You would never catch me sinking a fortune into a run-down animal shelter on a whim, that much is certain." Olivia gave a slightly smug hint of a smile. "I planned the entire thing from the start."

In the background, Clark had loosened his grip on Herman long enough to hit the record button on his phone. Oblivious, Olivia continued on, eager to share her own cleverness.

"As soon as I realized that the situation was untenable, I set out to get Francine to the dog show. She was quite resistant, at first."

"She was afraid one of the professional dog people would recognize her," Herman said bitterly. "I persuaded her that she had changed her appearance so much her own mother wouldn't have known her. Olivia was offering Lois so much money to do this simple gig, we thought it was worth the risk." A tear slid down his cheek, following the pathway of his scars. "I wish I'd let her stay home like she wanted."

"I am *very* difficult to refuse when I sent my mind to something," Olivia said, head high.

"I'll vouch for that," Suz said. "So you lured her here on purpose, intending to kill her all along?" She sounded both appalled and fascinated.

"It was the perfect setup," Olivia said. "Hundreds of people milling around all day long, many of them from out of town. So much noise and confusion that the cops would have a hard time pinning down any one person's location at any given time."

Richardson shook his head in reluctant agreement. "She's not wrong about that. I'm *still* trying to figure out who saw Ms. Holden and when. Most of the folks I talked to only knew where their dogs were or when a certain competition was held."

Olivia glowed. "You see? It was the perfect plan. I convinced Francine to come to the show by telling her my regular handler had broken her leg and I'd pay double for Francine to step in at the last minute. I also told her that the only way I could possibly get her money was if Snowball won Best in Show, which would qualify us for Westminster and make him more valuable.

"Then I messed up Snowball's haircut myself, in a way I knew was easily fixable, dragged Francine to Suzanne's tent to make a fuss, then knocked over the tools and slipped the scissors into my purse with a cloth over my hand so I wouldn't get my fingerprints on them." Olivia waved a perfectly manicured hand in the air like a magician.

"Then all I had to do was lure Francine to the supply tent

on the pretext of handing over her first blackmail payment and stab her in her lying heart."

"That's not as easy as it sounds," the sheriff said. "Are you sure you didn't have help? Your husband, maybe?"

"Don't be insulting, Sheriff," Olivia said. "The only way my husband is going to help is by paying for the lawyers. Justifiable homicide. They'll get me off in no time, I assure you. You should see what they bill per hour." The sheriff gaped at her. "Besides, I didn't need help. I am surprisingly strong. You don't maintain a figure like this at my age without working out every single day, I'll have you know."

Richardson shook his head. "I see. But your perfect plan seems to have gone a bit sideways." He gestured at the other cops standing around the clearing. Herman had finally stopped struggling and was standing dejectedly next to Kent. Clark had slowly been moving closer to Olivia, one hand hovering near his still-holstered sidearm.

"That Miriam. I never liked her either," Olivia said. "Really, the class of people they let into these kennel clubs, I don't understand it. And her dogs always won."

"Did you pick Ms. Holden's leash on purpose, to cast more suspicion on her?" the sheriff asked.

"Why not?" Olivia said. "It worked so well with the scissors. I just strolled into her tent when I knew she would be out dealing with an issue and plucked one off a rack with a dozen others. She never even missed it." She turned to Suz. "You really ought to be more careful with your tools, you know." Then she swiveled to look at Richardson. "You were allowing yourself to be distracted by too many other suspects. Ex-husbands. Ridiculous protesters. I couldn't have that.

"So I strangled Miriam—it was easy. She might have been a force to be reckoned with in the dog show community, but she was still just an old, tiny woman. I left the leash around her neck where you'd be sure to find it, then stuffed her in that disgusting Porta Potty." She wrinkled her nose. "Honestly, that's the only part I'm really sorry about. Such an undignified place to be found. But I couldn't have you discovering her body too soon, could I? I learned that trick with the string when I was in Girl Scouts, if you can believe it."

"I'd believe just about anything right now," Richardson said. "But for starters, I believe I am going to read you your rights. Olivia Weiner, you are under arrest for the murders of Francine Carver and Miriam Rosebaum. I think you are definitely going to need that lawyer of yours." He handcuffed her, finished reading her rights, and led her off, followed by Clark and Kent, who both looked a little shell-shocked, Kent holding on to Snowball's leash as if it were a snake that might bite him.

Queenie hissed as Olivia went by. Kari didn't blame her. She felt a little bit like hissing herself.

Suz shook herself like a wet dog. "Good grief," she said. "That was one hell of a confession. Does she really think having an expensive lawyer is going to save her from going to prison for premeditated murder?"

"You'd be surprised at what people get away with if their lawyers are good enough and the prosecution screws up somewhere along the line," Herman said. Kari guessed he was speaking from experience earned in his previous life.

"I'm sorry about Francine. I mean, Lois," Kari said. "What she was doing was wrong, but she didn't deserve to be killed for it."

He picked up his hat and put it back on his head, pulling the brim down to cover as much of his face as possible. "I'm going to give the cops all the records I can find about the dealings Lois had with that woman. Maybe it will help them with their case. It's the least I can do for Lois. She wasn't perfect. Her parents were brutally poor when she was a kid, and she was obsessed with money because of it. But I loved her from the first moment I saw her, and I always will."

Kari thought sadly that his feelings had probably never been returned and his beloved Lois had just been using him like she used everyone else. But you never knew.

"Mr. Blue, it would really help the AKC if you could give them the records of the dogs she sold that were registered under false parentage," Suz suggested gently. "It could untangle some of the mess she made. Maybe help give you some closure."

Herman shrugged. "I don't care much one way or the other," he said. "But you two helped to figure out who really killed my Lois, so if that's what you want as thanks, I'll do it." He sighed. "My handler is going to give me yet another identity and move me somewhere far away, because of all the publicity this case is going to generate. I'll be happy to leave. I never want to see this place again."

He walked slowly out of the clearing, head bowed.

"Wow," Suz said. "This day didn't go the way I expected."

"You can say that again," Kari said. "But look on the bright side. Now we can unpack all your stuff and you can finish out the show."

Queenie let out a huge purr, so apparently she approved of that idea too.

❦ Twenty-Two

Kari and Suz left the Picnic Table of Doom for the last time and walked back to the Serenity Sanctuary tent, Queenie perched triumphantly on Kari's shoulder.

Once there, they were happy to discover that all the kittens they'd brought to the show had been adopted (although they mostly wouldn't go to their forever homes until the people who wanted them had been checked out first), and many of the animals whose pictures were on the board had "adoption pending" stickers next to their names.

The stack of tee shirts they'd started out with had dwindled down to just a couple, and there was a long list of names on the sign-up sheet for volunteers. If even a quarter of them actually showed up to clean cages or walk dogs after the thrill of the show wore off, it would be a huge help to the existing staff.

Sara was perched on a stool behind the table with the cages on it, playing with one of the little yellow kittens inside, an adorable long-haired boy with extra toes. She'd poked the end of a feathered toy through the mesh, and the kitten was chasing it back and forth. Kari couldn't tell which one of them was more entertained.

Bryn, on the other hand, was pacing back and forth, chewing on one fingernail, and checking her cell phone for messages with a furrowed brow. She dropped the phone on the nearest table as soon as Kari and Suz walked into the tent and ran over to greet them.

"You're not under arrest!" she said to Suz. "You'd been gone so long, and one of the show attendees came through a few minutes ago and said she saw the cops leaving. I was afraid they were hauling you off to jail!"

"Not today," Suz said with a grin, giving the younger woman a hug so powerful it made her braids bounce. "I'm completely cleared, and in fact, if you are willing to give me a hand, I'm going to get all my stuff out of my car and set back up for the rest of the day."

"Why is all your stuff in your car?" Sara asked, abandoning the kitten to play with his siblings and coming over to join them.

"Olivia ordered her to leave earlier," Kari said, putting her tote bag down on one of the tables and setting the kitten down next to it. "That's part of why we were gone so long. We were packing up all Suz's supplies. But then Queenie gave us a clue to solving the murder, so we had to go talk to the sheriff."

"Then things got kind of complicated," Suz said.

Sara shook her head. "It already sounded complicated. Olivia kicked you out of the show? Why? The nerve of that woman."

Suz waved one hand. "It doesn't matter. She doesn't get to tell anyone what to do anymore, since she's the one going to jail."

"What?!" Sara and Bryn shouted in unison.

Bryn gaped at them. "*Olivia Weiner* killed two people? You've got to be kidding me. The wife of the Used-Car King is a murderer? I wonder how he's going to work that into his commercials."

"I suspect he is going to be a little too busy hiring lawyers to worry about it," Kari said. "Olivia actually confessed to the whole thing: luring Francine here in order to kill her, stealing Suz's scissors so she'd get the blame, then murdering poor Miriam too when she got in the way."

"Holy crap," Bryn said. "That's nuts."

"Very possibly," Kari said in a wry tone. "I'm pretty sure Olivia is more likely to end up in a room with padded walls than in a prison cell. Although the woman is awfully canny. I wouldn't be surprised if once she figured out she'd been caught, she decided to try for an insanity plea on purpose." She shook her head. "Thankfully, it isn't our problem anymore."

"Seriously," Suz said. "I am looking forward to grooming a few dogs, watching a couple of competitions, and finishing out the day with a feast of *all* the fried foods, and possibly some ice cream."

She looked at her friends. "It's my treat. Why don't we all meet up around five and grab dinner before they shut down the food trucks? Kari and I can tell you all the gory details over jalapeño poppers, onion rings, and burgers."

"Sounds perfect," Sara said. She turned to Kari with a sly smile. "Why don't you invite that nice vet Dr. McCoy to join us?"

"Oh, I don't think so," Kari said, feeling her cheeks heat up. "I'm sure he'll be busy with last-minute show stuff."

Queenie let out a meow and stuck one black paw into the tote bag next to her. She knocked Kari's phone onto the ground and pounced on it.

"Oh, you little monkey," Kari said, going over to rescue the cell phone. "What did you do that for?"

A faint voice could be heard, and Kari put the phone to her ear.

"Oh, hi, Angus," she said. "I'm sorry to interrupt whatever you're doing. Queenie accidentally hit the call button when she pushed my phone off the table." Kari narrowed her eyes at the kitten, who was looking innocent as usual. "Apparently she thought I should ask you to join us all for dinner so you can hear how everything turned out. Oh, you would? Okay, five o'clock by the food trucks. I'll see you then."

Kari ended the call and tucked the phone safely into her back pocket. "I suppose you think you're smart," she said to the kitten.

Her friends were trying not to laugh, and not doing a very good job of it.

"We all think she's smart," Sara said. "After all, she solved a murder and got you a date, both in one day. That is one special kitten."

Kari had to agree.

Acknowledgments

The only thing harder than writing the first book in a completely new series in a completely new genre, as it turns out, is writing the second book (especially during a pandemic). Huge thanks go out again to my wonderful agent, Elaine Spencer, and my brilliant editor, Jenn Snyder, for all the encouragement and for believing in me. All the folks at Berkley have been amazing, but extra special thanks to Natalie Sellars and Dache Rogers, for helping to promote and market the book so it got to as many readers as possible. You ladies were awesome, and I would have thanked you in the first book if I'd gotten the chance. Immense gratitude to my mystery writing guru and cheerleader: author extraordinaire Donna Andrews, and to Judy Levine, Karen Buys, Skye Hughes, and Lisa DiDio for first-reader duties and/or promotional assistance. This book took a village to create, and I am so blessed with the village I've got. Most of all, thanks to Ellen Dwyer, my real-life Suz, who shared her experience with dog shows and explained all about naming purebred dogs and the AKC. Any mistakes are my own.

*Keep reading for an excerpt from the next
Catskills Pet Rescue Mystery by Deborah Blake*

Claws for Suspicion

Coming in May 2022 from Berkley Prime Crime

One

Kari Stuart gazed around her kingdom and smiled with satisfaction. Okay, it wasn't really a kingdom, it was an animal shelter, and a small golden retriever puppy had just piddled in one corner of it, but still, it had come a long way from the rundown, nearly defunct rescue she had taken over a few months ago.

From her position behind her desk at the back of the room, Kari could see the usual low-keyed hum of activity you might expect on a relatively quiet Wednesday in early October. Over by the new top-of-the-line wood-framed cages against the wall, her friend and head volunteer, Sara, was showing a young couple some kittens, and trying to persuade them that two would be better than one. From the looks on their beaming faces as they cuddled a pair of little tiger-striped siblings, Kari suspected Sara had been her usual convincing self.

Of course, after more than forty years teaching English to ninth graders, the feisty seventy-two-year-old could get almost anyone to do what she suggested. Kari called Sara her secret weapon. Only the turquoise streak in Sara's gray hair hinted that she might not be the mild-mannered retiree she appeared to be. She had been working at the shelter long before Kari bought it, under its previous owner, Daisy, and had stubbornly refused to give up on either the place or their few remaining misfit animals.

Bryanna Jenkins, another dedicated volunteer and now a part-time employee when not attending vet technician classes at the two-year college in neighboring Perryville, was over in the corner cleaning up after the puppy she'd been handing over to its new owners.

Bryn had dealt with plenty of puddles during her time at the shelter, so she was completely unfazed by the mess, laughing and joking with the tall man and his excited teen daughter as they finished filling out the final paperwork. Bryn's dark hair was pulled back into many tiny braids, all of them tucked neatly under a rainbow-colored bandana to keep them out of the way, and her bright red Serenity Sanctuary tee shirt looked good with her light brown skin.

She and Kari hadn't hit it off right away when Kari took over, but these days they mostly got along just fine. The younger woman was learning to trust Kari's genuine desire to improve the shelter, and it didn't hurt that Bryn got along so well with Kari's best friend, Suz, a local dog groomer.

The main room glowed in the sunlight that poured in from the large windows, showing off the gleaming new linoleum floors and the soft blue paint on the walls. The L-shaped wooden desk at the front had stools for the volunteers who greeted visitors, as well as neat stacks of applications and information sheets. On the corkboard behind the desk, there were pictures of that month's featured dogs and cats, along with helpful descriptions—*Gets along with other dogs and cats. Rides well in cars, but could use additional leash training*—along with the basics like age and breed. One adorable hound dog with innocent-looking brown eyes had a note that said, *Very sweet. Will eat your shoes.*

Kari couldn't help beaming with pride as she took it all in. She knew some people—most people, maybe—thought she was crazy when she used most of her unexpected lottery winnings to buy and refurbish the sanctuary. But they had desperately needed help, and she had needed to find a purpose in her life. So far, at least, she had no regrets at all.

The pen she'd been using suddenly rolled across the desk and onto the floor with a sharp *click*, jarring Kari out of her reverie.

"Queenie," she scolded. "How many times do I have to tell you that my pens are not your toys?"

The little black kitten perched on top of the pile of bills Kari had been attempting to pay ignored this reminder with the ease of long practice, yawning up at Kari and showing off a pink tongue and sharp white teeth. At seven months old, Queen Nefertiti, or "Queenie" as she was known, was small for her age, and likely to stay that way, according to Kari's vet. Probably a combination of heredity and her rough start as a stray.

In fact, Queenie was directly responsible for Kari buying the sanctuary. When she'd rescued the kitten at about three months old, Kari had discovered to her dismay that all the local shelters were at capacity and beyond. So she'd bought the sanctuary, and ended up keeping the kitten. Or more accurately, the kitten had kept her.

Queenie more than made up for her diminutive size with her stubborn determination to get her own way and a slightly uncanny ability to know everything that was going on. She insisted on going in to work with Kari every day, rather than staying in the farmhouse on the property with Kari's other two cats, Westley and Robert, and her mixed-breed dog, Fred. The kitten was as much a fixture around the sanctuary as Tripod, the friendly three-legged yellow tomcat who had been around so long he was practically their mascot.

"I need to get to that paperwork," Kari said to Queenie, who seemed unimpressed by this fact. "Now stop throwing my pens on the floor." Kari tucked her long brown hair behind one ear as she bent down to retrieve the writing implement. Naturally, the pen had rolled well underneath the desk, so she had to duck down and stretch her arm out to reach it.

As her fingertips touched the smooth barrel, she heard the brassy sound of the bell that signaled the front door opening and footsteps approaching her desk.

A pleasant tenor voice said, "Hi, honey, I'm home."

Kari straightened up so fast, she smashed her head against the bottom of the desk. For a moment she saw stars, and her eyes watered from the impact. She supposed it was too much to hope that she had given herself a concussion and hallucinated hearing that familiar voice. Unfortunately, she didn't think she could be that lucky.

Holding her head, she sat up slowly and looked across the expanse of paperwork and wood. A tall, attractive man with professionally cut dark brown hair, twinkling brown eyes, and a broad smile stood there, holding a small bouquet of red roses. He was impeccably dressed in a black suit that had clearly been chosen to show off his still slim and muscular body, and at forty, only a few silver hairs were visible amid the brown. No doubt women thought it made him look distinguished. That and a few tiny wrinkles around his eyes were the only things about him that had changed since Kari had last seen him—in court when their divorce was finalized four years ago.

"Hello, Charlie," she said in a calm voice. "Long time, no see. You look good. Don't let the door hit you on the way out." She pointed at the front door with a finger that she was pleased to see wasn't trembling at all. Her stomach, on the other hand, was doing somersaults, as if it had suddenly been taken over by a conga line of drunken mice.

Across the room, Sara's keen ears had clearly picked up on Kari's unaccustomed rudeness, and the former teacher raised one gray eyebrow in her direction. Kari just shook her head and focused on Charlie, who didn't seem remotely put off by her less than enthusiastic welcome.

"Now is that any way to greet your long-lost husband?" Charlie asked cheerfully. "Look, I brought you roses." He plopped them down on the desk, scattering the neat piles of paperwork in the process. "What a cute kitten, is it yours?" He reached out one hand to pet Queenie, who hissed at him.

Out of the corner of her eye, Kari could see Sara's other eyebrow go up, since normally the kitten was friendly with everyone she met, whether human or furry.

"You tell him, Queenie," Kari said, standing up so she wouldn't get a crick in her neck. At five foot six, she was still a lot shorter than Charlie's six foot two, but at least she wasn't at quite as much of a disadvantage. "And yes, she's mine. You, on the other hand, are not, and I'd just as soon you stayed lost. So if you don't mind, please take your flowers and get out. We don't have anything to say to each other."

"Oh, you'd be surprised," Charlie said, looking around. "Nice place you've got here," he said, not sounding like he really meant it. "I couldn't believe it when I heard from someone that you'd bought an animal shelter in this back-water town in the Catskills. What on earth possessed you?"

Kari tried to figure out who he could have heard the news from. She hadn't stayed in touch with any of their mutual friends, who had mostly been his friends and business associates anyway. His mother had hated Kari from the first Thanksgiving dinner, and Kari hadn't spoken to her since she'd left. Suz was about the only friend who had been around during their three short years of marriage, and she had despised Charlie from day one and begged Kari not to marry him. It definitely hadn't been Suz.

Oh well, it didn't matter how he'd found out. He was here now, and unless something drastic had changed in the ensuing four years, that meant he wanted something. The sooner she discovered what it was, the sooner she could say *no* and send him on his merry way.

"Believe it or not," Kari said, "I wanted to do something meaningful with my life. Helping animals who would have otherwise fallen through the cracks seemed like a good way to do that. And Lakeview is hardly a backwater town. We have a thriving tourist trade, especially now during leaf-peeping season."

She picked up Queenie, who looked like she was considering attacking the roses. Kari would have been happy to let her but not until after they'd been checked for thorns. Any gift from Charlie was likely to smell sweet and have hidden prickles. "Besides, the commute is short."

Charlie shook his head, giving her the kind of indulgent look you might bestow on a cute but not very bright child. "You always did have a soft spot for critters, didn't you?" he said with a chuckle. "Wouldn't it have been easier to just adopt a few? I doubt there's much money in the shelter business."

Queenie gave a quiet growl, and Kari did her best not to do the same. Charlie had never liked animals—he thought they were messy and smelled and took too much work. One of the many reoccurring arguments during their marriage was about whether or not to have pets. Kari never did win that one. Practically the first thing she'd done once she'd finally settled into her own apartment was to go out and get a dog. Feline brothers Westley and Robert had followed not too much after.

"Nope," she said. "No money in it at all. So if that's what you're here for, you might as well take your flowers and leave. In fact, no matter what you're here for, I can assure you, you're barking up the wrong tree." She nodded in the direction of the puppy, who was now attempting to gnaw on his new owner's sneakers. "Pun intended. I have no interest in anything you might have to say."

"Oh, I think you'll find you do," Charlie said. He perched familiarly on the corner of her desk and smiled up at her. "I have kind of a surprise for you."

Kari hated surprises. In her experience, they were very rarely of the pleasant variety.

"My birthday's not until April," she said. "And I'm not likely to celebrate our anniversary unless it is by burning you in effigy. So whatever it is, I don't want it."

"You may want to rethink that anniversary thing," Charlie said, a hint of smugness in his smooth tone. "Because it turns out, we're still married."

Kari's legs turned to jelly, and she sank into her chair before they gave out on her. This had to be a bad joke, right?

"What the heck are you talking about, Charlie Smith?" she asked. "We stood in a courtroom together, and a judge accepted the terms of the divorce. Which, if you'll recall, were mostly in your favor. There is no way we are still married."

"The divorce wasn't official until we both signed the paperwork and mailed it back in to the county clerk's office," Charlie said. "And apparently you never did that. I checked, and there is no record of our divorce being finalized and officially filed. We're married, all right."

Kari swallowed hard around the lump in her throat. Of course she had sent in the papers. Hadn't she? It was four years ago, and once everything was done with, she'd tried to put it as far behind her as possible.

The kitten jumped out of her arms and nudged at a piece of paper, as if trying to make a point. Over the last few months, Kari had figured out not to ignore her hints.

"Charlie," Kari said in a carefully neutral tone, "why would you have checked on that, after all this time? Are you planning on getting remarried?" She had been his second wife, twenty-two to his thirty-three at the time, and he'd never been one to be without a woman. Or a few women.

He threw back his head and laughed, making everyone in the place turn around for a moment and stare. His laugh was seemingly charming, just like the rest of him. "Not at the moment," he said. "And it turns out that's a good thing, since I'm already hitched to you."

He straightened the crease on his perfectly pressed pants. "No, I decided to double-check with my lawyer when I heard your good news. Just in case I was entitled to something. He was the one who found out the paperwork had never been properly filed."

Kari's heart sank into her sneakers. She was pretty sure she knew which good news Charlie meant. "The good news about my buying the sanctuary?" she said.

"Don't be silly, Dumpling," he responded, using the nickname she'd always hated. It sounded affectionate, but it had been his subtle dig at the extra ten pounds she constantly seemed to be battling. Charlie specialized in the art of the understated put-down. Too bad it had taken her so long to figure out how damaging that was. "I mean your good luck winning all that money in the lottery. Congratulations, by the way. Well done."

"Thank you," she said. "Ironically, I bought the ticket when I stopped at the convenience store on the way home from work so I could pick up cat litter. So if you think about it, if we had been together, I never would have won at all. And you do realize that the payout isn't nearly as big as the original prize. After taxes, and with the penalties for taking it all at once, there was only about three million dollars."

"Still a nice sum," he said. "My lawyer says that since we're still married, I'm entitled to half."

"That's ridiculous!" Kari said, trying not to panic. "We haven't even seen each other in four years. We are supposed to be divorced. Besides, I've already sunk a lot of my winnings into buying and rehabbing the sanctuary."

"No problem," Charlie said with a smirk. "I'll take that. I'm sure the land isn't worth much, but I'm sure I can do something with it."

Kari stood up again, aware that their discussion was now the center of attention from everyone in the room. She didn't have the energy to care. "Let me say this very clearly, so there is no confusion," she said through clenched teeth. "You will get this sanctuary over my dead body." She glared at him. "Or, if necessary, yours."

Charlie just laughed at her and rose from his perch. "Still my feisty little Dumpling, I see. I'll go now and give you a little time to adjust to the idea. I'm sure you'll see reason in the end."

He blew her a kiss and strolled out the door, leaving both Kari's desk and her peace of mind a lot more disturbed than when he'd arrived.

Two

Sara hustled the young couple through their adoption paperwork in record time, and Bryn got the new puppy owners out through the door right behind them. As soon as the place was empty, they moved in on Kari like sharks on a drowning surfer.

She was still sitting at her desk, staring blankly at the stack of bills while Queenie played with a stray rose petal. The rest of the flowers were upside down in the trash can next to her. Kari wished the rest of her problems could be disposed of as easily.

"Do you want to tell us what that was all about?" Sara asked, pushing a strand of turquoise hair out of her face. It was clearly a rhetorical question, much like when she had asked the same basic thing years ago after finding Kari and Suz standing in front of a locker with a screaming cheerleader locked inside. (Hey, Missy Carlyle had been making fun of Suz's height and flat chest. There was no way Kari was going to put up with that. The three days in detention were well worth it.)

"Yeah," Bryn said eagerly. "Who was that guy? He was seriously tall, dark, and handsome. Way too old for me, and you know, the wrong gender, but you should definitely hit that."

"You weren't paying attention," Sara said with a wry twist of the lips. "From what I could hear, she already did. And it didn't go well."

Bryn tilted her head, causing her braids to sway gently back and forth. A few of the tiny beads she'd woven into them clicked together musically. "Ex-boyfriend?" she said.

"Ex-husband," Kari replied, giving up on the bills and putting them to the side in a neat pile for later. "Or so I thought until five minutes ago. We may have a problem."

"I'll get coffee and those chocolate muffins Bryn picked up on her way in," Sara said decisively. "This sounds like it is too complicated to discuss hovering over your desk. And definitely an occasion that calls for chocolate."

She marched off in the direction of the small kitchen at the back of the shelter, which now actually had a tiny section dedicated to human needs, in addition to the stacks of canned cat and dog food, bins of dry chow, and the various bowls and dishes that went with them.

"If you're just going to throw these out, can I have them?" Bryn asked, plucking the roses out of the garbage. They were only slightly battered from their abuse, a condition Kari felt a certain sympathy with. "My aunt loves roses."

Since Bryn's aunt Izzie was both the town librarian and one of Kari's favorite people, she figured that was as good a place for them as any. "Sure," Kari said, getting up and going over to the front counter. She filed the adoption paperwork under *pending* before sitting down on one of the stools. They would phone the couple's vet and check to make sure that any animals they already owned were up-to-date on their shots and checkups, as well as calling any references they had listed.

Once the three of them had gathered around the counter, Sara fixed Kari with a piercing blue-eyed gaze. "So, are you going to explain why an ex-husband we have never heard of before has suddenly shown up at the shelter, and how exactly he is going to be a problem?"

Kari sighed and took a sip of coffee. "You never heard of him because I happily left that part of my life behind me when I moved back to Lakeview. And the problem is that he says our divorce was never finalized due to some kind of technicality and he is entitled to half of my lottery winnings."

"What?" Bryn said. Her mouth dropped open. "But, that can't be right, can it?"

Sara looked thoughtful, a crease forming between her eyebrows as she considered Kari's statement. "The first part of his claim should be pretty easy to prove. Or disprove. You must have a copy of the official divorce decree." Sara had been happily married to her husband Todd for over forty-five years, but she tended to know all sorts of random facts.

"I'm not sure I do," Kari said unhappily. "I don't remember seeing it, anyway, although that would have been four years ago. Things were a little crazy for a while after I left Charlie. I moved around from one friend's house to another for about six months, sleeping on people's couches with everything I owned packed into the back of my old Toyota."

She still thought of that car fondly, even though she'd finally given in and bought herself a newer model with her lottery winnings, one with a hatchback that was large enough to haul animals or supplies around in if necessary. It was a lovely shiny blue, and she almost liked it as much as its rusty, duct-taped-together predecessor.

"How did you end up in Lakeview?" Bryn asked.

"I actually grew up here. And Suz was here," Kari said. "We've been best friends since grade school, and once I was sure Charlie wasn't going to come after me, she convinced me to move back." She shrugged. "It's ironic, really. When I graduated from high school, I couldn't wait to go to college and get out of this town. Now I can't think of any place I'd rather be."

Sara put down the muffin she'd been nibbling on. "What do you mean, once you were sure he wasn't going to come after you? Was he abusive? Should we be concerned?" She pulled out her cell phone as if she was going to call one of the many useful people in her speed dial—a cop, maybe, or possibly a lawyer. It wouldn't have surprised Kari if there was a hit man in there too.

Kari waved her down. "He wasn't abusive in the conventional sense, if that's what you mean. Charlie never hit me, or did anything obviously cruel. He was just controlling and emotionally manipulative. It wasn't so much that he wanted me back as that he didn't like losing. He only consented to the divorce after I agreed to walk away from the house and everything in it that I hadn't owned before the marriage."

Both women looked indignant on her behalf, but Kari just shrugged again. "Hey, he was the one earning most of the money, and he owned the house before we got married. I wanted out a lot more than I wanted to hang on to any stuff. Most of it wasn't my style anyway. I even let him be the injured party, to salve his ego. So I didn't *really* think he'd try and find me afterward. But after three years of feeling progressively more powerless, it took me a while before I could relax and stop looking over my shoulder."

"That sounds rough," Bryn said.

"It wasn't that bad," Kari said, not quite honestly. "But it did mean that I was so focused on surviving, I didn't really think about things like divorce paperwork. And honestly, I moved around so much, some of my mail never did catch up with me." She bit her lip. "I suppose it's possible that I missed something important."

"Well, you'll just have to look and see if you can find it," Sara said in a decisive tone. "What about your safe-deposit box?"

Kari laughed so hard she startled the kitten as she was trying to get a little black paw onto a crumb of muffin. "Safe-deposit box? Up until the time I won the lottery, the most valuable thing I owned was a twelve-year-old car and a sterling-silver locket handed down from my grandmother. I don't have a safe-deposit box. I have a file labeled 'Important Papers' stuck somewhere at the back of my filing cabinet, in between 'Healthcare Bills' and 'Insurance.'"

Sara pursed her lips and snagged the last muffin before either of the others could grab it. "Well, I guess you'd better go look in that file then. Because if you can't find your divorce papers, we might have to consider that your ex is telling the truth. And if he is, the shelter could be in a world of trouble."

Ready to find
your next great read?

Let us help.

Visit prh.com/nextread

Penguin
Random
House